Mapping
the
Night

iBooks
Habent Sua Fata Libelli

iBooks
Manhanset House
Shelter Island Hts., New York 11965-0342

bricktower@aol.com
ibooksinc.com

Library of Congress Cataloging-in-Publication Data
Bethel, John David
Mapping the Night
p. cm.

1. FICTION / Thrillers / Psychological. 2. FICTION / Thrillers / Crime.
3. FICTION / Crime
Fiction, I. Title.
ISBN: 978-1-955036-72-6 Trade Paper

June 2024

iBooks are published by iBooks, an imprint of J. Boylston & Company, Publishers
Manhanset House, Dering Harbor, New York 11965 •www.ibooksinc.com•

Mapping the Night

John David Bethel

Also by John David Bethel

Evil Town
Sirens
No Immaculate Conceptions
No Country Loved
Blood Moon
Little Wars
Unheard Of
Holding Back the Dark
Wretched

To my daughter Katie Bethel Orgeira.

The sweetest soul and best mother one could know.

"She emerged from the shadows of the recently dead."

—Anonymous

Table of Contents

Glossary of Major Characters

Jim Broaden	Detective, 19th Precinct, NYPD
Jane Levitt	Detective, 19th Precinct, NYPD
Nadine Robinson	Commanding Officer, 19th Precinct, NYPD
Eileen Prado	Special Agent, FBI
Ira Fisher	Special Agent, FBI
Warren Winston	Resident, The Plaza Residences
Maddy Broaden	Resident, The Plaza Residences
Eloise Fletcher	Winston family house manager
Regina Wozniak	Victim
Fiona Davis	Victim
Dorothy Provine	Victim
James Braddock	Superintendent, The Manchester Residences
Dr. Willow Briggs	Psychologist
Geoffrey Panday	Surinamese businessman/Regina Wozniak's father

Glossary of Recurring Characters

Officer Pendrage	Police Officer, NYPD
Officer Lattimore	Police Officer, NYPD
Cecil	Concierge, The Gramercy Residences
Dick Warner	Retired Detective, 19th Precinct, NYPD
Lorna Miley	Surviving Victim
Annie Real	Surviving Victim
Mike Wilson	Detective, Philadelphia Police Department
Willis Reasoner	Governor, State of New York
Raymond Sims	United States Senator, State of New York
Leonard Kinney	New York City Police Commissioner

Acronyms

AD	Assistant Director
ATF	Bureau of Alcohol, Tobacco, Firearms and Explosives
BAU	Behavioral Analysis Unit (FBI)
CI	Confidential Informant
CSU	Crime Scene Unit
Interpol	International Criminal Police Organization
OAS	Organization of American States
SAIC	Special Agent in Charge
ViCAP	Violent Criminal Apprehension Program

Chapter 1

Regina Wozniak

Pendrage and Lattimore slowed to a stop under the red and yellow canvas porte cochere in front of the Gramercy Residences. Pendrage leaned forward and studied the wide flight of stone stairs leading to the glass double-doored entrance.

"Here?" Pendrage asked incredulously.

"You heard the call," Lattimore answered as he pushed open the passenger side door and rolled his round body to a standing position. "Fuckin' cold," he said, the words coming in white puffs.

Pendrage walked around the front of the cruiser and stood next to his partner. The long, lanky officer was a distinct contrast to his short, stout companion.

As the officers walked up the staircase, flanked on either side by marble statues of lions depicted alert and ready to spring, Lattimore pointed at a man in tails and top hat standing behind the closed doors. "Gotta be the doorman. Must be the guy who called it in."

The automatic doors swung open with a hiss as the men approached.

Inside, Pendrage shook off the cold as he rubbed his arms.

"Are you…?" Lattimore started to ask the gaunt, hollow-cheeked man holding his hands tightly together in front of him exposing boney, white knuckles. The question went unfinished as the man nodded toward two women seated on a floral cloth couch to the left of the entrance.

The officers maneuvered around the setting of furniture in the lobby, which was tastefully decorated with an arrangement of couches and chairs surrounding a low-slung table that held a Baccarat crystal vase and a box of tissues. They stopped in front of the women; one standing, the other folded into herself, shoulders shaking.

Hair pinned up in a bun, the more composed of the two was draped in an unbuttoned cloth overcoat exposing plaid flannel nightwear and silk slippers. The thrown together ensemble fell in clean lines on the tall, attractive woman who stared at them blankly. The face of the other was hidden by a tissue pressed to her nose. Shoulders slumped, she was a mess in black yoga pants, white, long-sleeved pullover, running shoes and a goose down vest.

"Ma'am," Pendrage said, nodding at both women as he removed his hat. "Did you make the call about a body in an apartment?"

The woman behind the tissue came up for air saying, "Yes, well, no." She raised her red, swollen eyes to the man who had followed the officers from the door and stood opposite the women, behind a facing couch. "Cecil did."

The officers turned their attention to Cecil. "You did?"

"Yes," came a deep-voiced, rumbling response sounding like it emerged from the back of the man's throat.

"We asked him to," the cloth coat draped woman said, bringing the attention of the officers back to the huddled pair.

"So," Pendrage continued, "you were the ones who found the body."

"I did," the tissue crushing woman choked out. "I went into Regina's apartment as I do every morning to help her with Jason and…." She closed her eyes tightly squeezing out a rush of tears. She reached for the box of tissues, shaking her head. "I can't. It's too awful."

"Lily came to my door," the comforting woman said. "She was hysterical. I live across the hall from Regina. Regina Wozniak. Lily is one door down from her."

"Your name, ma'am?" Pendrage asked.

"Katherine Miller. Kate." She tilted her head toward Lily. "Lily Banbridge." She put her arm around Lily and brought her close. "She said something was wrong and we went back to Regina's. Lily wouldn't go inside. I did." She shook her head. "We came down here and asked Cecil to call 911."

"Who's Jason?" Lattimore asked.

"Regina's son," Cecil answered.

"Her son," Pendrage said, an edge to his voice. "He's still in the apartment? Alone?"

"We tried to bring him with us," Katherine said, "but he wouldn't come. He held onto Regina's legs and I couldn't get him to leave."

"I think I'm going to be sick," Lily said frantically and shot off the couch. She ran toward the back of the lobby, Katherine in tow.

"How old is the boy?" Lattimore asked, turning toward Cecil.

"He's in second grade, so, what? Seven?"

"What's the apartment number?"

"Ten seventeen."

Pendrage and Lattimore walked across the lobby, past portraits of men in high collars standing stiffly behind large desks. They were identified by brass plates on the wall as the architect and financier responsible for building the Gramercy. The portraits were dated 1923.

As the elevator doors slowly shut, enclosing the officers in a dimly lit, dark wood-paneled, brass railing lined box, Pendrage said, "I thought I was through with this shit. Escaped five years in Brownsville. A few arrests. Some armed robberies, but no bodies. I come to the Upper East Side and now this."

"Yeah, well, into every life a little rain must fall," Lattimore said, the sarcasm dripping.

When the elevator doors parted, the officers were accosted by a trio in various stages of morning dress. The first was a short, bald man, his open robe exposing black, silk underwear. His hairy upper body on display. "What the hell is going on? I heard screaming."

"Please back up," Lattimore said, maneuvering past the man whose place was quickly filled by an older woman pushing a walker into his path.

"It was Lily," the older woman said, bouncing so agitatedly on the bars of her walker that her glasses fell from her nose and clattered to the floor. "She was yelling something about Regina."

Lattimore picked up the glasses and handed them to the woman.

Lattimore and Pendrage weaved past the walker and toward another man in an NYU stenciled sweat shirt and black running shorts, who stood in a doorway.

"Didn't ask for the keys," Lattimore said, his frustration evident. "That was monumentally stupid."

"No, need," Pendrage answered, pointing ahead, where the NYU man stood, his shoulder resting against the jamb of the open door to apartment 1017.

"Ray Willis," the man said, pushing away from the door and holding out his hand. "Former cop, chief of police actually, in Gambier, Ohio. Keeping everyone out. No contamination."

"Thanks," Pendrage and Lattimore said as the man stepped out of their way. They shouldered through the opening, careful not to touch any surface and stood at the head of a long, wood floor hallway. The bare walls were covered in woven beige grass cloth. An open sliding glass door was visible at the end of the hallway which led to the living room. Sheer lace curtains were billowing into the room.

"It's freezing," Pendrage said.

The officers made their way down the hall and stopped at a door open to a large kitchen dominated by an island over which hung a wrought iron rack displaying copper pots and pans. A double-doored refrigerator and stove flanked by pantries filled the facing wall.

They stood a moment, exchanged glances and approached the only other door along the hall.

"Help," pleaded a high-pitched voice, forced through a sniffing sob.

"Fuck," Lattimore whispered as he preceded Pendrage into a large bedroom. A boy was kneeling next to a bed and the body of a young woman. She was covered from shoulder blades to upper thighs by a white towel. Her shoulders, arms and legs were bare.

As the officers approached, a towheaded, red-faced boy turned toward them. He was pressing a plastic refrigerator bag of green peas to the forehead of the woman in the bed. "Please help her," the boy said, his eyes going back to the body. "I can't make her wake up." He raised the bag slightly to show it to the officers. "I can't make her wake up."

There were three other bags around the woman's head. The melt left rings under each one. There were no signs of a struggle. The room was neat and tidy. The body showed bruising around the woman's throat and there was swelling around her left eye.

***

"CSI's been here, right?" Detective Jim Broaden called out before entering the apartment.

"Yeah," Officer Pendrage called back. "Been here."

"Great," Broaden said, walking down the hall. "I hate those damn booties and that plastic shit."

"PPE," his partner Jane Levitt said.

"What?"

"That plastic shit is called personal protective equipment."

"Really?" Broaden said sarcastically as he walked into the bedroom. Levitt lagged behind talking to the officers.

Broaden stood over the bed, hands on his hips. "Looks like she was strangled," he said to Levitt who he felt at his side.

"Ya think?" she answered, leaning over the body. "ME will make it official."

The five feet tall, five feet wide Detective Jane Levitt and six foot, six-inch Detective Jim Broaden had been a team for seven years. They could complete each other's sentences. Her shape, dark bangs and hair cut short to the bottom of her ears, made her look like a Russian Nesting Doll in a floral, Batwing dress. She carried a large leather purse the size of luggage. Broaden, the opposing image, elegant in an Italian-cut suit and pocket square, the colors always matching his tie. Lanky. All arms and legs.

Levitt straightened. "She's on top of the covers. The bed is undisturbed."

Broaden said, "Sad, really sad."

"Aren't they all?

"'Course," Broaden answered as he walked to the far side of the bed and studied the room. "This place is immaculate. Like she just cleaned it."

Levitt leaned close to the face of the woman. "Black eye. There was some kind of struggle."

"Then someone must've tidied up," Broaden said as he came around the bed and stood next to his partner. "Anything from the kid?"

"According to the officers, and the two women who found her, he didn't say much, other than he came in this morning, ready for school, and found her like this."

"Anyone ask him about the towel?" Broaden waved his hand over the bed. "It looks out of place. Like it was put there to cover her up. The kid, maybe?"

Levitt shook her head. "Kid's at the station. We can get into it then." She took a deep breath and backed away from the bed. "Fuck. The kid finds his mother like this and tries to help her with those," she said, pointing at the vegetable bags sitting in puddles on the bed. "Fuck," she repeated and walked out of the room and down the hall toward the living room. Broaden followed.

Pendrage and Lattimore, looking out the floor-to-ceiling bank of windows at the early morning joggers and walkers in Central Park, turned toward the detectives as they came into the room.

"I think this would be called minimalist," Levitt said, scanning the space. A cream-colored couch faced two similarly designed metal-framed linen armchairs. A large black rug covered the floor, leaving a frame of space revealing a wood floor. A Boahaus Kashley bar cart was centered against the wall opposite the windows. Two shelves were lined with a variety of rums, a bottle of vodka and gin. Bottle racks for wine on either side of the cart held a selection.

Lattimore offered, "Did you notice how" – he raised his chin – "clean and tidy everything is?"

"We're noticing," Broaden said. "The bedroom too."

Levitt gestured toward a door to the left of the cart. "Boy's room?"

"Yeah," Pendrage answered. "Doesn't share a wall with the mother's room. Guess that's why he didn't hear anything."

"He didn't hear anything?" Broaden asked as he and Levitt walked toward the door. "He tell you that?"

"We asked if he heard or saw anything last night or this morning," Lattimore said, "and he said 'no.'"

Levitt stepped on a baseball as she walked into the room and pitched forward. "Shit," she blurted as Broaden caught her by the elbow. Steadied, she glanced around at a typical boy's room. Bunk beds, a toy box at the head of the bed. A chest of drawers to the right of the door, the drawers open with clothes spilling out. A closet door ajar, clothes on the floor, along with a variety of single shoes and more toys. "Whoever kept the rest of the house so tidy didn't spend much time in here."

As they walked back into the living room, Lattimore volunteered that, "The sliding door to the balcony was open when we came in. It was freezing."

Broaden approached the sliding door. "This was open?"

"Yes, sir," Lattimore answered.

"You close it?"

"Didn't touch it. CSI dusted it and closed it."

Broaden opened the door and stepped onto the balcony. He peered over the side and studied the surroundings. Coming back into the living room he said, "That wasn't the way in."

Pendrage said, "Maybe he opened it to keep the place cold to preserve the body."

"If he was trying to do that, why leave the front door open?" Lattimore said.

Broaden asked, "The front door was open?"

Lattimore and Pendrage both nodded.

"Then, no," Levitt said. "Leaving the door open invites people to stick their noses in, check out what's going on. Preserving the body would mean the perp wanted to keep them out. For a while anyway."

"Not to mention there was the boy who would find the body as soon as he got up," Broaden said.

"Could be he didn't know about the boy," Lattimore answered.

Levitt shook her head. "Whatever. It isn't about preserving the body. There's gotta be another reason."

***

"Well, that was useless," Levitt said as she followed Broaden out of an interrogation room.

"These are 'ladies who lunch' and consider it a catastrophe when they break a nail," Broaden answered as they walked down a dingy corridor, the floor sticky with spots of spilled coffee and soft drinks; the walls yellow and still holding the faint smell of cigarettes. "Finding a body isn't part of their world. That's for other people."

"Like us." Levitt screwed up her face in disgust. "They left the kid alone with his dead mother. How fucked up is that?"

"Not being able to get the kid away from his mother...okay, I can see that, but one of 'em should've stayed with him."

They walked into the break room. "Fuckers," came from Broaden as he held up an empty coffee pot. He opened doors in a cabinet lining one wall, eyed the empty space and slammed them shut. "Where are the Goddamn filters?"

"Underneath the sink," Levitt said. She sat in a bright yellow plastic chair at a Formica topped table in the center of the room and read from a piece of paper. "Regina Wozniak. Home is Kalispell, Montana."

"A world away," Broaden quipped as he lined the drawer of the coffee machine with a filter. "Wozniak? In Montana? I always thought of cowboys and stuff, not Wozniaks."

"You'd prefer Earp or, uh...?" Levitt said, waving her hands in a circle as she struggled for a name. "John Bonham, maybe."

"John Bonham was the drummer for Led Zeppelin," Broaden said, scooping ground coffee into the filter. "You're probably thinking of Bonney. William Bonney."

"Who was?"

"Billy the Kid."

Broaden filled the machine with water and pressed a red button at the base.

"Okay, then Earp or Bonney. Just not Wozniak. Doesn't fit."

Broaden drummed his fingers impatiently as the coffee pot filled.

"Pendrage and Lattimore are doing a door-to-door in the building," Levitt said. "Maybe they'll come up with something useful. I'll call out to Kalispell and see what I can find."

Broaden brought two cups of coffee to the table and placed one in front of Levitt who wrapped her hands around the cup. "How do you want to handle questioning the kid?"

"There will be someone from Child and Family Services with him. They usually know how to frame the questions so we get what we need."

"This is my first with a kid," Levitt said. "We just sit there and listen?"

"Pretty much, but what I've done before is pass notes to whoever is with them and they know how to ask the right way."

"The 'right way'?"

Broaden shrugged. "Yeah, so it doesn't scare the kid. Shut'em down. Let me guess. You don't have any children."

"Fuck you. You know I don't."

***

They stood in front of the two-way glass looking into a room set up for children. Legos and colorful blocks were strewn across the rugged floor. Boxes of games and iPads were arranged in a bookcase that also held toy trucks, Matchbox cars, and an assortment of dolls.

"No TV," Levitt observed.

"Too much of a distraction, maybe," Broaden said.

"Could turn it off."

"Try that when it's got a kid's attention."

The boy sat in a child's chair at a short-legged table and fiddled with crayons, occupying himself with random strokes across the page. A woman sat cross-legged on the floor next to him. She watched him attentively.

"Here we go," announced Broaden and opened a door into the room.

As soon as Levitt and Broaden entered, the boy's eyes saucered. He asked, "Is my Mom okay?"

Broaden and Levitt looked to the woman, a question in their raised eyebrows and tilted chins.

She laid her hand gently on the boy's back. "These people want to ask you some questions."

"But is she okay?" the boy asked insistently looking from the woman to the detectives, his chest heaving.

"There are other people who we can talk to you about that," the woman answered, her hand now stroking the boy's back.

Levitt and Broaden looked around the room. The woman saw the question in their eyes and said, "There aren't any chairs you'd be comfortable in. Sit down next to us." She lowered her hand, palm down, and mouthed "Intimidating."

Levitt gathered some pillows and reached a hand out to Broaden who helped her settle. He took off his suit jacket and folded it carefully, hitched his pants and sat. He tried to find a comfortable position for his long legs, opting to extend them straight out in front of him and leaned back, his arms supporting him.

"Well, that was fun," Levitt said, catching her breath. To the boy: "I'm Jane and this is Jim."

The boy stared at them, expressionless.

Levitt nodded at the woman, a signal to begin the questioning.

"Can you tell them what happened at home this morning?" the woman asked.

"I found my Mommy on her bed and couldn't wake her."

"From the beginning," the woman said. "From the time you woke up."

"I always get up by myself. I have an alarm clock and it wakes me up at seven. I wash and brush, get dressed and go to the kitchen where my Mommy makes me breakfast. She wasn't in the kitchen so I went into her bedroom. She was lying there not moving. I couldn't wake her so I went to the refrigerator and got the bags she puts on my head when I don't feel good. I put them on her head, but she didn't wake up."

"Then your friends came and saw what happened, right?"

"Lily first. She ran away and Katie came. She wanted me to go with her, but I didn't. She left."

"They went to call the police to help your mother."

The boy lowered his head and his shoulders began jerking as he tried to hold back his tears. "They came and took her away."

The woman offered the boy a bottle of water and a tissue.

Levitt passed a note to the woman, which she read, nodded, and asked, "Did you hear anything last night or this morning?"

The boy cocked his head in question. "Like what?"

"Like anything you don't usually hear in your apartment," Broaden asked. The woman stared at him.

"No," the boy said, shaking his head, his brow knitted.

"Did your mother have any visitors last night or this morning?" the woman asked, her eyes on Broaden, letting him know she had this.

"No, we watched a show about elephants and went to bed. Lily comes in the mornings to take me to school."

"She does that every morning?"

The boy nodded.

"Can you tell us about her other friends? Give us their names?"

"No."

Broaden craned his neck toward the boy, then looked at the woman, eyes wide, his arms raised in question.

The woman asked, "Why can't you tell us about her other friends?"

"She doesn't have any. Just Lily and sometimes Katie."

"Nobody else?"

"Not like them. Sometimes a man comes to give her stuff."

"What kind of stuff?"

The boy raised and dropped his shoulders. "I don't know. Mommy told me once it was stuff she did for work. That's all."

Levitt scribbled a note and passed it across the table as the boy was talking.

The woman asked, "Does your mother always sleep like you found her?"

"In her bed?" the boy asked, obviously confused by the question.

"On top of the covers."

"No, she never sleeps like that, and she has pajamas."

"So, she always wears something when she goes to sleep?"

The boy nodded. "I put a towel over her this morning. She would never want anyone to see her like that."

The woman read a note from Broaden and asked, "She really keeps your house clean. Is it always like that?"

The boy shook his head. "I'm messy. That's what she says and I leave things around the house."

"Does she always clean up before bed?"

"No, Martha does that."

"Who's Martha?"

"The lady who puts my stuff away and cleans all the rooms." The boy smiled, which caught everyone by surprise. "My mother is like me. She's messy."

"Martha must have been there recently," Levitt said, directing a look of apology toward the woman.

The boy folded his hands together and stared at the paper with his crayon-painted lines. A beat before he answered. "No, we left things on the couch last night and we didn't clean up after dinner." He let his eyes shift from Levitt to Broaden. "The kitchen was clean this morning and nothing was on the couch."

***

"Before we get to the cleaning part...," Broaden said. "That kid looks exactly like his mother, right?"

"He's going to be a stunner," Levitt replied.

"I didn't want to say anything before, you know, like it's 'too soon', but she was gorgeous. And I'm not saying that it's worse when someone like that is..."

Levitt raised her hand. "I know. I get it. I get the same vibe whenever it's someone young. And this lady was young, and what you said, gorgeous. Plus, she has...*had* a kid. A deadly trifecta."

"Okay, how does someone get into the apartment," Broaden asked, "kill her, then – it looks like – clean up the place, all without the boy hearing anything?"

"Someone who's done this before," Levitt answered. "Probably a lot. I asked Pendrage and Lattimore to get a copy of CCTV recordings for the night of and the morning after."

"You saw cameras?"

"In the lobby. None in the elevators or public hallways. I don't know about outside the building."

"Now begins the dreaded slog. Going through hours of CCTV recordings and all the rest of it. Talking to her employer, friends, and I'm sure there are more than just those two ladies."

"I'll start with a call to Kalispell," Levitt volunteered.

"I'll start with the CCTV."

Chapter 2

Walkabout

He checked his phone. He had about five hours of dark.

He walked down the steps of the Plaza, stood on the sidewalk facing 5th Avenue, and surveyed his domain. Which way tonight? Left toward Museum Mile or right to Carnegie Hill? Would it be the Guggenheim, the Metropolitan Museum of Art, the Goethe Cultural Center or the upscale neighborhood and hip bars and restaurants?

He stared across the street at Central Park and opted for a different direction altogether. He would visit Tavern on the Green on the edge of the park's 15-acre Sheep Meadow. Close by and it offered the opportunity to wander through the park.

His choice proved entertaining. At the valet station in front of the restaurant he watched a man who had one too many attempt to hijack a horse drawn carriage. Cold-cocked by the carriage driver, abandoned by his date, the man was tossed into a cab by a security guard.

He went against the grain when it came to spending time in Central Park during the darkest hours. Too dangerous according to conventional wisdom; when bad things happened; when muggers hid behind rock outcroppings and monuments ready to pounce. Not true. Or at least not that he had ever experienced. It was true that people not fit for the light roamed the park after dark. The kind who could not or would not mingle. The kind who renounced the "day people" whose rituals they found impossible to accept, or they simply could not deal with the crowds, the noise, the turmoil. It created anxiety – shattering them sometimes – chasing them away to hide during the day; when they slept with the rats and feral animals behind dumpsters in the grimy alleys slick with detritus produced by the throngs, or in the darkened nooks deep in the bowels of the subway.

Night people like 'feather man' who appeared from the grove of lilac trees surrounding the Sheep Meadow. He collected bird feathers, mostly from pigeons, and pasted them all over his clothes, braided them into his hair. He glided around the park whistling and chirping, waving his arms, running, his knees high. He did that all night, and he was not a young man.

There was also the clan that gathered on top of the rock outcroppings in the dense vegetation of the Ramble; the base from which they "patrolled and governed" the park every night. They had a code. Anyone could be there, but no one could be mean. They defined "mean" as fighting, yelling angrily, intimidating others, annoying the animals in the zoo or making a mess in the restrooms. They were tolerant of those who talked to the voices in their head, sometimes loudly. They understood. If they did not want someone in the park, they would swarm them, walk them to the 59th or 110th Street exit, or sometimes one of the avenues, either 8th or 5th, and deposit the person onto the sidewalk. It was forceful but rarely violent. He was approached periodically and interrogated, which was how he came to know the "governors." It was because of how he was dressed, neat and clean, newer clothes. Expensive walking shoes. Sunglasses and always a hat with side and back panels. *Where are you from? Where do you stay during the day?* The answers surprised them.

He left the park after his usual walk around the Bethesda Fountain where he came once during the day with his father – and only once. It was a good memory, which was why he always visited the fountain on his trips into the park. His father had pointed at the statue of the angel on top of the 26-foot sculpture and told him that the lily in the angel's left hand symbolized the purity of the water, and the four figures arrayed around the base represented Peace, Health, Purity and Temperance. There was so little else he remembered about his father, he had no idea why he remembered that so vividly, other than it was one of the few times he was allowed out during the day. Those day trips, in fact all day trips, stopped when he was seven.

The other day trip he recalled was to D'Agostino's market. He went there with Eloise before he was shut away. After that he visited with her at night, just before Bert D'Agostino closed at eleven. In recent years, he visited alone. Bert always offered a smile, a nod. He had seen the boy grow up. Knew about him. Now a man, he walked around, enjoying feeling where people *had* been, without having them around. And he relished the vibrant colors of the vegetables. The greens. The reds and yellows of the peppers. His world otherwise was mostly dark colors and just plain darkness.

This night, he made his way from the park to the theater district. A bit of a hike, but he enjoyed the activity of the stagehands bustling in and out of the buildings, busy doing whatever it was they did after every show. The front doors to the theaters were usually open when he passed by as cleaning crews came and went allowing him a peek inside. He strode past the Eugene O'Neill Theater, Henry Miller's, the Longacre, Lunt-Fontanne, the Majestic and the Music Box. His favorite was the Al Hirschfeld Theater. It had a free-standing ticket booth like the ones in old movie theaters, and columns with ornate Moorish designs. The line of glass doors were framed in bronze. He could picture huge spotlights piercing the heavens and limousines depositing women in gowns and men in top hats and tails at the curb as people crowded the sidewalk waving bits of paper seeking autographs while reporters with flash cameras and small notepads rushed forward for a word or two. To him, it was magical.

He prized his walkabouts; an opportunity to hike the empty streets, take in the wealth of window dressings behind the glass of closed storefronts, walk through the canyons of buildings where the stars were permitted only slivers of the sky.

The beeping of his phone alarm warning him of the coming daylight caught him in the middle of the block across from the 5th Avenue entrance to the Plaza. There a man stood erect, not moving a muscle, staring up at the building. The figure remained stock still as if cemented to the sidewalk. He remained with his arms pressed to his side for some time before stretching his arms wide and beginning a cross-legged dance down the block, his attention riveted on the building. At the end of the block the man bowed deeply and walked away.

He felt himself smiling. Could be the strange man was paying homage to a celebrated piece of the city's history. There were few who truly appreciated the roots of the Plaza as part of that history. He did. He had lived in the building all his life, where his father came as the chief architect and overseer for Western International's acquisition and renovation of the Plaza, a position he retained as the property changed hands a number of times. His father earned a share in the ownership of the Plaza while supervising countless renovations as well as guiding the conversion of the property to a hotel and residence. His father was among the first purchasers of an apartment, a penthouse on the 21st floor acquired for an attractive sum – a bow to his special connection to the property.

The conclusion of the evening took him across 5th Avenue to his usual spot in the Grand Army Plaza across from the building's front entrance. He leaned against the base of the statue of William Tecumseh Sherman and took in the ornate façade. It never failed to impress with Tuscan-style columns supporting a wide balcony on the second of twenty-one floors. The facing was a riot of columns, pillars, balconies and elaborate towers, spires and steep roofs.

Built in 1907, the Vanderbilts, Goulds, Harrimans and Guggenheims were among the first guests, a fact his father always included in his lectures about the Plaza, which he would deliver to anyone who would listen. He absorbed his father's regard for the hotel, doing his own research and learning that F. Scott Fitzgerald and his wife Zelda, along with Enrico Caruso and Frank Lloyd Wright stayed there. Peggy Lee, Liza Minelli, Robert Goulet, Dusty Springfield, the high society bandleader Eddie Duchin, and whoever was the hot ticket of the day, headlined in the various salons. He spent hours watching films shot or set in the hotel. His favorites were *North by Northwest, Barefoot in the Park, Plaza Suite* and *The Way We Were*.

As dawn announced in ribbons of purple and pink lacing the spires of Manhattan – his unique last call – he took in the elaborately lit Pulitzer Fountain, before heading to the Central Park South side of the building. He went into the entrance here, never the front. Though early, the activity there was hectic at that hour with hotel staff preparing the restaurants for breakfast. The smell of bacon wafted. The clattering of dishes, pounding footfalls and shouting was too much for him. That, and he preferred not to be seen, although he knew most of the employees by sight, many by name. When employed at the Plaza, people tended to remain for a lifetime of service. It was a prestige position. Over time, he ran into them on elevators, in corridors, even sometimes at night when he was beginning or returning from his walkabout. Individual encounters he could handle. It was the collection of people and the din of their voices that unnerved him. He preferred the solitude.

The Central Park South entrance was originally the main lobby. A mezzanine loomed over the foyer which was a showroom of veined Italian-marble, gold trimmings, and a mosaic floor overseen by a glittering crystal chandelier hanging from an ornately designed ceiling pocked with sunken panels.

As was often the case, he could not help himself and peeked into the Oak Room just beyond the foyer. Though closed as a restaurant for years, it was well kept and used for special occasions. According to his father, the Oak Room was a faithful reproduction of German Renaissance design. The oak walls – decorated with frescoes of Bavarian castles and faux wine casks carved into the woodwork – shined with care. The most impressive feature, for him, was the brass chandelier and its large hanging, grape-style ornaments. The fabled Oak Bar was a few steps beyond and he peeked into the space where Dorothy Parker, Ernest Hemingway, Truman Capote, Jimmy Breslin and others drank and pounded down the famed platters of oysters.

In nearby rooms, the morning activities were becoming frantic as daylight filtered in and ate the shadows. Most of the increasing noise and clatter came from The Palm Court in the center of the ground floor. The showpiece of the restaurants in the hotel with its stained glass ceiling and colorful mosaic floors would soon be overrun by the breakfast crowd.

As the bronze elevator doors closed behind him he felt a sense of relief the enclosure always provided. No matter how invigorating his time out, he was on a timer, a warning signal when to turn around. The feeling of safety brought in full relief a reminder of the consequences of getting caught out in the daylight.

The elevator whisked him to the 21st floor and the penthouse apartment. His was among the largest of the 181 condominiums occupying the eleventh through twenty-first stories. Always a magnet for the rich and famous, the Plaza became a coveted residential option after the conversion. This was a problem for him as it meant attention from the paparazzi who too often found ways to evade building security. There was a special entrance to clear visitors. No one was allowed in without an "okay" from a resident. There were regular sweeps of the hallways. All doors that permitted an entrance to the residences were double locked and alarmed. Still, it was not uncommon for someone to come knocking hoping for an ambush photo, or attempting to find a source for a story or exposé.

Still and all, the Plaza was worth it. He loved his home.

***

A very loud and harsh "Mr. Warren Winston" assaulted him as he pushed through the heavy walnut front door. He was in trouble.

Pinch-faced and angry, a small woman, hurried toward him, waving a pair of sunglasses. "If I've told you once...."

Warren completed her sentence. "'I've told you a thousand times.'"

"Don't get sassy with me," she said. "You could go blind, you idiot."

Eloise Fletcher stood five feet tall and weighed ninety-five pounds. She stared at Warren, hands on her hips, mouth pursed. Angry she was fearless and formidable. "You're too old to punish, but please," she said, her face relaxing. "Please," she pleaded, holding up the sunglasses, "take these whenever you go out."

Warren took the glasses from her and kissed her gently on the cheek. "I'm sorry. I promise I will."

She inspected him closely. "Is that UPF 50 material?" she asked, pointing to a long-sleeved pullover under his quilted goose down vest.

Warren nodded and raised his leg. "And so are these joggers."

Eloise cupped his face in her hands. "How are you feeling?"

"Good." And he did. Despite his condition, and the challenges it presented, he was a broad shouldered, robust, tall man. A lock of thick black hair fell across a broad forehead, his skin not pale, but a shade with less melanin than average. He maintained a toned figure, working out in the well-appointed resident gym late on those nights he was not walking about.

Eloise considered him a moment before dropping her hands from his face. She turned and walked away from the front entrance toward the living room around which the 3,700 square foot, three-bedroom, three-

and-a half bath apartment sprawled. Walls extended to 11-foot ceilings on three sides. A panel of heat-strengthened, half-inch glass faced the living room and would have offered a stunning view of Central Park were it not behind thick blackout curtains. Persian rugs covered most of the walnut herringbone flooring. A Swedish modern couch, love seat and chair were surrounded by artwork, both wood sculptures and paintings, which Warren knew little about except they were expensive and admired by people who knew about such things.

He followed Eloise into the chef's kitchen where she commanded a central island on which sat a mixing bowl, cutting board, vegetables – finely sliced tomatoes, green peppers, onions and radishes – and a slab of uncut bacon. Butter was melting in a copper pan over a low flame on the Viking stove that occupied the wall behind her.

"Omelet or scrambled?"

"And now I'm going to say something I've told you a thousand times. 'You don't....'"

It was Eloise's turn to complete his thought and she did in a sing-songy cadence: "'Have to wait up for me.' Well, I didn't. I got up an hour ago and couldn't get back to sleep."

"You don't seriously think I believe that, do you?"

"I don't care if you do or not." She waved a hand. "Now, go wash up."

"Omelet," Warren called over his shoulder as he walked out of the kitchen and crossed the living room toward his bedroom.

The apartment had been the perfect size when his parents were alive but since they passed – his father seven years ago and his mother two years after – he felt as if he was rattling around in the space. He moved into the master suite complete with fireplace, expansive walk-in closet and an ensuite bathroom with double vanity. He sometimes joked with Eloise that since he could not fill the closet with his clothes, he was going to convert it into a basketball court.

But they could not move. The apartment was outfitted to accommodate his special needs. Not only the blackout curtains, which could be replicated anywhere, there were other conveniences. A dumb waiter traveled from the penthouse kitchen to the Palm Court restaurant kitchen making it possible to order meals and deliver groceries, and anything else that would otherwise require a trip outside the building.

There was also the valued location of the apartment directly across from an elevator making Warren's comings and goings as convenient as possible. He never had to navigate distances in the lighted hallways. Most significantly, Warren's father had attracted the family physician to the Plaza making him an offer on an apartment he could not refuse. Two floors below the Winstons, Dr. Engberg was available to make house calls. Although the need for this attention was rare, the occasional bump or bruise had to be tended to with urgency, and there was the time or two when accidental exposure to light aggravated Warren's skin and required attention.

Plus, there was Eloise. She had dug in and would not be open to a move. It took Warren almost a year to convince her to move from her small bedroom behind the kitchen into his larger one after he took the master suite. Initially she argued that being steps from the kitchen was more convenient than in a bedroom down the hall, but that argument fell apart when she heard her own words. The difference between ten and twenty steps was no difference at all. "I'm comfortable where I am," came next and then "there's no need to change after more than 20 years." She argued determinedly that she had made the room her own with Native American wall hangings and other personal touches, including multiple shelves displaying a collection of antique German Bisque Dolls. She finally agreed to move after an intense campaign by Warren that included her agreeing to stay in the room for a week, as a test. She could not deny the comfort.

It took the death of Warren's parents for Eloise to fully understand and accept her indispensability to the household. Without her, Warren would lose his Praetorian Guard. Acceptance brought a "new" Eloise to the fore. She took greater initiative and made her voice known on matters she had previously held her tongue. The sunglasses being the most recent, if somewhat trivial, example.

Eloise had been hired by Warren's mother after he spent two miserable years in school. Granted it was a private school, and very exclusive, still his condition prevented him from bonding with the other students. He could not participate in activities other than classroom instruction and he had to be accommodated for his special needs. It set him apart and the reminder of his 'otherness' was in his face every single day. He wore hats when other students did not. He had to apply special ointments that were not only visible, they also smelled. He remained behind in the classroom when others went outside for recess or physical education. He could not go on much coveted field trips to museums, the theater, the New York Library, and, once, to a baseball game at Yankee Stadium. He was different and it hurt.

Eloise was more than a nanny. She was a tutor as well as a nurse educated to attend to Warren's unique situation. There was not a subject she could not help him master, except, initially, trigonometry. For that he had a special tutor and Eloise sat in on every class during which she became proficient enough to teach him herself. The tutor was gone within a few months. She was Warren's minder, setting his schedule, one that fit his needs. That included finding ways to keep him safe and active. Teacher. Nurse. Chef. Coach.

Over time, Eloise's role expanded beyond what she did for Warren. She assisted Mrs. Winston organizing annual employee appreciation occasions such as the Christmas and Easter parties. She also managed charity events that Mrs. Winston sponsored, the most important was for Jimmy Carter's Habitat for Humanity during which she served as the liaison between the NYPD and the Secret Service. She also took on work for Mr. Winston, keeping his "confidential" schedule of meetings with residents of the Plaza who did not want – or who Mr. Winston did not want – to be listed on his public schedule. One such occasion involved arranging for Princess Diana to dine with the Winstons and a select few Plaza residents. Eloise was often called on to organize and secure the privacy of events for other residents.

Showered and hungry, Warren returned to the kitchen and a fully packed omelet replete with cheddar cheese, vegetables and a side of bacon.

"I saw the strangest thing tonight," he said between mouthfuls.

"Just tonight?" Eloise quipped as she wiped down the stove. "Wandering around New York in the middle of the night you should be seeing a lot of strange things. I've never been comfortable with you doing that, and never will be."

"I know, I know, but – and I'm going over old ground – it gets me out. I'd go crazy spending twenty-four hours a day, seven days a week cooped up in this apartment."

"I do. I manage. You could find a way."

"No, you can go out whenever you want. And you do. There's a big difference. Again, we've talked this to death."

Eloise stopped her cleaning and smiled. "I said I wasn't comfortable with these walkarounds of yours, not that..."

"'Walkabouts.'"

"Walkabouts," she said with a nod. "Right, and I am not comfortable with them, but I understand why you need to get out. Now" – she said with a dramatic swipe of a cloth across the top of the island – "what about this strange thing you saw?"

"As I was coming back, I saw a man doing, uh, well..." Warren shook his head. "I'm not sure what the hell he was doing. It looked like it was some sort of dance of praise to the Plaza."

"A dance of praise?" Eloise leaned forward resting her elbows on the island. "Like what? Bowing or something?"

"Yeah, kinda like bowing and" – he raised his arms – "doing this and looking up at the building. Then he danced up and down the sidewalk. Doing some kind of Irish jig or something."

Eloise straightened and returned to her cleaning. "Yes, that is strange, but I'm betting it isn't the strangest thing you'll see if you keep up your walkabouts."

"I'm going to keep them up and, yes, I agree. I'll see stranger."

Chapter 3

19th Precinct

Broaden followed Levitt into Nadine Robinson's office where they stood, hands resting on the backs of two chairs facing her desk. Robinson did not acknowledge their presence. She was focused intently on a document she held in her hands. The moment extended into a quiet that was becoming uncomfortable when Robinson looked up, sighed heavily and declared, "This" – she waved the pages before laying them on her desk – "is from the mayor. She has a lot of friends living in the Gramercy." Robinson stared at the detectives. "Oh, for Christ's sake, sit down," she demanded.

Commanding Officer Robinson had been in charge of the 19th Precinct for three years, an area covering the Upper East Side of Manhattan, one of the most densely populated residential neighborhoods in the city. She was the first woman, and the first African-American to hold that position. Often considered an easy assignment, it was not. On the plus side, the Upper East Side was the home to some of the wealthiest people in the city. They were the best educated; attended the best schools; patronized the best restaurants; and shopped at the high end stores in the city along Lexington, Madison and 3rd Avenue all gracing the Upper East Side. Crime was low and law enforcement officers were at lesser risk than almost anywhere else in the city. That also meant the expectations of the residents living in a cocoon of privilege were very high. Any crime, no matter how incidental, was inexcusable, and murder was cause for outrage.

Robinson, her hand on top of the pages she had been reading, said, "She also has friends living everywhere else in the 19th. Friends as in people who support her with huge campaign donations and have tremendous influence within city hall. They are very unhappy that someone was murdered in their neighborhood."

"Really?" said Levitt. "Imagine that."

Broaden cringed waiting for the blowback.

Robinson leaned forward – her eyes slits of intensity – placed her elbows on the desk, and looked down at the document in front of her. "The mayor says she's considering asking CSU and other NYPD bureau detectives 'to provide us with assistance.'" She took a deep breath and stared hard at Broaden and Levitt. "I don't want that. Do you want that?"

Her question was met with silence.

"That wasn't rhetorical."

"No, ma'am," Levitt answered.

"Then stop with the wise ass remarks and do your job."

Commander Robinson inspired and also frightened her officers and detectives. A large woman, more than six feet, broad shouldered, with the hard body of the Olympic rower she was not so many years ago, she caused heads to turn and people to step out of her way.

"Tell me about the progress you're making on the Wozniak case."

Levitt said, "The ME confirmed she was strangled and has ruled it a murder."

Robinson smiled without any joy reaching her eyes. "I know that."

"Officers Pendrage and Lattimore conducted interviews with almost everyone in the building and...."

Robinson interrupted. "Almost everyone?"

"They need to complete the process. Some people were not home or..."

"Okay, okay," Robinson said with a dismissive wave. "What'd they find out so far?"

"The victim was not well known by anyone. Even the woman who was her neighbor and took her boy to school every day didn't give us much. Wozniak rarely went anywhere and worked from home."

"What kind of work?"

"Freelance writer."

"Who'd she write for?"

"She had a couple of clients. PR firms."

"Talk to those people."

"Did that," Levitt said. "Not much there. They corresponded almost entirely by email or in Zoom meetings."

"She never met with any of them in person?" Robinson asked incredulously. "Never?"

"Not that we've been able to establish," Broaden pitched in. "We've scoured her computer and phone. All of her correspondence with the people she wrote for, clients of the PR firm, went through the firm."

"There was no direct correspondence with the people she wrote for," Levitt clarified. "But we did find out that she was recommended to the firm by a man who lives in her building."

"So, go talk to him."

"We have. Phone interviews. He said he met her in the business center in the building. The Gramercy has a pretty large business center," Levitt added. "It was where a lot of the residents worked during the pandemic."

Robinson scoffed. "Might as well have gone into their offices."

Levitt continued, "He said he found out she was a writer. She let him read some things she wrote. He recommended her to the firm she did the work for."

"What about whoever was her intermediary with the clients she wrote for? She must've reported to someone who dealt directly with them. Right?"

"Nothing there. All Zoom meetings and phone calls. Some emails. No personal connection," Broaden said, adding, "The vestiges of the pandemic live on. You'd have thought it would end when the bug died down. It hasn't. Phone and Zoom reign supreme. "

"Forensics?" from Robinson.

"The scene was compromised by the kid and...."

"The kid?"

"She has...*had* a kid. He was trying to revive her when we got to the scene. Other people had been in the room before CSI got there. Rape kit. Nothing. The perp used a condom and probably wore gloves."

"Any thoughts?" Robinson asked expectantly.

"There are a lot of things that don't make sense," Levitt said. "She was living in one of the most expensive buildings in the city. Her son went to an expensive private school, but from what her bank records show..."

"You got a warrant for those, right?" Robinson asked.

Levitt made a face. "Of course we did. From what we could find, there's no way she could afford any of that on what she was making. No deposits into her account other than what she earned, which wasn't much. And I thought cops were underpaid."

"What's next?"

"There's some other stuff that doesn't wash."

"Like?"

"Like the woman who took her son to school every morning said Wozniak was from Kalispell."

"Where?" Robinson asked.

"It's in Montana. I checked that out with the major crimes unit there."

"Kalispell has a major crimes unit?" Robinson asked.

Levitt nodded. "Yeah, and there's no one living there named Wozniak. Not now, not ever."

"Could be her married name," suggested Robinson.

"We tried to trace that back," Levitt said, "and we can't get any information on her past beyond eight years ago. Her driver's license, social security number and her bank accounts all begin then. Nothing we can find any further back than that. Like she dropped to earth then."

Robinson drummed her fingernails and nodded her head. "Send the information we have on Wozniak's murder to that crime data gathering unit in the FBI. The, uh...?"

"ViCAP," Levitt interjected.

Robinson squinted in question. "The Violent Crime Apprehension Program? I thought that was used to track serial killers."

"It is," Levitt agreed, "but it also compiles information on sexual assaults. Might get lucky."

Robinson nodded. "Follow up with your buddies around town. Maybe there are similar cases we can glean something from."

"We did that," Levitt said. "We sent out a questionnaire asking for feedback on similar crimes, similar MOs. Murders in upscale apartment buildings. Strangulation with a kid in the residence where the scene was basically undisturbed."

"More than undisturbed," Levitt said. "It looked like the entire apartment had been scrubbed."

"Yeah, I heard," Robinson said. "One of the officers who was first on the scene caught me in the break room. Perplexed him. That and the open door to the balcony. Any thoughts?"

"Not yet," responded Levitt.

"Which brings us to this," Broaden said, lifting a handful of files from his lap. "Answers some of the questions we sent around on that questionnaire. Probably should have dug these up first. Anyway," he said and placed the files on Robinson's desk, "it ain't good."

Robinson eyed the files. "You don't have anything for me except stuff that 'ain't good'?"

"I went through the system looking for similar cases," Broaden said. "Went back five years and didn't find anything. I decided to dig around in the morgue. The boxes. Hard copies. There are boxes of files that have never been entered into the system." He tapped the files on Robinson's desk. "Like these. They were in a box dated 2015. That's after everything was supposed to be in the system. These should've been. They weren't."

"Why not?" Robinson asked.

"You're not going to like the answer," from Levitt.

"I'm already not liking this," Robinson hissed. "What's in the files?"

Broaden opened one of the jackets. "In 2015 a woman was found strangled and naked in the Hampshire House." He looked up at Robinson. "She had a kid asleep in another room." He leafed through the pages of a second file. "In 2016, in the Ritz Carlton. Same MO." He turned the cover of a third file. "2017, in Trump Parc. Same MO."

"Holy shit," Robinson let loose.

Levitt said, "We're thinking he might've controlled his victims by threatening to harm their kids."

"All of them were single mothers?" Robinson asked.

Broaden and Levitt nodded.

"You're saying we have a serial killer rampaging through the Upper East Side."

"That's the last thing in the world we want to say," Broaden answered. "There was a person-of-interest in each case, but the names have been redacted."

"What the fuck?" Robinson said loud enough to draw attention from the squad room. Eyes went to the glass wall separating her office from the rows of desks and clattering computers. "What were the files doing in the morgue? And why the hell wasn't the information entered into the system?"

"Can't answer that. The name of the investigating officer is there. It's the same detective in each case. He should've entered them."

Robinson flipped through the jackets, running her finger down the pages. "Dick Warner. I know him. He was a good detective. Retired three years ago when I was coming onboard. I asked him to stay at least a year. He didn't." She sat up straight and handed the files back to Broaden. "Go talk to him. Find out what the hell this is all about."

"One other thing," Levitt said. "We have CCTV from the night Wozniak was killed."

"And?"

"The only people coming and going are residents of the building."

"Are there cameras on the outside of the building?" Robinson asked. "In the elevators?"

"Not in the elevators. Residents thought it was intrusive."

"Bet they'll reconsider that now," Robinson said.

"There is CCTV around the side of the building, in the alley," Levitt said. "Caught some homeless people squatting there. Our guy could be one of them. Pendrage and Lattimore are on it and will track them down, see if they have anything for us."

"That it?"

"Pretty much," Levitt said as she and Broaden stood.

Broaden stopped at the doorway. "There is that guy the concierge saw dancing around the building."

"What?"

"The concierge said when he was coming into work that morning...."

"'That morning' being when the body was discovered?" Levitt clarified.

"He saw a guy dancing is how he described it. Dancing around in front of the building. Bowing and stuff like that."

"Can he describe him?" Robinson asked.

Levitt shook her head. "We asked and he said he didn't think much of it. Just thought it was another crazy and he avoided him."

"Every detail," Robinson said. "I want every detail covered. Go back and talk to the concierge. Get more." She waved a hand at Broaden. "Stay a minute, Jim. Close the door on your way out," she instructed Levitt.

"Sit," Robinson said. She waited until he was settled before asking, "How's Maddy doing?"

"As well as can be expected."

"Anything new?"

"She's undergoing something called Gamma Tile Therapy. Supposed to be tougher on the tumor, but easier on the patient."

"Is it easier on Maddy?"

Broaden stared past Robinson and waited a moment before responding. "Hell, I don't know. She's the bravest little girl I've ever seen." He cleared his throat. "Rachel and I spend half our time crying and Maddy cheers us up. Can you believe that?"

Robinson winced. "Jesus, I'm so sorry."

"There is some decent news, I suppose. Maddy is gonna graduate at the top of her class at Erasmus Hall and was in line for a National Merit Scholarship. John Leopold...you know him?"

"I know of him. A developer. Lots of money."

"That's the one. He graduated from Erasmus. Every year he pays for four years of college for the valedictorian. That's Maddy, and Leopold found out about her. He's paying for her treatment at Sloan Kettering. He set her up in one of his apartments at the Plaza so it's easier for her to get to the hospital. He has a car take her to the treatments and back out to Brooklyn for school."

"She has treatments every day?"

"No, not every day, but she stays in the apartment. It's easier on her. Rachel stays with her sometimes."

"Look, Jim, you should probably take some leave yourself. Be with your daughter."

Broaden shook his head vigorously. "No, if I did that, Maddy would know how bad it is."

Robinson pulled back her head in surprise. "She doesn't know?"

"She knows it's bad. She knows it's brain cancer."

Robinson closed her eyes and sat back in her chair. "I'm about to step way over the line here, Jim. I know I'm doing it, so hold your fire." She took a deep breath and exhaled. "My mother had breast cancer and no one told us kids. There were four of us. I was the youngest. Like with Maddy, we knew it was bad. You could take one look at my mother and see that, but we were never told how bad. When she died it was like someone ripped my guts out. I wasn't ready. I felt I'd been betrayed, and I resented my father for years for not saying anything. I know there isn't a direct correlation between what I went through and Maddy's situation, but not leveling with her...is that really the best way to go?"

"We want to keep her dreams alive. Give her some hope. A reason to fight to live. If we say something, well, that hope is gone because the God's honest truth is she's not ...." Broaden stopped and shook his head.

"I appreciate that, and I respect it, of course, but I'm guessing she knows and isn't letting on to save you and Rachel from knowing she knows. I'm talking in circles a little bit here, but maybe she's strong enough to share the truth with, and still keep hope alive."

Broaden stood. "You're probably right and she does know. I'm just not strong enough to find out that she does."

Chapter 4

Ball and Crow

"Thanks for seeing us Detective Warner," Levitt said as she and Broaden were met at the front door by a diminutive, thin, dour-faced man.

The pedigree of this middle class neighborhood was captured in the clapboard home; the second story wrapped in aluminum siding. A chain link fence surrounded a tidy, postage stamp size yard. Trash cans lined driveways up and down the block.

"Not Detective," Warner said as he ushered them down a short hallway, the walls garnished with family photos. "Thankfully retired," he said pointing to a cloth covered, green and blue patterned sofa. He sat opposite them in an overstuffed recliner. The surface around a cup holder showed signs of rot from spilled liquid.

The house smelled of cigarettes and cooked meat, the kitchen visible behind Warner.

"So," he said, pushing himself into a slightly reclining position. "What can I do for you?"

Broaden opened one of the file folders he had placed on a coffee table in front of the couch and handed Warner a sheaf of pages. "What can you tell us about this case?"

Warner reached into his shirt pocket and lifted out thick-framed reading glasses, which he settled near the tip of his long, thin nose. He lifted his eyes to Broaden and Levitt after a quick glance and handed the pages back to Broaden. "Sorry, can't help you. I don't remember much about that case."

"'Don't remember *much*?'" Levitt said slowly. "Tell us what you *do* remember."

Warner removed his glasses and stared hard at Levitt. "What's this about?" Suspicion in his voice.

"A woman was recently murdered and" – Levitt retrieved the pages from Broaden and waved them at Warner – "it has all the earmarks of this case, and others you investigated." She glanced at the files on the coffee table. "Those."

Warner shifted his weight, snapping the recliner forward, bringing him to his feet. "You want some water or anything to drink?"

Levitt and Broaden shook their heads.

"I do," Warner said. He walked to the refrigerator where he fiddled with a water dispenser. "Tricky," he said over his shoulder as he filled a shiny, green metal container. "Been meaning to get it fixed." His voice quavered. He made a slow return, settled on the recliner and took a long sip of water.

"What can you tell us?" Levitt said.

"We had a person-of-interest. Didn't pan out."

"Why didn't it pan out?" Broaden asked.

"It's been a long time. I don't remember the details, but I gotta think it's because the guy had an alibi, or something."

"Or something?" Broaden said, a challenge in his response.

Warner took another pull from the container and sat a moment before responding. "Like I said, it's been a long time."

Broaden opened another file. "Can you tell me why the name of the person-of-interest has been redacted in all of these reports?"

Warner shrugged. Having been on Broaden and Levitt's side of similar discussions many times, and knowing what signs of deceit or nervousness they were looking for, he fought to control his body language, maintain eye contact and not fidget. "Don't know. Probably because we had nothing and were closing it out."

"Was that a thing then?" Levitt asked, moving forward on the couch. "To scratch out the name of someone you cleared?"

"Wasn't *my* thing," Warner replied with insistence. "I didn't do that."

"We figured that or you would've scratched out your name also," Levitt said. "Someone did a sloppy job of covering up. Or maybe not. Threw you under the bus. Maybe that was the aim."

Warner screwed up his face. "What do you mean, 'threw me under the bus'?"

"We have an unsub and his MO is exactly like your guy's. Single mother. Strangled her, cleaned up the scene, and probably threatened to kill the kid to control his victim." She took the files from Broaden and placed them in Warner's lap. "A serial killer."

The three sat in silence, Broaden and Levitt staring at Warner, who let his head drop against the back of the recliner. The only sounds came from the kitchen. A faucet dripped and the second hand on a wall clock ticked.

Warner broke the silence, snapping forward in the chair, grabbing the files to keep them from sliding off his lap. "My guy was convicted of rape. He had his sentence increased because of previous convictions for assault and all kinds of other shit. He was a fucking psycho and the last I heard, he was gone. Would never be out. Ever. Life."

"Okay," Levitt said approvingly, "but that doesn't explain the redactions."

"First," Warner said, "you tell me how he got out."

Broaden let out a noise, a sound of exasperation. "We don't even know who the fuck he is, thanks to you. And that's assuming we're talking about the same person. How the hell would we know how he got out?"

Warner bent forward, arms on his legs and bobbed his head. "All I got is a pension and some Social Security. Barely making it. Had to refinance the house to cover my wife's health costs. She has MS." He paused a beat. "I feel like a real loser heaping this on you, but I can't lose my pension."

Levitt glanced at Broaden, then back at Warner. "That's a helluva start."

"Yeah," Warner said, "and there's a real 'wow' finish, but you gotta promise me you won't go after my pension."

Broaden said, "We're detectives. We can't promise shit. You know that. What we do know is if you didn't get rid of that name that means someone else did. Someone who it looks like protected a serial killer. Might still be doing it today, and just like we found you, we'll find them. And when we do, they'll throw you under the bus so fast you won't even feel the wheels grinding you into jelly."

Levitt pressed, "We're giving you a chance to get on the right side of this and if we don't have to bring you into it to get the job done, we won't." She jabbed her finger on Warner's leg. "But if you don't help us out, for sure we'll be back when someone points the finger at you. And, like Jim said, they will. We can dismiss what they say as BS and keep the focus where it belongs. Now where does the focus belong?"

"It was Willis Reasoner," Warner said through an extended exhale.

"Reasoner?" Broaden and Levitt blurted simultaneously. Levitt added, "The Governor?"

"He was police commissioner then," Warner said. "Reasoner was a big supporter of Ray Sims when he was running for the Senate. As I heard it, Sims promised to support Reasoner when he ran for mayor, before he ran for Governor, if he did this."

Levitt held up her hand. "Stop. Did *what*?"

Warner nodded at the files. "That."

"You're saying Willis Reasoner, when he was police commissioner, was responsible for the redactions?" she said, gesturing toward the files. "And he did it for Sims when he was running for the Senate? Why?"

Warner nodded. "Remember Sims was Governor then and he was catching a lot of shit from his opponent...."

"His opponent in the Senatorial race?" Levitt asked.

"Yeah, he was catching it from him and from the press for his budget cuts that stripped mental health programs of state funding. That forced a lot of people out of state psychiatric hospitals. Ended up moving them from state hospitals to nursing homes, group homes, boarding houses, whatever, but most didn't stay. They just walked out. Sims also supported some kind of bill that got rid of involuntary hospitalizations. Part of the budget cuts and that moved most of the really serious crazies out of state hospitals. That was when the homeless thing went nuts. I remember seeing a lot more of 'em on the streets after that.

"Anyway, Sims was getting pounded. The crime rate exploded and he was getting called on it because a lot of it was from mentally ill people. Sims disputed that and he had all kinds of experts who said it wasn't what he did that caused the spike. That it was from other stuff. I forget all the details. Anyway, the point is that Sims was panicking. He was way ahead in the race until the hits on his mental health stuff starting coming and he was fighting to stay ahead. That's when James Braddock began his one man crime spree."

"Who?" from both Broaden and Levitt.

Warner put his hand on the files in his lap. "The man whose name is crossed out. James Braddock. He was one of those people who walked out of a halfway house after he was released from a mental health hospital. Just left. He was one of a lot of 'em. He was about the worst, but there was a bunch." Warner eyed Broaden. "These were all you found?" he asked, lifting the files.

"They were in a box. I pulled them out because of the MO. Matches what we're looking at."

"Take a close look at what else is in that box. All those jackets are people who were mental health patients. You got assaults, robberies, indecent exposure. Rape. And with Braddock, murder."

"All the names in those other files have been redacted?" Broaden asked. Warner nodded.

"Reasoner pimped for Sims" Levitt said. "Fuckin' incredible."

"Actually, what Sims asked was that we get Braddock put away, but not on the murder thing. Something else. Less sensational. Something that wouldn't attract much attention. Something the press wouldn't want to look at too closely and maybe uncover way too much shit. Sims didn't ask Reasoner to let Braddock go or anything like that."

"You waited until you could get him on the attempted rape and assault charge?" Levitt asked, pinching her face in disgust.

Warner shook his head. "No, we didn't wait. We knew what he was, what he would keep doing. We went and got him."

"Made up some shit?" Broaden asked.

"The shit was there. We just had to fill in some blanks. Bottom line he was put away. We never thought he'd get out."

"And the others?" Broaden asked. "What happened with them?"

"You mean that are in that box. The others in that file box?"
Broaden nodded.

"If it was petty enough, we just let 'em skate. If it was serious like armed robbery or assault, we charged 'em, but never let on about their past; about having been in the nut house. Kept that off the radar so no one would start putting two and two together and figure out that all these people who had been put on the street could be tied to Sims. That was the concern."

"We need to get hold of Braddock's parole officer ASAP," Levitt said, grabbed the files from Warner, jumped off the couch, and headed for the front door, Broaden in her wake.

Warner followed them out the front door. "What about...?"

"You better hope you never see us again," Levitt called to him over her shoulder.

***

As soon as Broaden and Levitt were in the cruiser, she got to work on the computer. "Braddock's PO is Mel Carp."

She tapped hurriedly on the face of her phone.

"I don't know how you do that," Broaden said. "I think I'm hitting the right key and three of the wrong letters pop up."

"Mel Carp? This is Detective Jane Levitt with the 19th Precinct. I'm trying to track down James Braddock."

Carp's voice came through the speaker. "Yeah, he's one of mine. Bad dude."

"How long has he been out?"

"Three years."

"When was the last time you met with him?"

"Never have. He never reported in. I put his name in the system for pick up but it's been crickets. The guy has gone to ground. He could be anywhere."

"We think he's in the city."

"Really? What makes you think that?"

"Fuck," Carp spit after Levitt briefed him.

Broaden asked, "How the hell did this guy get released?"

"Overcrowding. Believe it or not, he was a model inmate. Took college courses. Even graduated with an associates' degree and tutored other inmates."

"Terrific," Levitt said. "A psychopath with smarts."

"Get him off the streets," Carp said insistently, "or you'll have more bodies."

As she tapped off the call, Levitt suggested, "We need to re-interview that guy who recommended Wozniak for her job." She shoved an arm into her purse.

"How do you ever find anything in that black hole?" Broaden asked.

"Like this," Levitt answered, pulling out her notebook. She ran her finger down a page. "Daniel VandenHeuval." She shook head, closed the notebook and waved it in front of her face. "He seems to be the only one who actually dealt with her face-to-face."

"There's also that thing about the man dancing around the Gramercy," Broaden said. "What the doorman saw. We can hit him up on that when we're there."

***

"Cecil, right?" Broaden said to the deadpan scarecrow of a man standing behind the desk in the Gramercy lobby.

"Not SEE-cil," the man huffed. It's CEH-cil."

"My bad," Broaden said. "Got a question for you. You said you saw a man acting strangely the morning Ms. Wozniak's body was discovered. Right?"

Cecil nodded. Broaden and Levitt waited for more. They got a blank stare.

"Can you tell us a little about that?" Broaden asked.

"He was skipping around on the sidewalk in front of the building. Bowing too. I avoided him."

"What did he look like?"

"Like I said, I avoided him. Couldn't tell you."

"Short or tall?" Levitt prodded. "Skinny? Fat? How was he dressed?"

"He was tall, looked like maybe medium build and wore dark clothes."

Again, they waited. Again, they got nothing more.

"Can you tell us which apartment, uh...?" Levitt rummaged in her suitcase of a purse and fished out the notebook. "Mr. VandenHeuval lives in?"

"I have to call and let him know you want to visit," Cecil droned.

"Sure," Broaden said. "In the meantime," he turned toward the bank of elevators, "we'll head up. Apartment?"

Cecil held up a finger as he brought the phone receiver to his ear. "You have two officers who..."

"Detectives," Levitt said loudly enough to be heard by the person on the other end of the line.

"Detectives," Cecil said. He placed the receiver in the phone cradle. "Mr. Daniel VandenHeuval is in 1209."

Walking toward the elevators, Levitt offered, "That's one weird dude."

***

Broaden nodded to the right as they stepped off the elevator. The plush red rug, thick navy blue border, sank and sprang with their footsteps. A door opened as they approached.

A man stepped into the hallway. "Come in," he said, a slight accent evident. Germanic. "Daniel VandenHeuval," he said, offering his hand as they passed him and walked into a foyer.

Broaden and Levitt stopped a few steps into the apartment and waited for the man to pass them. A slight almost petit person, narrow shoulders and hips giving him a shapeless silhouette. His pallor very pink, slight features topped by a thick head of graying blonde hair. VandenHeuval was dressed comfortably in khakis, a robin's egg blue cashmere sweater over a collared white shirt and loafers, no socks.

"This way," he said, leading them through the first door along the hall. Bookshelves lined three of the four walls. The fourth was a bank of windows. The room was warmer than the hallway and smelled of a hint of vanilla, which Levitt commented on. "I've had many people tell me that," VandenHeuval said. "I was curious about it and asked the owner of a book store who said it is from Lignin, which is present in all wood-based paper, and is related to vanillin. As it breaks down, the lignin grants old books that faint vanilla scent." He guided them to an arrangement of leather armchairs in front of a large fireplace. "I'm sure that is way more information than you needed or wanted."

As they sat, he said, "I'm not sure how much more I can tell you about Ms. Wozniak." He squinted, bringing his barely visible blonde eyebrows together in a display of concern. "Of course, I'm happy to help in any way I can."

"We're hoping you can fill in some blanks," Levitt said. "No one seems to have known her very well. Even her neighbor who took her son to school most mornings couldn't give us more than that her family was from Kalispell, Montana. And that has turned out to be a problem."

"A problem?" VandenHeuval said. "How so?"

"We called Kalispell and came up empty. No Wozniaks live there. Never have according to city records."

"Yes," VandenHeuval agreed with a nod, "that is curious."

"You seem to be the only one who had any personal contact with her."

"That wasn't much more to it than what I've already told you."

"You recommended her for a job," Levitt said, reading from her notebook. "Cushman and Styles Strategic Communications."

"I did, yes, as we have discussed. I know Mr. Styles and he is always looking for writers. Ms. Wozniak was a writer and I pointed her in his direction."

"You must have been confident she could fit the bill if you felt comfortable recommending her."

"This goes back to what I've told you about our running into each other at the office center in this building. I found out about her writing. Read some of it. It was good. She seemed like a nice person, so, yes, I was comfortable making the recommendation."

"Did you have any other contact with her?"

VandenHeuval shook his head. "Not really."

Levitt asked, "What does 'not really' mean?"

"I'm sorry, I should be more specific given the circumstances." VandenHeuval crossed his legs and folded his hands together, resting them in his lap. "I saw her occasionally after she began working and asked how things were going. She told me she was writing articles for CEOs and other senior executives with companies that used Mr. Styles' services. Those articles were placed in internal publications mostly, but also in professional journals. I read them. Mr. Styles told me he was satisfied with her work. He thanked me for the recommendation. That was pretty much it."

"We're baffled by a few things," Levitt said. "She lived at this expensive address and sent her son to a very exclusive school. Do you know if Mr. Styles paid her well enough to afford this?"

VandenHeuval smiled broadly. "No, that is definitely not anything I would know. Frankly, I assumed she came from a wealthy family."

"Did she ever discuss her son with you?"

"Other than responding when I asked how he was doing, no."

"Nothing about the boy's father?"

VandenHeuval shook his head. "No."

Levitt and Broaden looked at each other, their signal to wrap things up, and stood.

"If I can think of anything else," VandenHeuval said, as he walked with them into the hallway, I'll be in touch."

As they stood waiting for the elevator, Levitt glanced at Broaden. "You get the feeling he was leaving out stuff?" Then, both their cell phones vibrated. Levitt's "Oh, shit" was overlaid by Broaden's, "Fuck, that's where Maddy is."

***

Broaden used the speaker megaphone and flashed his grille and dashboard lights to open a lane through the crush of press and onlookers in front of the Plaza. "What the hell?" he said as they coasted to a stop behind an ambulance and fire engine, and a black and white cruiser.

"It's the Plaza," Levitt said, leaning a shoulder against the passenger side door, pushing it open. "As soon as word got out over the scanners that something was going on here, where the rich and famous live and play, all the antennas went up."

Levitt and Broaden climbed the stone stairs, where they stopped and took in the nest of satellite dishes poking from the top of the mobile video trucks parked outside yellow police tape.

Levitt said, "This is going to be a circus," as they walked into the lobby of the Plaza. They crossed the colorfully designed marble floor, under the Swarovski chandelier, around a marble table holding a two-foot high floral decoration and approached the registration desk. Their attention was diverted to two officers standing in front of a bank of elevators.

"You the first ones on this?" Broaden asked.

Pendrage nodded.

"You were at the Gramercy scene, right?" Levitt asked.

"Our neighborhood," Lattimore answered.

"All we know is that a body was found," Broaden said. "What's the deal?"

"Dorothy Provine," Lattimore answered. "Single mom. Strangled. Don't know any more than that."

"Scene look like the one at the Gramercy?" Levitt asked.

"Carbon copy," Lattimore said with a nod. "Crime Scene is up there now. Apartment 1100."

"Why don't you check in on Maddy," Levitt said to Broaden, "and meet me after?"

"She's at school," he said, gesturing toward the elevator. To Pendrage and Lattimore: "No one but our people upstairs. Ride with whoever wants to use the elevator and make sure they stay off the 11th floor, unless they live there. If they do, escort them to their apartment."

As the doors closed, Lattimore said, "Ball and Crow."

"What?" Pendrage asked.

Lattimore thumbed toward the elevator. "Ball and Crow." In response to the question in Pendrage's eyes, he added, "Bowling ball and Scarecrow. Levitt and Broaden."

Pendrage snorted out a laugh. "Never heard that before. Perfect."

***

"Maddy doing okay?" Levitt asked as the car jerked into motion.

"She's getting the best care possible."

The elevator doors opened to a riot of noise and crush of bodies. Radios chirping, PPE-clad bodies checking IPads, EMTs standing idle next to gurneys, emergency fire response in full regalia.

"I thought we are talking one body," Broaden said to no one in particular as he threaded his way toward an open apartment door.

"I'm guessing we are," Levitt responded, "but like I said, this is the Plaza. Fire and rescue. EMTs. They're like everyone else. Curious."

As they started into the apartment a woman held up her hand. "This isn't your first rodeo." She pointed to a box holding PPE coveralls, booties and a head cover.

"What's with the cast of thousands?" Broaden asked as he struggled into the outfit that did not cover his limbs entirely. He wrestled with his booties, wobbling and falling against the door.

"More on the way. Got word your CO is in the building."

"Cue Flight of the Valkyries," Levitt said, holding Broaden by the elbow as he fitted his second bootie. She could not fully close the PPE across her chest and stomach.

"*Ride* of the Valkyrie's," said Broaden.

"Fuck you," from Levitt.

"And these," the woman said, offering masks. She watched as they covered their mouths before turning and leading Broaden and Levitt down a hall, past a kitchen, to the other side of a living room, and toward a bedroom.

Shuffling half in and half out of the PPEs, they looked like a comedy team in a slapstick movie.

The crowd thinned as they neared the bedroom where two investigators, and a body on the bed, occupied the stillness.

The CSI hovering over the body held out her arm. "Stay where you are. When we're done you can do your thing. I can tell you with some certainty that she was strangled and raped."

"Probably the other way around," Levitt said, drawing a cold-eyed glare.

"We were told there's a kid," Broaden said.

"He's with a neighbor. The one who found her," the CSI said with a nod toward the bed.

"Room's immaculate," Levitt said with a sweep of her arm.

"Yeah, it is," the hovering CSI said and straightened, looking around as if noticing the surroundings for the first time.

"Looks like it's just been cleaned," Levitt added, turned and walked into the living room. A white leather couch and matching chairs were the focal point. A wine cabinet stood against the far wall. A large china cabinet sat outside a dining area to the right of the living room where a small table was set with chargers and a cornucopia centerpiece spilling wax fruit. "Same in here. Bet there's no dust on any of the surfaces."

Broaden walked to the sliding glass door leading to a porch. "Was this open when you got here?" he asked, turning to the investigator who had followed them from the bedroom into the living room.

"Yes. It was freezing in here."

"Can I?" Broaden asked, pointing at the door handle.

"Knock yourself out. We got nothing from it. If it was opened by the perp, he musta worn gloves."

Broaden slid the door aside and walked to a clear plastic barrier, looked up, down and to either side. Back in the living room he shook his head, saying to Levitt, "That was definitely not a point of entry or egress."

"'Egress,'" she said teasingly. "You mean he didn't leave that way?"

"Fuck you."

"Egress," Levitt said, scoffing. She ducked her head into the bedroom. "Which apartment is the kid in?"

"Across the hall," from the CSI.

"It would have been useful to know we couldn't do anything in there," Broaden said with a glance at the bedroom, "before trying to fit into these." With that he started shedding the PPE.

"Detectives," got their attention. Nadine Robinson stood at the apartment door crooking her finger at Levitt and Broaden.

"What do we have?" Robinson asked as they approached. She backed into the hallway, which was now empty. Her doing, no doubt.

"From what we know, a single mother, probably strangled," Levitt reported. "I'm going to go out on a limb and say she was raped."

Robinson took a deep breath. "Like what we had at the Gramercy, right?"

"Yes, ma'am," Levitt said, "and when you factor in what we found out from Warner...."

"You talked to Dick Warner? Robinson interrupted, her eyebrows arched.

"Yeah, and given that in there," Levitt said, turning her shoulders toward the open door, "and what he told us, we have a big fucking problem."

"A *big fucking* problem," Robinson said and blew out a sigh. "Like this" – she looked past Levitt into the apartment – "isn't bad enough? You can brief me on Warner later, but right now, we have a pack of hungry wolves downstairs who I have to feed. Not just locals either. We've got national media ready to pounce. We're already hearing 'serial killer' and 'maniac' and that kinda shit."

"Who linked this to the Gramercy?" Broaden asked. "We haven't released any details have we?"

Robinson shook her head. "Just the usual two or three paragraph press release. No details. I don't know how anyone linked them. My guess is that some ambitious son-of-a-bitch looking for a Pulitzer took an interest in what happened at the Gramercy, got a leak on those details, made some guesses about this one," – she nodded at the apartment – "and is drawing their own conclusions." She crossed her arms and stared at her feet. "Hell, *we* don't even know what we have yet." She looked up, staring down the hallway. "There have to be three bodies before we can begin talking about a serial killer."

"That," Broaden said, jerking his head toward the hall, "plus the Gramercy, and what Warner told us, means it's likely we *do* have a serial killer."

"Fuck," Robinson said, turning away from Levitt and Broaden and taking a few steps down the hall. Returning, she asked, "What exactly did Dick tell you?"

"That's gonna take a while to explain," Broaden answered.

"And we don't want to do it here," Levitt added.

"My office in an hour. For now we aren't going to even hint anything about a serial killer. That freaks everyone out." Robinson looked from Levitt to Broaden. "That is the *real fucking problem*, right? The serial killer?"

"Part of it," Levitt answered.

"Really? *Part of it*?" Robinson said. She began moving toward the elevator, drawing Levitt and Broaden with her. "I'm not going to feed the wolves. I'm not going to engage. I'm going out through an employees' exit." She tapped a text on her phone. "If my driver doesn't see this and you see him in front when you leave, tell him where I am. What's next for you?"

"Talking to the kid," Levitt said.

"Okay," Robinson said. "Nothing to the media vultures when you leave. Wade through the horde and be gone. I'll tell comms to issue a statement. Figure out how to say nothing that sounds like something. Maybe 'It's an ongoing investigation and we will provide information when it is appropriate. We have two of our best investigators working this.' We'll include your names and some of your 'greatest hits' to support the 'two of our best' thing. No mention of the Gramercy. No way do we want to link them." With that, Robinson got on the elevator and smiled stiffly as the doors closed.

Levitt and Broaden stood a moment staring ahead. Levitt broke the silence declaring, "Well, fuck me."

"Christ," Broaden added. "We're gonna be the faces of this...uh, whatever *this* is. Shit rolls downhill, and with what we found out, plus the pressure that's gonna come once everything is on the table, we're gonna get crushed."

"I guarantee you that 'everything' will never be on the table," Levitt said, turning away from the elevator door. "But what ends up on the table will be bad enough. Now, let's go talk to the kid."

"We can't do that until someone from Child Services is with him."

"Do we know it's a 'him,'"? Levitt asked.

"There's a 50/50 chance."

Levitt indicated a door across from the victim's apartment. "Let's go see."

***

The door opened and an elderly woman, her round face tight with worry, tried for a smile, her thin lips stiffening into an awkward grimace. Her eyes, a faded blue, were rheumy. Full cheeks had melted into jowls.

Broaden flashed his most reassuring smile. "I'm Detective Jim Broaden and" – turning to Levitt – "this is Detective Jane Levitt. We understand that you're watching Ms. Provine's son."

"Yes, please come in," the woman said, moving away from the door allowing Levitt and Broaden past her.

"Larry is in my sitting room," she said, moving into the hallway. She squeezed her terrycloth bathrobe closed around her throat. "He's a delightful young man," she said and stopped at the entrance to what Levitt and Broaden could see was a kitchen. "I haven't told him anything." She pressed a crumbling tissue to her mouth. "I heard someone say that Dorothy was dead. Terrible," she said softly. "Awful."

Levitt reached out and put a hand on the woman's trembling shoulder. "Could we get your name, please?"

"Lois Chandler," the woman replied.

"You're very kind to look after Larry, Ms. Chandler."

"Of course, of course," she replied, her eyes wide. "It's all such a shock. Finding her like…." Chandler's knees buckled.

Broaden grabbed Chandler's arm and led her to a bench seat in a breakfast nook. Levitt searched cabinets on either side of a stove finding a glass that she filled with water from a dispenser on the refrigerator door.

Broaden sat down next to Chandler. Levitt stood in front of her. They waited until she sipped from the glass and regained her composure before Levitt said, "We'd like to talk to Larry but we have to wait for Child Services before we can do that."

"She's here."

"There's someone here from Child Services?"

"Yes, she told me she got the call from someone doing whatever it is they're doing to Dorothy." Chandler collapsed into tears.

Levitt glanced at Broaden who raised his eyebrows. She sat down on the other side of Chandler and put an arm around the woman's shoulder. "We've been doing this for more years than I'll admit and it's always a shock. Always sad and tragic." She stroked the woman's back and pointed Broaden toward a box of tissues on a ledge beneath the cabinets. "Before we talk to Larry, we'd like to ask you a few questions whenever you're up to it."

Broaden handed Chandler the box of tissues.

"Do I have to go with you to the police station?" Chandler managed through sniffles.

"No, we can do it here where you're comfortable."

"Okay," Chandler said, uncertainly. "I'm not sure what good I'll be to you."

"Whatever you can tell us will be helpful," Broaden said. "Start at the beginning, from the time you went into the apartment."

Chandler blew her nose, retrieved another tissue and wiped her eyes. She sat up straight and cleared her throat. "I got up like I do every morning, thank the Lord, and after washing and brushing, went across the hall and knocked on Dorothy's door, as I do every morning. She is… . Oh, God." Chandler took a deep breath, and fought off another crying jag. "She *was* an executive at a publishing company. We have coffee together and then she gets Larry ready to be picked up for school. Dorothy has a car service for that. I usually walk him downstairs and wait until he's picked up. This morning no one answered her door. That is very unusual. Dorothy gave me a key to her apartment for emergencies. I would never take advantage," she said earnestly, "but this worried me so I got the keys and let myself in."

Chandler fell silent. Her shoulders began to tremble and she gripped her hands together tightly. She let a moment pass, cleared her throat, and resumed. "I found her lying on her back in her bed. She was nude and cold to the touch. I called 911 and brought Larry here."

"He's doesn't know what happened?" Levitt asked.

"He was fast asleep. I hustled him out of there. No, he has no idea what happened."

Levitt asked, "Did it look like anyone had broken in? Was the lock tampered with?"

Chandler stared ahead and shook her head slowly. "No, there was nothing like that. The door was locked, and after I let myself in, I called out for Dorothy and got no reply. Then I went into the room and found her."

"Any sign of a struggle?" Broaden asked.

Chandler shook her head. "No, but it was very cold. The door to the balcony was wide open."

"Anything else grab your attention?"

Chandler paused a beat before answering, "Her room was very tidy."

"And that was unusual?" Levitt asked.

"It was out of character for Dorothy," she said with a touch of embarrassment. "She was a lovely person and a wonderful mother, but not a very good housekeeper." Chandler squinted in concentration. "Now that I think about it, when I went to check on Larry, the living room was also unusually clean. Dorothy and Larry used to eat dinner in front of the TV and when I came in every morning, there were dishes all over the place. I would pick them up while she got Larry ready and put them in the dishwasher. This morning the kitchen was very neat." She lowered her head, stared into her lap. "Yes, that was different."

Broaden and Levitt waited a moment to allow Chandler to add to her recall. When none came, Levitt asked, "Do you know any of Dorothy's friends? Did she have a steady boyfriend?"

Broaden gave Levitt a look.

"She went out occasionally, and I would sit with Larry, but nothing steady. She always said she was too busy whenever I asked about that kind of thing. I didn't pry."

"What about Larry's father?"

Chandler shook her head. "All she ever said about that, and I never pressed her, was that he wasn't in the picture. That's exactly how she described it. 'Was not in the picture.' Oh," she said, stood, walked to the kitchen counter, opened a drawer, lifted out a business card, and handed it to Levitt.

Levitt read, "Dorothy Provine, Executive Vice President, Trident Publishing Company." She handed it to Broaden. "Thanks. We'll be in touch with her people there. Now, would you take us to Larry?"

"Yes, of course," Chandler said, pushed her hands against her thighs to prop herself up, but faltered. She raised her arms toward Levitt and Broaden. "You're going to have to help an old lady up. This shit..." She looked embarrassed. "So sorry. A slip of the tongue. This is weighing on me. Sapping my strength."

Helped to her feet, she took a moment to steady herself and shuffled forward a few tentative steps before declaring, "I'm good. The bedroom is toward the front door."

"A boyfriend? Broaden whispered as they trailed. "What was that about? We know who it is and I doubt he's boyfriend material."

"Habit," Levitt said. "The questions come from a permanent script tattooed somewhere up here," she added, tapping her forehead.

Chandler stood in the doorway, a forced smile crossed her lips. "Larry, there are some detectives who would like to speak to you."

A dark haired boy in Spider Man pajamas was sitting on the floor in front of a flat screen television. High-pitched voices came from pink and green cartoon images. He turned his attention to Broaden and Levitt as they walked into the room.

"Hello," Levitt said.

"Can I see your badges?" Larry asked.

"Of course," Levitt said.

Broaden pulled his suit coat aside at his beltline revealing his silver shield. Levitt knelt next to the boy, dumped the contents of her purse on the rug and sorted through a mound that included her phone, a compact, crumpled tissues, takeout menus, pencils and pens, her notebook and a keyring. "Here it is," she declared triumphantly. She raised the emblem in front of Larry, who nodded approvingly.

"I'm Jane," Levitt said, as she swept the contents of her purse back into storage. "And this is Jim. Can we ask you a few questions?"

A woman sitting in an armchair in an alcove at the far end of the room muted the television volume and stood. "We've met before," she said. "All too recently."

Levitt nodded her recognition and asked, "Would you mind if we...?"

The woman motioned Levitt and Broaden to her. Talking softly, she said, "You can try but I don't think you're going to get anything." She nodded at the boy who was staring at the silent screen. "He's been sitting like that for an hour without moving. The only words he's spoken were to ask you to see your badges. If we can't find a relative soon, I'm going to take him to the hospital. I think he's either in shock or on the way there."

Levitt sat down next to the boy. "We need your help with something."

The boy looked at her. His thousand-mile stare told Levitt she was not going to get anything useful. She placed her hand on the boy's shoulder and squeezed gently. She got no reaction.

Levitt pushed off the floor and gestured at Broaden and the woman to follow her into the hallway. "What happened to the other kid?" she asked the woman. "The one from the Gramercy?"

"Out of our hands."

"Out of your hands? What does that mean?"

"It means the boy is not in our system."

"He's with family?"

"I honestly don't know. I was 'asked'" – the woman curled her fingers – "to sign release papers. That's all I know."

"The child has disappeared?"

"I noticed the name VandenHeuval on the signature line next to mine."

Chapter 5

A Stalker

"Please, stay home," Eloise pleaded. "A person was found dead in this building yesterday afternoon. There's a mad man running around out there."

"That mad man is far away from here," Warren replied. "He's not going to stay anywhere near the scene of the crime."

"Oh, well, thank you for that Sherlock."

"Elementary, and just common sense."

Eloise put her hands on her hips, feet planted wide, and stood in front of Warren. "This is crazy." But she knew he was out the door no matter what she said. "Do you have your sunglasses?"

Warren wagged them in front of her face. She slapped his wrist and tugged his long-sleeved UPF-protective pullover down over his wrists. She lifted the hoodie onto his head and touched his cheek. "SPF-70?"

Warren nodded. "Slathered."

"This is your Christmas run, right?"

"The first one. I'll probably make a couple more. Can't see everything in one night. This is New York," Warren said, arms raised.

"Saks has the train set running. I saw that today, and Bergdorf Goodman has most of its window decorations up. Don't know about Macy's. Didn't get by there."

"I'll catch FAO Schwartz along the way."

"My favorite," Eloise said. "That giant nutcracker says Christmas."

"See, you have the spirit," Warren said as he slid past Eloise and headed to the front door. "I'll probably do Radio City Music Hall and Rockefeller Center too."

"That means lots of lights," Eloise said, pointing at the sunglasses. "Wear those." She interrupted Warren, who she knew was going to complain about 'looking strange with sunglasses on at night.' "No, excuses."

"No excuses," Warren agreed. "Since it's the first Christmas run" – he said, opening the front door – "I'll cut it short...a little." He stood in the open doorway. "To make you happy. Consider it an early Christmas present."

He was tempted to stop on the eleventh floor for a quick peek, but stayed the course. The Central Park South entrance to the building was free of police and press, who were still congregating around the corner on Fifth Avenue.

Warren walked to Madison Avenue, down to 57th Street, and turned onto the block with the crème de la crème of retail shopping in the city. Chanel. Dior. David Yurman. St. Laurent. Louis Vuitton. All with elaborate window displays beckoning a celebration of Christmas in the most expensive manner possible.

It was invigorating for Warren. The colors. The imaginative displays of clothing, jewelry, accessories of every shape and size. His enjoyment was tempered with caution. He zig-zagged from one side of the street to the other keeping a careful distance from the lights, taking it all in from a safe distance, which is how he viewed the lively activities at Rockefeller Center. The giant Christmas tree annually topped out at 100 feet and was strewn with three million crystals. Pretty but dangerous.

This being "the happiest time of the year," and celebrated in New York City as nowhere else in the world, or so New Yorkers told themselves, people were out late in large numbers, especially at Rockefeller Center. The skating rink was packed.

Warren found a secluded spot overlooking the rink and began his classification of the holiday skaters. There were the "see me" types, twirling, skating backward, leaping and maneuvering figure eights. There were the "young lovers" who propped each other up, likely an excuse to manhandle one another. And Warren's favorites, those who had no idea what they were doing and appeared to be having the most fun trying to stay upright, especially the children who managed the most spectacular falls and popped right up, sprawling again and again.

From Rockefeller Center it was a short distance to St. Patrick's Cathedral, another stop along his annual Christmas tour. As he approached, Warren began to feel an uncomfortableness in his shoulders. It was almost like a weight, a heaviness. He worried that he had triggered an aggravation of his XP. Maybe he had not been as careful as he should have been. Had he gotten carried away by the goings-on and not taken the proper precautions? Gotten too close to the lights, or spent too much time near them?

Standing in the shadows of the park behind the Cathedral, eyes closed, concentrating, he conducted an inventory. No tingling in his limbs. No unusual sensitivity – such as itching – anywhere on his body. His eyes did not ache or feel irritated. Warren opened his eyes and took a deep cleansing breath. None of the symptoms had flared.

It must be the excitement. He rarely spent time where people were congregating. Long ago, he had cut himself off from interactions with others; actually that had come as a consequence of being sheltered due to his XP. Over time, Warren discovered he was not comfortable in social situations. He had not honed his social skills which made interactions – when they occurred – uncomfortable. Plus, his recollection of the experiences he had with others as a child were negative. Ridicule. Pity. He was often considered off-putting as he got older. He heard 'Asperger's' whispered more than once. He never bothered to respond. It would have provoked a conversation. He was most comfortable alone.

He felt movement behind him. He turned. Nothing. Was he being targeted by a mugger? "Shit," he said under his breath and hustled from the shadows of the park to the front of the spired cathedral. Warren walked up the stairs to the front doors and stood watching from the shadows of the recessed entrance. No one had followed. He relaxed and turned toward the massive doors, reached out and ran his hand along the surface decorated with images of various saints. He was always amazed at their size. Almost 17 feet high and 6 feet wide – cast in bronze – they weighed more than 9,000 pounds apiece.

He walked down the stairs to the sidewalk and stared up at the 156-foot tall central gable flanked by soaring towers. Thirty seconds of this and his neck began to ache.

He decided to keep his promise to Eloise and cut the walkabout short.

About the time he passed the Museum of Modern Art, Warren again felt that heaviness. The discomfort in his shoulders. This time he identified the feeling. Someone was watching him. He was certain of it. Had it been a mugger, there were plenty of opportunities for the person to strike. They had not. It was not a mugger. He did not feel threatened. He was curious. How to play it? He decided to march ahead. Not give any indication that he was on to the game, if it was a game. It had to be. Had someone noticed his wandering and become curious? That had to be it. He would plow on and see if he could find a way to ferret out the tracker as he neared the Plaza. Double back on them or dart down stairs below curb level near a basement apartment and hover.

He made his usual pilgrimage to the Grand Army Plaza, leaned against the base of the Sherman statue and studied the surroundings. Movement near the neighboring Pulitzer Fountain caught his eye. He pushed away from the statue and walked slowly toward the fountain. As he neared, a body darted away toward the hotel.

Warren ran toward the figure which turned in his direction. It was a young girl. "Stop following me," a high-pitched voice called. Whoever it was, was scared, and Warren stopped as the person disappeared around the side of the Plaza.

Chapter 6

Déjà vu

"Aren't you joining us?" Eileen Prado asked Ryan Linden, Special Agent in Charge of the FBI's Manhattan office.

"I was asked to provide space for a meeting and then make myself scarce," Linden replied, closing the door to a small conference room. His footsteps echoed as he walked away.

"What the hell?" Ira Fisher blurted seeing ATF Director Jonah Rhodes seated at an oval table.

"Good to see you again too," Rhodes said, stood and offered his hand to Fisher and Prado.

"Do you have any idea what's going on?" Prado asked as she and Fisher sat down opposite Rhodes.

"I got a call from the NSC and...."

"Wait," Fisher interrupted. "As in National Security Council?"

Rhodes nodded. "A deputy there, uh...." he consulted a small notebook. "Lyle Regent asked me to be here. That's all I got. I had no idea you'd be here. Did you know about me?"

Prado shook her head. "Nope. We got the same type of request. Ours came from the Bureau AD. No details, just be here."

A flat screen on the wall at the head of the table flickered to life. The screen filled with dark blue, and a cheerful voice bid them a "Good morning" before an image materialized.

"Fuck me," came from Fisher.

"No can do," exclaimed Alex Chandon, "but I appreciate the sentiment. How is everyone this morning?"

"Good," Rhodes said tentatively.

"Thanks for joining me this morning," Chandon said.

"Why are we here?" Prado asked flatly. "The last time we talked, you told us to shut up and go away."

Chandon smiled. "That's harsh, and if that's the way you interpreted my meaning, I apologize. I simply meant we were taking over the operation from Blanchard and you could stand down."

"No," Rhodes said aggressively, "I distinctly recall you telling us, me in particular, to shut up and go away."

"Again, my apologies," Chandon said. "When we took over distribution from Blanchard, we had to ensure that the Bureau and ATF kept a distance. There can't be any interruptions."

"Weapons trafficking by the CIA," Fisher blurted. "Gotta love it."

Chandon stared ahead without responding.

"We have stayed out of your business," Rhodes said. "Has there been a hiccup? Is that why I'm here?"

Chandon shook his head and sat forward, his face filling the frame of the screen. "No, we're good. The product is getting delivered. I appreciate your cooperation."

"You and I came to an understanding," Prado said. "I made sure you were protected by planting a story that resulted in Eddings' resignation from the Senate. That shifted the focus far away from what you're doing. I sure as hell hope we're not getting dragged back into any of your shit. We stepped into it by accident while we were investigating something entirely different. I don't want to revisit any of it."

"Your help was appreciated," Chandon said with a nod. "The reporter's original interest in Blanchard would have created serious problems. Diverting attention to the Senator's covering up his wife's hit-and-run was brilliant. Thank you." Chandon joined his hands together and gave a quick bow of his head.

"Okay," Prado said, "so, if all is well, what are we doing here?"

"We're here to make certain things stay copacetic," Chandon responded. "Let me bring you up to date on a few developments and then we can move ahead." He paused, scooted back on his chair and cleared his throat. "Ambassador Wheeler is back home in Montana. She has been appointed to fill the seat of the recently deceased Senator Homan."

"I missed that," Fisher said. "I mean, I knew Homan died. That was almost a month ago. Wheeler just got the call on this?"

"Not 'just'," Chandon said. "It's been about three weeks. I'm acting ambassador and have been told I'll be nominated for the position."

"Congratulations," came from Rhodes without any sincerity.

"Now you'll be using the office of ambassador to Suriname as cover for weapons trafficking," Fisher said. "Priceless. That has to be a first. I can't believe you convinced the State Department that it makes sense. Sensitivities to sharing diplomacy with the CIA sure ain't what they used to be."

"I'll pass along your observations," Chandon said coldly. "Back to why you're here. The distribution operation continues to various countries and it's going smoothly, with a complication I'll get to in a moment. Our plans are to expand given the growing instability in a number of democracies here in Latin America. You must be aware of what's going on in Ecuador. Add that to Bolivia, Venezuela, Chile and others on the brink."

"The script has always been the same," Fisher said. "Our response is always the same. Nothing changes."

Chandon moved toward the screen, again filling the space. "We firmly believe conditions require us to move beyond "ant smuggling" to a more sophisticated, larger operation. We can no longer count on individual mules to deliver the volume we need."

Prado asked, "Why do we need to know any of this? We're out. We did what we needed to do."

"It's been easy for us to overlook the trail of individual mules carrying one or two weapons across the border," Rhodes said. "Stopping ant smuggling is not a priority. No one cares. The U.N., Interpol and OAS have bigger fish to fry, but if you start a larger operation that's going to ping on everyone's radar. We'll be asked to work with these international organizations. It's going to be impossible to ignore this."

Chandon said, "Keep it off ATF's radar and we're good. That's your charge. I will work with my colleagues to keep it off their radars. Away from Interpol and the others."

"That explains what he's doing here," Prado said with a quick glance at Rhodes. "How does any of this involve the Bureau?"

Chandon smiled broadly. "You and Mr. Fisher have a huge role to play."

"Can't see it," Fisher responded. "We're domestic. Our responsibilities end at the border."

"Did you forget about your soirée here in Suriname?"

"That was an extraordinary situation," Fisher countered. "We were investigating a crime here in the U.S. and a lead took us there. International weapons trafficking is way out of our jurisdiction."

"I agree," Chandon said with a nod. "I wouldn't think of asking you to violate your charter."

"Get to the point," Prado demanded.

"There have been a series of murders in New York City. One of the victims is, *was,* the daughter of a businessman here in Paramaribo who is critical to our operation."

"Let me guess," Fisher said. "He's part of that one percent who runs Suriname."

Chandon touched his nose. "Right."

"And you want us to find out who killed his daughter to keep this guy happy," Fisher said.

"That would be nice, but I have other concerns."

Prado sat up stiffly. "We haven't been told anything about a serial killer, if that's where you're going with this."

"Let me be the first to tell you then," Chandon said. "There is a serial killer in New York City and you're going to be called in to help the NYPD."

"How many murders?"

"Two."

Fisher shook his head. "Need three to be classified as serial murder."

Chandon's face hardened. "Mr. Fisher, I don't give a damn what the official definition is. Two, three, twelve. We're going to identify the perpetrator as a serial killer because we need to get you involved to assist me with a situation."

"We *are* getting dragged back in," Prado said, frustration in her voice.

Chandon took a deep breath. "Not in the way you're thinking. Please, let me finish."

Prado nodded and waved him ahead.

"As I was saying, one of the victims is the daughter of a man important to what we're doing. Although it would be terrific if you could discover who killed his daughter because of who he is, what I'm about to ask has much broader implications."

Fisher let his head drop. "I don't like where this is going."

Chandon raised his hands. "You have no idea where this is going."

"Tell us," Prado said.

"This man, Geoffrey Panday...."

"The Attorney General?" Fisher asked.

"He was when you were here. He has since retired from government and is running his family's construction business. Suriname is awash in petrodollars with the discovery of offshore oil and Mr. Panday is taking advantage of the growth opportunities. He is also running our payments through his accounts; payments to those whose eyes we need to keep averted from what we're up to."

"Payments as in 'bribes,'" said Fisher.

"Panday is laundering your payouts," Prado added.

"Yes," Chandon agreed, "that explains it succinctly. Therefore, we can't have New York City's finest poking around during their investigation and landing on anything embarrassing. That is where you come into the picture. Given your background investigating serial murder and ...."

"And our experience in keeping people away from you," Prado said.

"Yes, given all of that, who better to make certain the investigation remains focused on finding out who killed her, and the other woman, and not on who Regina Wozniak is...*was*; who her father is and what he does?" Chandon shook his head. "You will build a firewall for us."

Prado asked, "Does the fact that her name is Regina Wozniak and not Regina Panday have anything to do with this 'keeping a distance' thing? A name change to protect the family enterprise?"

"More to protect the family," Chandon answered. "When she became pregnant, her family was not happy. The baby's father is, oh, shall we say, not acceptable. But that's another story. Anyway, she was sent to New York for an abortion, which she didn't have. She had the child."

"Why 'Wozniak'?" Fisher said. "What's the story behind that?"

"I have no idea where that came from," Chandon answered, "but it is a long way from Panday. She chose to remain in New York given her parents' attitude. They continued to support her and had people in New York watching out for her."

"They weren't very successful with that," Fisher said.

"Not that kind of 'watching out'," Chandon said. "More like an extended family. Not security."

"And the baby's father?" Prado asked.

"We're told he was given a choice. Take a suitcase full of cash and disappear or be disappeared. He chose wisely."

"What's happened to the kid?" Fisher asked.

"He's with the Pandays. The former ambassador from Suriname to the U.S., Daniel VandenHeuval, lives in New York and used his connections to make that happen."

"Wouldn't that have happened anyway?" Fisher asked. "With or without Vandenwhatever? The grandparents are the next of kin."

Chandon answered. "It happened faster with his intercession."

"Was he one of the people in New York watching out for her?" Prado asked.

Chandon nodded his answer.

"And the Pandays are okay with that? With taking in the kid?"

"They had no choice. We couldn't have the child floating around the system in New York and attracting attention. Now," Chandon said, "we need to concentrate on the task at hand. I'll send you what you need to know about the investigation and about the people you'll be contacting."

"Our job is to keep information about the daughter on close hold?" Prado said, skepticism draping her words.

"In a nutshell," agreed Chandon.

"You really think the people already investigating this are going to step aside and let us take over?" Prado asked.

"I am counting on you and Mr. Fisher persuading them to do that."

"The Bureau can't walk in and take over an investigation, or even get involved as a partner unless our assistance is requested."

"Not to worry. I know the rules and have a call into the Commissioner of Police, Leonard Kinney. He is an old friend. We went to boarding school together. The place you have to go is the 19th Precinct, where the case is being handled. The red carpet will be laid out by the time you get there."

"Not a chance," Fisher declared. "Even when we get invited, it's begrudgingly. No one likes to ask for help. With this one, we're being forced down their throats."

"Make it work," Chandon demanded.

"To summarize why I'm here," Rhodes said. "You're planning to expand the CIA's weapons trafficking operation and you want the ATF to ignore it."

"Yes, ignore it and dismiss any intelligence that comes your way. Ignore anyone who comes to you with a request, or even a suggestion, that you investigate. That includes all your own personnel, of course, but also anything and anyone from Capitol Hill."

"That includes our oversight committees?" Rhodes asked. "And yours?"

"You will not be hearing from them. I promise."

"The NSC must know all about this," Rhodes said. "That's who I got the word from to be here today."

"The NSC is a White House operation. The White House, NSC, and those with a need to know in Europe and South America have all pledged their support."

"They all know what you're doing?" Rhodes asked incredulously.

Chandon snorted a laugh. "Of course not. Not the details. Everyone stays in their lane. The same sort of understanding exists with our counterparts abroad. Essentially, it's blinders on. They don't meddle in our sphere of influence and we don't meddle in theirs. As I said, I'll make sure that etiquette is respected."

"And we'll be guiding the investigation to keep Regina Wozniak's identity in the dark," Prado said. "Very organized."

"But you won't mind if we find out who killed her?" Fisher asked, not attempting to conceal his disdain.

"I'll assume that's rhetorical," Chandon said. "It's nice to touch base with everyone again. We'll be talking."

As soon as the screen went blank, Fisher exploded. "You have to be kidding me. This is ridiculous. We're being told by a CIA operative masquerading as a diplomat to control an investigation into multiple murders. Bullshit."

"At least you can do your job," Rhodes said. "I have to ignore my job completely and then likely lie to Congress. I don't care what he says, someone on the Hill is going to ferret this out. No one can keep a secret in Washington, especially when it can be politicized. This is ripe for that. One whiff and empires fall."

Prado sank down in the chair and covered her face with her hands. "I can't wait to tell New York City cops that they have to step aside and let us take over the investigation." She sat a moment before popping out of the chair. "That's not happening. Not if we want to get anywhere with the investigation." She shouldered her purse and computer bag and pushed through the conference room door into a long hallway, offices open on both sides. Fisher at her side, she announced, "We'll work with them. Maybe divvy up what we do so you and I are the ones looking into what happened to Wozniak, but I sure as hell am not going to tell a New York cop to step aside. That could be life threatening."

Chapter 7

A Division of Labor

"Levitt, Broaden," Robinson called out as she hurried into the squad room, her voice cutting through the chatter. "With me, now."

She peeled off her patchwork design brushed wool coat as she walked into her office and tossed it on a metal pole rack. "Sit," she demanded as the detectives stepped across the threshold. She paced behind her desk sipping coffee from a to-go cup.

Robinson placed the cup on her desk and leaned forward, arms supporting her. "I got a call at home from Kinney...."

"The commissioner?" Broaden asked.

Robinson glared. "Yes, *that* Kinney. He has asked the FBI to help us and...." She stopped and lowered her head. "Fucking *help us* with our investigation into the apartment house murders." She looked up, her face distorted with anger. "*Help us* for fuck's sake."

Robinson sat heavily causing her chair to slam against the wall behind. "By the way, that's what they're calling it. 'The Apartment House Murders.'"

Levitt mouthed "who" to Broaden.

Robinson caught the movement and said, "The press. Read this morning's papers, or turn on your television to any channel. It's actually a very tame label, even unimaginative. I'm betting it'll get a lot more colorful."

Broaden raised a handful of pages. "Wanna hear what we got on the second one?"

Robinson frowned. Her attention shifted past Broaden. "It looks like our saviors have arrived."

"We've been called worse," Prado said with a tight smile. Fisher moved from behind to her side. "Special Agent Eileen Prado." She turned toward Fisher. "Special Agent Ira Fisher."

Standing, Robinson offered her hand. "Commanding Officer Nadine Robinson. Detectives Jane Levitt and Jim Broaden."

"I'll grab a couple of chairs," Broaden said.

Robinson pointed to a door behind the coat rack. "In my closet."

Broaden disappeared behind the door, shuffled around the closet, and emerged, handing Prado and Fisher folding chairs.

Everyone seated, Robinson asked, "Comfortable?"

Prado nodded and offered, "Cards on the table. We are as surprised as you are to be here."

"It's your job," Robinson said, a sharp edge in her voice.

"The usual protocol is for someone to reach out from a jurisdiction and request our assistance," Prado said. "My understanding is that it went the other way this time, which is unusual. Your commissioner was asked to make the request and here we are. Like I said, 'cards on the table.'"

Robinson considered Prado a moment before replying. "Well, that's refreshing. Feds without an attitude."

"Thanks, I think," Fisher said.

Prado followed with, "We'll help any way we can, but this is your investigation."

"I assume you have experience with this kind of thing," Robinson said. "Multiple murders. Generally we request help from the BAU in cases like this. That's not you, right?"

"No, that's not us. We aren't profilers but we have worked closely with the BAU. We have some experience in this field."

"Not exactly like this," Fisher added.

"No," Prado agreed. "Not anything like this, really."

Fisher said, "Our experience was a little more rural. Like out in the hinterlands of Iowa."

"That was you?" Broaden said, excitement in his voice. "That guy who kidnapped girls and kept them in his basement. I thought I recognized your names. Shit, I read about that. Awful, awful stuff."

"That was us," Prado said, "and it was awful."

"We don't have a lot of experience with this kind of thing," Robinson said. "I'm not happy with how you ended up here, but you are here and we'll gladly mine your expertise."

Prado nodded. "We have a few details on what you're dealing with. Read some background material. Two women raped and strangled. Both single mothers, but we didn't get any information on forensics or anything else."

Robinson gestured toward Broaden. "Detective Broaden was about to bring me up to speed on the latest developments in the second murder when you arrived. Let's start with that."

Broaden scooted his chair forward and read from a sheaf of pages he placed on Robinson's desk. "Dorothy Provine, 36, was found in her bed. She was nude and the ME determined she was killed by ligature strangulation. She had been dead about three hours when she was discovered. Ruled a homicide. No DNA evidence was found." Broaden raised his eyes. "No *useful* DNA was found." He returned to what he was reading. "There were no signs of forced entry or of a struggle. There was no evidence of defensive wounds. Nothing found under the victim's fingernails. Rape kit found nothing. The perp likely wore a condom and gloves. The window to the balcony was open and it appeared the bedroom, kitchen and living room were cleaned postmortem."

"Excuse me," Fisher said. "The scene was cleaned postmortem meaning the unsub cleaned up everything?"

Broaden nodded. "That's what it looks like."

Fisher continued. "Not only in the area of the murder but the entire apartment?"

"All except the bedroom where Ms. Provine's son was asleep, yes."

"The child didn't hear anything?" Fisher asked. "None of the neighbors either?"

Robinson leaned forward. "Why don't we let the detective run through his briefing and I think most of your questions will be answered."

"Sure," Fisher answered. "My bad."

Broaden turned over the page he had been reading from, placed it on the desk and went to a second page. "The son, Larry, didn't hear anything." He looked up. "We're thinking the unsub threatened to harm the son if the victim resisted and that kept her quiet. Probably explains why no one heard anything." His attention back on the file, he read, "Interview with the neighbor who found the body didn't provide any useful information, neither did any other interview within the building. Ms. Provine didn't have much interaction with fellow tenants. A review of the CCTV was not helpful."

Broaden pushed away from Robinson's desk, taking the pages with him.

"Thanks, detective," from Robinson. She gestured toward Prado and Fisher. "Questions?"

"You said the CCTV was not helpful," Prado said. "Why?"

"The only people seen for a 12-hour period before and an 8-hour period following the murder are tenants and all have iron clad alibis. Delivery people are not allowed any further than the concierge's desk, and all other visitors have been interviewed and cleared."

"What about people at her job?" Fisher asked. "And friends?"

"We thought of all that," Robinson answered, smiling tightly. "Dead ends."

Prado said, "I'm guessing the first victim was killed in the same way."

"Yes," Levitt responded, "and everything else Detective Broaden described, that is, the condition of the apartments and the uselessness of the CCTV and interviews. Got nothing."

"There is one thing we have to follow up on," Broaden said. He turned quickly toward Robinson. "We're going to take care of that today."

"Which is?" Robinson asked.

"When we were talking to the Child Services person who came to look after Provine's son we found out that the son of the first victim, Regina Wozniak, was claimed." Broaden put his hand up. "That's the wrong way to put it. He was placed in the custody of a neighbor of Ms. Wozniak. Daniel VandenHeuval, who didn't mention this when we talked to him. We have to cover that base."

"VandenHeuval?" Prado said, hoping the unintended surprise in her voice was not detected. "You talked to him?"

Broaden nodded. "We need to get back to him."

"Could that be because he hadn't taken custody of the boy when you interviewed him?" Prado asked.

"Could be," Broaden agreed. "We haven't checked any dates on this, but that aside, don't you think the guy should've mentioned he had a relationship with this woman? I mean, he must have. He was granted custody of her son. When we talked to him he acted like he barely knew her."

"He did say he recommended her for a job but acted like it was no big deal," Levitt added. "We both came away from our interview convinced he was not telling us everything he knew."

"He recommended her for a job?" Prado asked.

"He begged off of any connection to her other than knowing she could help a friend of his with some work," Broaden explained. "Denied any other knowledge about her."

Robinson said, looking from Prado to Fisher, "Any thoughts?"

"Not a lot," Prado answered. "I'd like to make a suggestion if I could."

"That's why you're here."

"We" – Prado cocked her head toward Fisher – "don't know the city. Serial offenders usually stick to a given area. A comfort zone. They rarely range far afield. Even if we determined what that area is, we'd have no familiarity with it. No way of ferreting out the obvious nooks and crannies he would seek out."

Robinson nodded. "Right now it looks like he's sticking to the Upper East Side."

"And we don't know anything about the locality," Prado said. "I'm guessing there are...uh...for lack of a better way to put this – 'hidey holes' – that you all are intimate with."

Robinson bobbed her head. "And?"

"We can best help by digging into the backgrounds of the victims. Find out what types the unsub prefers. Bundy liked brunettes who parted their hair down the center. The Son of Sam went after couples. It looks like the one Long Island guy, Heuermann, targeted prostitutes. My point is they often have a type. Studying the victims and establishing a type should give us some direction on 'why' he selects them. We can build on that lead, maybe even come up with enough to develop a profile to point us in the direction of persons of interest."

Robinson sat up in her chair and eyed Prado a moment before offering, "You're proposing a division of labor."

Prado nodded.

"You would be doing a deep dive on the victims and" – Robinson looked at Levitt and Broaden – "what exactly would they be doing?"

Prado reached into a computer bag she had placed on the floor next to her purse. She lifted out an accordion file and handed it to Robinson. "When I found out we'd be doing this, I asked the elves at the Bureau who peck away at their computers collecting data on all the nasty people in the world if you'd been in touch. Sure enough, you had and they gave me this to give to you. A response to what you sent to ViCAP. Other incidents with like MOs and similar victims."

Robinson took the file and leafed through the contents. "We can read all this later." She handed it to Broaden. "Give me the broad strokes."

"The MO for our guy," Prado started, and paused. "I say 'guy' theoretically, it could be a woman, but only about one percent of serials are women. Anyway, the MO for what is going on here matches a few events in New Jersey and Pennsylvania. It's all there," she said pointed at Broaden.

"You're saying he's moving back and forth among various cities?" Robinson asked.

Prado shook her head. "No, he's gone from those other cities. He was active a few years back. Never apprehended but the investigators had persons of interests."

"Persons?" Broaden said. "Like they thought more than one person was active?"

"That could be, of course," Prado answered, but "I'm thinking it was the same person who had aliases. If we can confirm that and then find out where he lived and worked back then, that could help us define places and people to look at closely here. Finding out what his comfort zone looked like in those other places could give you some areas to...."

Robinson waved Prado off. "Thanks, I think we've got the idea. So, this division of labor? Explain."

"We concentrate on the victims, you use what ViCAP came up with to tell us more about the person we're looking for. Talk to the investigators who worked on the cases in Philadelphia, I think it was. Don't recall where in New Jersey." She raised her eyebrows in question and let her attention go from Robinson to Broaden to Levitt. "Okay?"

Broaden and Levitt turned to Robinson, who nodded.

"We will need your help with some of the grunt work to find out more about the victims," Prado said.

"The 'slog,'" Broaden said.

"Excuse me," from Prado.

"Grunt work. I call it 'the slog.'"

"Okay, then. We need help with that. We're going to need cell phone records. Need to know what's on their computers. We'd appreciate having some extra hands to grind through that stuff."

"We've already done some of it," Robinson said. "Bank records for one." To Levitt and Broaden. "Who were the first officers on the scene?"

"Pendrage and Lattimore," Broaden answered.

Robinson nodded. "Tell them I authorized overtime and get them moving on what they" – she gestured toward Prado and Fisher – "need. If they can't handle some of that, like the computer stuff, tell them to find someone who can." To Prado: "Anything else?"

"We'll start our end of things with this VandenHeuval person," Prado said and stood.

***

Robinson, Levitt and Broaden watched Prado and Fisher walk through and out of the squad room.

"We're not going to tell them about Braddock?" Broaden asked, disbelief in his voice.

"They suggested the division of labor," Robinson responded. "It makes sense. They'll be focusing on the victims and you two do your job. You have a head start. You know who you're looking for. Find him." She handed the ViCAP files to Broaden. "There's stuff in here that can help."

Levitt shook her head. "I don't know," she said doubtfully. "It's a big city. That bit about the comfort zone. I didn't know that? Did you?" she directed at Broaden, who shook his head. "Those two know what they're doing."

"And we don't?" Robinson asked challengingly.

"She has it right. Find out why he picked his victims and we have better insight on Braddock. Could tie us to who his friends are. Where he hangs out. Where he works. Lives. Basic police work we can't do without access to the victims."

"I'm expecting to get briefed regularly," Robinson said. "I'll make sure of it. That should give us what they have."

Levitt bobbed her head. "Okay, but I gotta say, I'm not comfortable with this way of doing business. Withholding information."

"Noted, Robinson said. "It's the way it has to be for now, but I am curious. How would you go about telling federal agents that we know our Governor and Senator colluded to keep the identity of a serial killer hidden?" She sat forward. "Think that might create some problems? Some noise? Some distractions?" She held her hands up. "How would you weigh how we go about doing our job against blowing up the state's political delegation? Any suggestions?"

Silence.

"I didn't think so."

***

"Do you have a death wish?" Broaden asked as they walked away from Robinson's office.

"Thought she was gonna come across her desk and rip my heart out."

"I have no idea what kinda words she's had with the commissioner and what other pressure she might be dealing with, but she has a point about keeping the focus on finding Braddock. Avoiding distractions."

"Yeah," Levitt agreed. "Enough of that," she said, sitting down at her desk which faced Broaden's. "You ever notice that all of these FBI agents look like they stepped out of a recruiting brochure?"

"Smooth change of subject and, yes, I have noticed. Prado. She's perfect. I'm guessing Hispanic. Ticks that box on the quota sheet. Pretty, but not model pretty. You know, regular human being pretty. He's the same. All American boy, and 'Ira Fisher.' Jewish. Check another box."

"If we were any more cynical, we'd be useless," Levitt said. "In the meantime, what the hell are we supposed to be doing? I'm not all together clear on that."

"Dig into this," Broaden said, tossing Levitt half of the files Prado handed over. "See if anything in here adds to what we already know, and go from there."

"We have James Braddock."

"We don't *have* have him."

"Aren't we right back to our conversation with Robinson?" Levitt asked. "I don't think these files are going to be the answer to putting our hands on him."

"All this" – Broaden waved a hand over his half of the files – "might give us something. We have to prove our case. We need to find hard evidence that it is Braddock. That he's our guy. We've kinda skipped over that part. We can't rely on what a bad cop and worse politicians have left us."

***

"That was clever," Fisher said as he and Prado walked out of the precinct building and stood on the sidewalk.

"Kinda fell into my lap. It makes sense to go in that direction anyway. We don't know the city. We do know how to do our job. Plus, it has the advantage of putting us right where Chandon wants us. Shielding Regina Wozniak from them." She jabbed her thumb over her shoulder.

"I hate that our strings are being pulled by a CIA agent masquerading as a diplomat. It's ridiculous. It's embarrassing."

"No, our strings are not being pulled by that asshole. We are free agents now – no pun intended – and can get on with what we need to do. There is a sicko running around who's killed at least two women. Let's find him before he finds another victim."

"Look around," she said indicating the canyon of buildings to her left and right. "This is as foreign to us as Olatha was. Let's narrow our focus and concentrate on doing what we know how to do. Okay?"

"Fine," Fisher answered, grudgingly.

Prado stepped in front of him. "Fine?"

"I'm good. I'm good. Really. Let's do this."

"Van. Den. Heuval." Prado drew out the name. "Chandon forgot to tell us a few things about this guy. Let's see how far he's been read into this. Find out what his deal is."

***

"Facetiming are we?" Willow Briggs said as soon as Prado's image materialized on her computer screen. "Are you avoiding an in-person session?"

"You know better than that. I've popped up on your doorstep unannounced so many early mornings even the coffee I brought wasn't an adequate apology."

Briggs laughed. "So, what is it? You have a problem with making an appointment and showing up when you're supposed to?"

"Hey, what can I tell you? I need to talk to you when I need to talk to you. I'm in New York. This is the way to go. Not ideal but it'll have to do."

"You know I'm kidding. I always have time for you. What's up?"

"Can we just talk like two friends, not psychologist to client, and you don't ask 'Well, what do *you* think about that'?"

"Oh, it's been one of those days."

"Not as bad as some, but..." Prado hesitated a moment before continuing. "You remember when we were trying to get information on the murder of Senator Eddings' daughter? See if he was tied to it somehow?"

"I do. Hard to forget."

"We put some pieces together that told us it was a sick plan to mug his daughter, raise hell, show his determination as a law and order guy and cement his 'tough on crime' campaign plank. It went off the rails, but we couldn't put all the pieces together. The daughter died for a career boost and we couldn't do anything about it. As fucked up as it gets."

"Chilling stuff, but you're not giving yourself credit. You forced Eddings out of office."

"A door prize, kinda. We found his former lawyer and campaign treasurer...."

"In Suriname, right?"

"Yeah, he'd run off after he figured out what was going on. He fit some of the pieces together for us. Not enough, but he did turn everything on its ear. He told us that Eddings had been covering up the details of a fatal hit-and-run by his wife. He hid it for thirty years and let her slide into a nervous breakdown to protect his political career, one that started with the murder of his daughter. What a shit person." Prado held up both hands. "That's a story for another day. Got something else I want to talk to you about."

"Fire away."

"I don't think I ever told you that we turned over another rock while we were in Suriname."

"On top of the hit-and-run thing?"

"Yeah, and out crawled all kinds of slimy characters, mostly our own people. U.S. corporations buying off public officials, politicians; anybody who needed to be bought off to keep their businesses going. There was the added bonus of finding out that the CIA is weapons trafficking to 'save democracy' in South America." Prado closed her eyes and shook her head. "I shouldn't be so cavalier about that one. I know there are serious problems that well-meaning people are trying to deal with."

"Jesus, there are a lot of rocks in that country."

"The guy who crawled out from under the CIA rock dragged us into a case here in New York. The daughter of the man at the center of the corrupt politics in Suriname was murdered in Manhattan. The father funnels money from the CIA to whoever has a palm out and is willing to turn a blind eye to the trafficking. The daughter is one of two, and given other information we've dug up, it's likely a serial killer case, which means the killing is going to continue until we find the guy."

"Jesus, Eileen, again? The one in Iowa was the worst thing I've ever heard of. A serial sexual sadist. Little girls." Briggs shook her head. "Just thinking about it makes me...." She raised her arms. "I have goosebumps."

"It's my job."

"That is a cop out. Before Iowa you had the Dooney Boys. There isn't a bone in your body they didn't break. A surface left unmarked."

"Actually, they didn't break my nose. Not that they didn't try, just keep missing it. Got my orbital bones and jaw instead. Silver lining though. No more undercover assignments with drug gangs. FBI found me."

"And they haven't given you a break."

"I'm not trying to push any of that aside. Iowa or the Dooney Boys. Hell, I've just gotten used to my new face and body after being put back together. Life goes on."

"I know, I know. You've handled it all incredibly bravely."

"Bravely, is it?"

"That's a technical term only really talented psychologists are allowed to use. Seriously though, putting the physical challenges aside, I'm deadly serious when I say that I didn't expect you to be right back at it after Iowa. It's not only the physical challenges. It's the mental part. I've talked to profilers who take years to recover."

"Truthfully, I haven't given my timeline any thought. I was pointed in this direction and here I am."

"So, how can I help?"

"Not sure you can, which is why I asked that we talk like friends not psychologist and client. I need someone to listen."

"Okay, whaddya got?"

"I've agreed to limitations on how I do my job. We have to keep a shield around the daughter of that middle man. Protect her identity."

"I'm confused."

"Chandon, the CIA agent in Suriname is concerned that if there is a lot of digging into the background of... Let's start by giving her a name. It's Regina Wozniak. That's not her real name. And that's the point. We have to protect her identity. Like I said, her father is funneling money to the powers that be in Suriname making the CIA operation possible. Too much attention on Wozniak and the cover might get peeled back."

"Convoluted, but I got it."

"Essentially, then, we're looking for a multiple murderer while protecting an unlawful international operation. I'm not feeling good about this. Not sure I'm on the right side of things."

"My first observation is that it sounds like you're going to be able to do your job, just in a workaround kind of way."

"I think we'll be able to do what we need to do. My partner is not happy with all of this and his visceral reaction got me wondering if we should've refused to take it on."

Prado stared at her keyboard. Briggs nodded thoughtfully. The women were accustomed to sitting together in silence and neither exhibited any discomfort. Both recognized that the quiet was a positive. Useful contemplation.

"I say go ahead and do your job," Briggs said. "Find the sick asshole. If along the way you get asked to do something that gets in the way of that result, you refuse."

More quiet.

"Almost verbatim what I said to Ira."

"Great minds and all that," Briggs said.

Chapter 8

Xeroderma Pigmentosum

"I'm leaving," Warren announced as he stood at the front door.

Eloise appeared from the kitchen drying her hands with a dish towel, an apron tied at her waist apron embroidered with: *My kitchen. My rules.* "You're walking across the park. That's why you're leaving a little earlier than usual."

"You know me too well."

"Wait," she demanded and walked hurriedly toward Warren. She inspected him from head to toe. "Hold this," she said handing him the dish towel. She pulled the bill of his cap low on his forehead and patted the pockets of his down vest. "Gloves?"

"Yes."

She backed up a step and looked at his feet. "Wool socks? It's going down well below freezing tonight."

"Wool socks," he confirmed.

Eloise retrieved the dish towel. "I'd tell you not to walk across the park, but I know that would do no good."

"I promise not to walk all the way back through the park. I'll leave at 90th Street and come back along the West side. I want to walk over to the Lincoln Center anyway."

"Stay away from the lights."

"Of course."

"Pilgrimage to the Dakota?"

"Always," Warren said, opened the door and stepped into the hallway. He waited until she closed the door behind him before moving toward the elevator.

Warren crossed 59th Street and headed toward the Columbus Circle entrance to Central Park. Traffic was heavy given his earlier than usual start. He kept his head down, hands in his pockets. There were people walking into and out of the park, another product of the hour. He headed toward the carousel and could see the lights of the Tavern on the Green. Sitting on the edge of the Sheep Meadow, Warren tried to imagine what the restaurant looked like when it was the sheepfold, where the animals were sheltered and fed.

He crossed the Bow Bridge leading across the lake near the Bethesda Fountain and headed for the woodlands of the Ramble, the closest anyone could get to a forest landscape in the city – and where the night guardians of the park hid. Warren skirted the edge of the Ramble and set on a path toward Belvedere Castle. As he neared the landmark, his attention was diverted by the scuffle of feet behind him and a voice demanding "Let me go. Stop."

Warren turned toward a knot of bodies about 20 yards behind him.

A high-pitched, "You fuckers better let me go" came from the center of the knot.

Warren recognized the voice and approached. He pushed through the huddle and saw a small, very pale, very delicate looking girl turning in a circle, fists raised in front of her face. She was bouncing on the balls of her feet. "Let me go you creeps," she screamed. "My Dad's a cop. He'll get you."

"She's with me," Warren said and held out his hand, which the girl considered, but did not take.

"If she's with you," a large man said as he approached from the opposite side of the group, "why isn't she *with* you?"

Eyes of the others turned toward Warren. At least 20 bodies. Warren recognized some from other nights in the park and a few from alley ways and street corners near the Plaza. Vacant stares. Some angry faces. Tattered and dirty figures in ratty clothes. A few with shards of cloth wrapped around their feet in place of shoes. Salvation Army blankets were draped around shoulders.

Warren took a step back feeling threatened and because the man coming toward him smelled sour and putrid. He wore a rug fashioned into a poncho, a hole cut in the center. His face was covered by a scruffy beard, bits of food and what looked like grass and twigs hung from long hair that draped his shoulders. The frame of hair and beard obscured every feature of his face except for his light eyes, the color unclear in the dark.

"We got separated," was all Warren could think to say.

The man considered Warren for a moment and turned away. The others trailed in his wake and the lot disappeared into the trees.

Warren and the girl faced each other. She backed away. He stared.

"I saw you the other night," he said. "You were following me."

"Yeah, that was me."

"Why?"

The elfin figure in front of Warren shrugged. "I didn't start out following you. It just kinda happened. Like tonight."

"You were following me?"

The girl nodded.

Warren tilted his head. "Just kinda happened?"

"I wasn't even going to go anywhere. Went outside to get some air. I don't know anything about" – she gestured in a circle – "where we are. I saw you leave the building and thought I'd follow for a little bit. You ended up going to some pretty cool places last time, so I followed tonight."

"You saw me leave?"

The girl nodded. "I live there too. Figured I'd do a better job this time so you wouldn't see me." She shrugged. "I guess I'm not very good at this."

"You live in the Plaza?"

"I'm living at a friend's apartment. Not *with* him. He's not there. Not really a friend."

Warren narrowed his eyes in question. "What does that mean? Not with him? Not a friend...who's not there'?"

The girl looked around. "I'm freezing. Can we walk and talk, maybe find someplace warm and go inside."

"Yeah, sure. The Dairy is near here. It isn't open but there's someplace to sit out of the cold."

"That's the Hansel and Gretel looking building, right?"

"Guess so," Warren said with a shrug and motioned them forward. "Never thought of it like that. It's a visitor center. Has chairs. Benches. Picnic tables. There are corners near the building that stay warm from the heat that's on during the day."

"That would be good. How long have you lived at the Plaza?"

"My whole life."

The girl stopped. "Really? You must be rich."

Warren laughed. "Not really."

"You hafta be to live there like all the time."

"Long story." He ushered them ahead. "Is the person you're living with family or something?"

"No, I hardly know the guy. Met him maybe three times. I have brain cancer and he's paying for my medicine and doctors and nurses."

Warren felt his face twitch in surprise at the girl's cavalier attitude. That did explain her appearance. The pallor and stick figure body.

"You want to know why, right? Why this guy I hardly know is paying for everything?"

"First, what's your name?"

"Maddy. Short for Madeline, but don't call me that. No one calls me that except my Mom. She can, but no one else."

"Okay, I'm Warren. Now, who is this man you're living with?"

"Not 'with,'" she responded firmly. "He's not there."

"Sorry."

"I'm smart," she answered with an offhand self-assurance. "I graduated first in my class, or I will this year, and this guy gives a scholarship to whoever does that. He graduated from the same high school I go to and made a lot of money. But when he found out I was dying..."

"You're dying?" came out of Warren's mouth unbidden.

"Yeah, I'm dying. You don't listen very well."

"You said you had brain cancer, but not that you're going to die."

"I didn't think I had to add that. Kinda self-explanatory, but no one says it. Not my parents or the doctors. I guess it's to protect me, but I know."

Warren stopped short. The girl was three steps in front before she realized he was standing behind her.

"You okay?" she asked.

"I'm sorry you're dying."

"So am I," she said and walked back to Warren. "How about you keep taking me with you whenever you go out like this." She gestured toward the park's Great Lawn. "Otherwise, I'm cooped up in an apartment 24/7.

Nice apartment. Way nicer than my house, but still. I gotta get out or I've got nothing else going on except homework and the smell of medicine and stuff, and the nurses running around asking all the time 'How do you feel?' and 'Did you take your pills?' And there are a lot of pills."

"Aren't you afraid that you'll get sicker? I mean" – Warren gazed across the 13-acre lawn searching for words – "with your system so compromised you could...."

"What? Die?" Maddy laughed. "If that smelly guy wearing the rug, and his gang of other smelly people, didn't give me something awful, I should live forever. And if I'm going to live forever, I need more in my life than just going to school, going to the hospital, and sitting around the apartment. I need something to live for."

"You live by yourself?"

"Yeah, except for the nurses, there's three of them. They're on shifts. Anyway, I can get out after the night one goes to bed. Just text me and I'll meet you at Columbus Circle." She stared at Warren, smiling hopefully. "Okay?"

"Come on," he urged her forward. "Walk and talk. What about this man who's helping you?"

"Okay," she answered, "so he found out about my brain cancer. Knew I'd probably not make it through four years of college and decided to pay for the doctors, hospital and...." A wave of her hand signaled a change of subject. "This is a downer. Let's talk about something else."

"We've passed the Dairy. You okay? Not too cold?"

"I'm okay as long as we keep moving."

Warren pointed to their right. "That's the West side. Lincoln Center. Metropolitan Opera House. Residential too. More like a normal neighborhood than where we live. A lot of trees and..."

"Hell's Kitchen is over there, right?"

Warren nodded.

"Always wondered about that name."

"Lots of different explanations," Warren said. "My favorite is that a reporter went to the neighborhood with a police guide to get details about a bunch of murders. This was in the 1890s. The cop called it 'Hell's Kitchen' and said it was 'the lowest and filthiest place in the city'."

"Are you some kind of expert on New York?"

"I've learned a lot walking around."

Warren directed them toward a break in the low stone wall surrounding the park and on to the sidewalk on 8th Avenue.

"Why are you walking around late at night?"

"Long story."

"I don't have a lot of time," Maddy said with a chuckle, "but I have enough for you to answer that question."

"Later," Warren said and stopped in front of a red brick apartment building. "The same man who designed the Plaza, designed this building. It was the tallest one in New York when it was built."

"That musta been a long time ago. Not even the tallest in the neighborhood," she said. "Kinda like a really big version of the Hansel and Gretel house in the park. Pointed roofs. Fancy carvings and stuff."

"Dormers, terracotta spandrels and panels, niches, balconies and balustrades."

"What?"

"Nothing. It's the Dakota. Where John Lennon lived and was shot." Warren looked up and down the front walk. "Right out here somewhere."

"That's awful. Who's John Lennon? Why was he shot? Was he killed?"

Warren stared at Maddy a moment before blurting, "Seriously? You've never heard of John Lennon?"

"No."

"The Beatles?"

"He was one of those guys?"

"Yeah, he was one of those guys," Warren said under his breath and started up the block. "And, yes, he was killed by some nut who said he hated Lennon because he was rich and famous. You ever heard of Strawberry Fields? It's near where we came from in the park."

"No, but I like the name. What is it?"

"A memorial to Lennon. It's named after a Beatles song."

"I think I've heard the song."

"How about Sergeant Pepper's Lonely Hearts Club Band?"

What's that?"

"Never mind."

"So, why do you walk around late at night?"

"Why don't we head back? I have a quiet place we can sit inside the Plaza. More comfortable than walking and talking and freezing."

As they walked past the corner of the Dakota, Warren pulled Maddy to a stop and backed them up against the side of the building.

"What?"

Warren peeked around the corner up 72nd Street. "That man." Maddy moved around Warren and followed his attention. "He's dancing."

"I don't know if it's dancing. It looks more like he's having some kind of fit."

"I saw him doing that same thing the other night."

"Here?" Maddy asked, flattening herself against the building.

"No, near the Plaza."

Warren and Maddy leaned forward. The block was now empty. They resumed up Central Park West.

"That was weird," Maddy said.

"That is New York according to Eloise."

"Who's Eloise?"

"I'll explain everything. Let's get out of this cold."

***

Warren led Maddy into the Oak Room, dark but with enough light to make out the size of the space.

"Wow," Maddy said, walking to the middle of the room. She stopped and stared up at the large chandelier. She moved to one side of the room, walked along the wall running her fingers along the polished wood.

"English and Flemish oak," Warren said. "Why it's called the Oak Room."

Maddy made a circuit around the room, a smile on her face. Warren motioned her to one side. "These are called frescoes."

"Paintings," Maddy said.

"Well, yeah, but the paint is applied so when it dries, it penetrates the plaster and becomes fixed, part of the wall." He tugged her arm, bringing

84

her closer to the images. "These are Bavarian castles." He guided her to a section of woodwork that extended from floor to ceiling and lifted her hand to the surface. "Feel that? Carvings of wine casks."

Maddy leaned close. "I can feel it but I can't see it very well." She turned toward Warren. "We can't turn on the lights because someone might come and we're not supposed to be here, right?"

Warren stared ahead a moment. "Yes and no. I'll get to that in a minute."

Maddy turned toward the open space. "No furniture. What is this place?"

"It used to be a restaurant. It's been closed for years. Started out as a bar just for men."

"What the fuck?" came from Maddy. "Only men?"

"That's the way it was years ago. Men used it as a place to talk business."

"Women couldn't talk business?

"Women weren't in business back then. Not a lot of them anyway."

"Maybe that's because they weren't allowed to talk about it."

"Starting in the late 1940s, women were allowed in the Oak Room during the summers. In the '50s, those hours were extended to evenings year-round. By the late '60s it was opened for everyone."

"How very generous," Maddy said. "What is this placed used for now?"

"Rented out for parties and weddings."

Maddy approached Warren. "Okay, now tell me why you walk around at night. You said you'd tell me when we got out of the cold. We're out of the cold."

Warren motioned to a corner of the room where a stack of folding chairs was resting against a wall. He set up two chairs facing each other and directed Maddy to, "Have a seat." He settled, crossed his legs and took a moment before saying, "I have a condition called Xeroderma pigmentosum."

Maddy leaned forward, her knees touching Warren's. "Pig what?"

"XP. Leave it at XP. It's an inherited condition making me sensitive to almost any kind of light."

Warren responded to Maddy's look of confusion with, "It's like being allergic to light. I don't have the ability to repair damage caused by light, primarily ultraviolet light. Light burns my skin."

"Okay, okay," Maddy said, absorbing the explanation. "Like you can get a really bad sunburn."

"Yeah," Warren said with a tight smile. "Like a sunburn only I never tan. The burns can get infected and it also means I'm susceptible to getting skin cancer. My eyes are also very sensitive to light. My skin can get dry, but not the regular dry where you can put lotion on and clear it up. The kind of dry where layers of skin peel off."

"So, no light. Even from" – she glanced up at the chandelier – "light bulbs?"

"Some light bulbs. The damage is not as bad as from sunlight, but even small amounts of UV light, especially from fluorescent lights and halogen lights, can be bad. I used to carry around a light meter but I've pretty much figured out what to stay away from."

"Had this since you were born?"

"Like I said, it's inherited and" – Warren held his arms out – "it's part of the packaging. My mother had a lot of tests done after I was born. They discovered it then."

Maddy's eyes widened. She inhaled sharply and raised her hands, covering her mouth. "So, you've never been out during the day?"

"I did when I was growing up. They sent me to school for a few years. It didn't work."

Maddy, eyes still wide, hands away from her mouth asked, "Because you got burned?"

"There was that but I was pretty much covered from head-to-toe in clothes and was slathered with gobs of sunscreen. That protected me pretty much. But I couldn't do stuff with the other kids. No recess. No school trips. That kind of thing. There was also some bullying so after second grade, I was home schooled."

"You've never been outside during the day since second grade? That means you were seven years old."

"That's why I'm out at night."

Maddy slumped forward, resting her elbows on her knees. "Wow."

"Yeah, wow, but I see things almost no one else does."

"And you know a lot about the city."

"I do."

Maddy sat up straight and smiled broadly. "So, you'll take me with you whenever you go out?"

"If you want."

"I want."

Chapter 9

Connections

Prado leaned forward to read the nametag of the uniformed man in front of her. "Cecil, we're here to see Daniel VandenHeuval." She displayed her ID.

"Popular fellow," Cecil responded. He walked slowly to the opposite end of the reception desk, lifted a phone receiver to his ear and jabbed at the face of the set very purposefully. "Yes, sir, it's Cecil and I have two…." As he listened, he raised his long, lanky arm and pointed toward a bank of elevators, mouthing, '1209.' "I'll send them up."

A man was waiting in the corridor as Prado and Fisher stepped off the elevator. "I'm Daniel VandenHeuval," he said, waving off their reach for credentials and ushered them inside the apartment. "Please. Straight ahead to the living room. I think we'll be most comfortable there."

A narrow hallway opened to a large room, a stairway to a second floor on the left.

Tile floors were visible where not covered by an intricately patterned green and blue wool Oriental rug. A gray fabric-covered couch with nail head accents faced them. Chairs in the same color and design completed the setting.

Prado stopped in front of a framed certificate on the wall to the right of the couch.

"You were at the UN?"

"I was my nation's representative there."

"As well as ambassador."

"You're well-informed," VandenHeuval said and waited for Prado and Fisher to sit before settling across from them. "It was a privilege to hold both positions. Not at the same time, of course," he said with a smile.

"Which explains your connection to Mr. Panday," Fisher said.

VandenHeuval nodded. "You are very well informed indeed. Yes, we were both in government service. I understand you spent some time in my country."

"And you have done your research," Prado said.

"I was ambassador here when you were in Suriname. Cable traffic informed me you were in Paramaribo. I hope you enjoyed it."

"We had a unique experience," Fisher said.

"'A unique experience'. I'm sure there's a story behind that observation."

"There is," Prado agreed and held her eyes intently on VandenHeuval.

"Perhaps you will share it with me some other time."

"I doubt there's anything more we can tell you than what you learned from that cable traffic."

"I'd like to hear your personal observations. Now, how can I help you today?"

"We know you've been interviewed about Regina Wozniak," Prado said. "We were briefed on that. We'd like to hear more about your relationship with her."

"We didn't have a relationship," VandenHeuval said.

"You found her a job," Prado countered. "Recommended her so there must have been more than a passing acquaintance."

"Not really. You said you were briefed on my interview. You know then that I found out she was a writer. I know people who employ writers. I recommended her. That's the sum and substance of it."

"We'd like to discuss a few of those details. It might jog some other thoughts you have
about her. Also, we want to make sure we don't have any bad information." Prado smiled.

"Okay?"

"Okay," VandenHeuval responded cheerfully. "Whatever I can do to help."

"We haven't been able to identify any of Ms. Wozniak's friends; it appears she rarely went out; and she worked almost exclusively from home. Does that track with what you knew about her?"

"Again, I knew very little about the woman so I can't answer."

"Did you two ever socialize?"

VandenHeuval crossed his legs and sat back in his chair. "Perhaps we can cut to the chase. Alex Chandon told me you know about my connection to Regina and her family, but I'll be happy to review it for you."

"Ah," Fisher said. "Good to know we have friends in common."

VandenHeuval shifted in his chair before continuing. "When she came to New York, her father asked me to look out for her. I was told she was going to get an abortion, which, as you know, she did not. After the child was born, I was asked to help keep a lid on things."

"What does that mean?" Fisher asked.

"At first it meant making sure the boy's father didn't try to contact her, which he didn't. The financial arrangement worked. Then, it meant finding her a job. She was an intelligent young woman who wouldn't have been content watching soap operas and knitting. If she got bored, that could have been a problem. What's the saying? 'Idle hands are the devil's workshop'?"

"Translated," Fisher said, "her family didn't want her to come home with the child so you found something that kept her here in New York."

"There was that," VandenHeuval agreed, "but also, she wanted to work. She was a skilled writer and she needed a job that wouldn't require her to spend much time outside the apartment."

"Your requirement or hers?" Prado asked.

"She understood the reasons," VandenHeuval answered. "Later, we had to enroll her son in school. I took care of those arrangements and anything else that made it easier to keep her out of the public eye."

"You were her jailer," Fisher said.

"I prefer 'protector'. I was keeping safe what needed to be kept safe."

"Speaking of that," Prado said, "no more games. When we ask you to level with us, we expect you do to precisely that if you want us to do our job. To make sure we're all on the same page, is there anything else, anything at all," she said leaning into the words, "we need to know?"

"About Regina?"

"About *anything*. We don't like surprises. We've worked out a plan with the NYPD that keeps them away from you and Chandon and all the shit you're in to. We don't want to be put in a position where we have to make up excuses or explain away something you should have told us about."

"If you don't want any more surprises, Alex is the person you should be having this conversation with."

Prado looked at Fisher. "Not a good answer. Why would I have to speak to him? What don't we know?"

"Again, best to talk to him."

"He's not sitting here with us. You are." Prado asked aggressively, "What the hell don't we know?"

Fisher said, "And remember we spent time in your country. We know the people you deal with. The way you do business. We know how things work. Tell us everything. Don't try to whitewash anything."

"Whitewash?" VandenHeuval spit out venomously. "We wouldn't be having this conversation if your country hadn't forced its 'holy wars' on us. You took advantage of a small, impoverished nation and here we are." He stood abruptly. "Water?"

Prado shook her head.

"I'm good," from Fisher.

"You touched a nerve," Prado whispered to Fisher.

As VandenHeuval returned to the room, Prado said, "If we've offended you, we apologize, but to make this work the way you want, we need everything on the table."

VandenHeuval sat down and took a long sip from his glass, which he placed on a small side table. He cleared his throat. "You asked for everything. I'm going to give you everything. I'm going to give you information you do not have, and you may be sorry you asked for it." A pause. "Alex will be expanding the trafficking program."

"We know that," Fisher said. "That was part of his rationale for tying us into this insane operation."

VandenHeuval directed himself to Fisher. "What you don't know is that many of us are not happy with this prospect. Alex is trying to tempt us with increased payments for our cooperation."

"So, you're negotiating with him," Fisher said.

"No," VandenHeuval spit back angrily. "There is a reluctance to continue, much less expand. We are on the cusp of a new economic direction for our nation and we should be redirecting our energies. We should be getting out from under the corruption that has been a way of life if we want to encourage solid, long-term investments."

"This new direction," Fisher said, "you're talking about the development of offshore oil."

"Yes, a number of international companies are bidding on leases and other companies are building the infrastructure to support the industry. We must clean up our act so we can demonstrate that we are governed by the rule of law. Ensure confidence in our government."

"I don't mean to be dismissive," Prado said, "but what does this have to do with our" – she glanced at Fisher – "involvement? With Regina and her story?"

"A great deal," VandenHeuval answered. "In a few days, I will be meeting with representatives from your State Department, ATF, National Security Council and CIA to ask that Mr. Chandon be removed from his post. We will also insist that the weapons trafficking program be scrapped."

Prado nodded thoughtfully. "That is big, and we didn't know anything about it, but wouldn't you still need to control the narrative about Regina?" She paused, gathering her thoughts. "If Regina's situation is discovered, that could open the book on her father's cooperation with Chandon, and, possibly, on the other corruption. Wouldn't that create complications and make it difficult for you to move forward with your plans? The extent of what has been going on could discourage investors even if Chandon is gone and his operation is scuttled."

"Yes," VandenHeuval agreed, "and what we're going to ask could cause Alex to blow everything up and that could affect what *you're* doing. We need to know you will line up with us as a counterbalance to Alex, for our mutual benefit."

"What the hell does that mean? Fisher asked snappishly.

"Simple. When I make my case, I would like to say you two would find your going easier if Alex was out of the picture."

Prado glanced at Fisher, who cocked his head in question, before responding. "Your thing is your thing. We can move ahead no matter what you do. Whatever it is Chandon is up to, whatever your plans are to change that are noise as far as we're concerned." She leaned forward. "We're going to continue doing what we do no matter what you and your friends cook up."

"Alex is not going to go quietly," VandenHeuval said. "He will push back and your agency might react by pulling you away, ending your involvement, unless we can find a way to work together."

"Not gonna happen," Fisher exclaimed. "Cut us out of this? That would raise a lot of questions and there are no good answers."

"Better than staying the course, getting discovered, and then trying to explain why the FBI was complicit in weapons trafficking. Not only did you say nothing, you protected the trafficker." VandenHeuval took a sip of water. "To some degree it's a Hobson's choice, unless we remove Chandon from the picture together."

"Seems more like you're dealing with 'mutually assured destruction," Fisher responded. "Chandon has the goods to embarrass not only the Bureau, but also the ATF, maybe the NSC and his own agency, if he has a death wish."

"You forgot a very important card he can play. The Panday family is very keen on keeping the details of their daughter's situation quiet. Alex could use that to pressure Geoffrey to stand with him. We need you as counterbalance. You say you will continue to keep what needs to be hidden, hidden. The Pandays would appreciate that."

"You're saying Chandon would blackmail Panday?" Prado said. "Over an illegitimate child, and even that whole 'illegitimate' thing is almost an anachronism these days."

"Maybe you didn't learn enough about my country when you were there. First of all, the problem is not with the child being illegitimate, although that is not ideal. The real problem is the boy's father. He's Maroon. Black. There has been a lot of social and racial progress in Suriname, but there is still a bias. And there has been an increase in racial tensions recently. The spotlight is on one's origins these days. We have our own 'one drop rule' in Suriname. Families within the very thin layer of influence and power in Suriname are mostly of Creole, Hindustani or European origin, and they will protect their positions vigorously. If you are in Geoffrey's position where the social standing of his family could be threatened...and without which one loses everything, what would you do?"

"Loses everything?" Fisher said chidingly. "It's not like the guy would be reduced to destitution. He's stolen millions."

VandenHeuval showed his tight smile. "No, you did not learn enough about my country. Money without 'distinction' – I think that is the best way to describe it – without the distinction of being one of the 'betters' translates to poverty in Suriname. Without a place in the proper circles, one becomes a non-person. A wealthy non-person, but without any status. No power. No sway in how decisions are made. In essence, a wealthy and useless mannequin."

"To repeat," Prado said, "we have a job to do and we're going to continue doing it. No more side deals."

"I am proposing a way to keep your investigation on track."

Prado stood. "Go ahead. Do what you have to do. I am telling you again, the clusterfuck you're describing won't keep us from doing what we have to do."

"There is so much more. You are either very naïve or simply fail to recognize the realities." VandenHeuval paused a moment and looked from Prado to Fisher. "You really don't know that Alex has been making a king's ransom from his venture?"

"*His* venture?" Fisher snapped. "Are we still talking about the trafficking?"

"Yes, under the cover of official business, it is his operation. Of course, the supply gets to its destination and the proceeds fund the purchase of more weapons, and pay the right people, but a good bit of the return stays with Alex. He is going to fight hard to protect his fortune, but we will get what we want. We hold the better hand."

"Look," Prado said, shaking her head, "we agreed to guide things so no one would stumble into what's going on in Suriname. That's where we are and that's where things will stay." She raised a cautionary finger. "Unless someone tries to interfere, then all bets are off."

***

Prado slathered chive cream cheese onto her bagel as she took in the activity boiling around her in the Stage Door Deli. A crowd gathered at a glass display case filled with white lox, prepared foods and large pieces of cheese. Another group hovered around baskets displaying an assortment of bagels and breads. The cross talk between customers and servers behind the food display was animated to the point of hostility.

"You're pointing at the lox but you're saying you want white fish. Which is it lady?

There's a line behind you."

"Yes, the chopped liver is fresh. What kinda question is that?"

"You get a Baker's Dozen with twelve. No, you don't get seven when you order six."

Round, linoleum-topped tables and red vinyl upholstered chairs filled the balance of the room which smelled like strong coffee. Waitresses hustled from a kitchen balancing trays piled high with thick sandwiches, steaming cups of soup and carafes of coffee.

"What a wonderful city," Prado said, smiling. "I'll bet you can find any kind of food or whatever else you wanted. You wouldn't have to travel further than Chinatown to get authentic

Lo Mein noodles, or go to Rome for good pasta. And the clothes. From rags to 5th Avenue.

Whatever you want."

Prado turned slightly in her chair. "And the people. Is this amazing, or what? Don't see this in D.C. The most buttoned up city in the world. Here, if it's on their minds, it comes out of their mouths. In D.C. it has to be vetted by a press secretary after it's written by a speechwriter, and that's after the words are tested by a focus group. This is refreshing."

"Yeah, fascinating," Fisher said, looking around at the chaos. "My mind is on the guy who just told us our investigation could be compromised, even fucked."

"It won't be," Prado said, biting into her egg bagel, depositing a dollop of cream cheese in the corner of her mouth.

"The point is he thought it could. There could be some discussion of what's going on, what we're doing, when the great minds meet. Right?"

"Could be," Prado said, wiping a tip of her napkin across the corner of her mouth. "But there's something off about what he told us. VandenHeuval said he's meeting with the ATF,

NSC, CIA along with State. Why? If the discussion is going to be about recalling an ambassador, why include those agencies? Why not just the State Department?

"'Cause he wants us to use us as cover. Include us as allies. And there are guns involved."

"Yeah, there's all that," Prado agreed with a thoughtful nod, "but I think VandenHeuval is feeding us a load of shit. All that stuff about corruption, the rule of law. I'm not buying it.

There's something else going on. Maybe he's pissed that Chandon is making bank and not sharing enough of the goods. And why did he tell us about it in the first place? Why take the chance that we'd give Chandon a heads up, or even go straight to the executive suite at the Bureau?

"All that was a show? Why?"

"I haven't put the pieces together. We're missing something." She took another bite of bagel and chewed deliberately, in thought. Swallowed " Okay, let's say he wants to get Chandon out of the way whether it's to get a bigger piece of the pie or for the reasons he gave. Rule of law and all that. He'd want us to keep following the script. Keep a lid on things. Wouldn't be good news to have someone figure out what the deal is with Regina's father if he's really trying to sell the 'let's get clean' direction. He never addressed that when I brought it up."

Fisher asked, "I wonder who we'll hear from when the dust settles?"

"Not from our people. We were told to report here without an explanation, and no one from the New York office took any role other than providing the meeting place. We get lent out and someone now owes someone else a favor. Interagency cooperation without any paperwork.

Handshake deal." Prado waved away her previous words. "There's paperwork somewhere to cover everyone's ass, just not a lot of detail."

"Or the right details."

"Or that," she agreed. "Here's the deal, if anything comes our way, anything that could compromise how we do our job, derail us, we'll ignore it." She looked intently at Fisher. "You good with that?"

"I'm good."

Prado picked up a large dill pickle from her plate and eyed it before taking a bite. "I had people in New York. Probably still do but most left for better opportunities. That's the way my family tells it."

"Every Jew who came to this country probably passed through New York, and most of us still have family here. I do. In Brooklyn. My grandfather complained about the Dodgers leaving Brooklyn every day until he died. After my parents left, the ties frayed."

"'NewYorkricans is what my people are called. Puerto Ricans from New York."

"So, we're related by city," Fisher said with a laugh. "Who'd a thunk it?"

***

"You gonna make the call, or should I?" Levitt asked as she directed the cruiser to the
curb. "This is their bailiwick. We're supposed to be concentrating on Braddock."

"We're here," Broaden said. "Dispatch called us in. Let's see what we have, then call." He opened the passenger side door, unfurled one leg, anchored it on the sidewalk, and pushed himself upright.

They made their way past the first line of defense, a plain-clothed guard standing outside the iron gates leading to The Dakota courtyard. They flashed their badges and were waved ahead.

"No greeting committee like outside the Plaza," Broaden said, surveying the surroundings. "This place carries as much weight with the beautiful people as the Plaza. No media. No crowds of the morbidly curious."

"Dispatch sent out the call as an address. No names attached like with the Plaza.

Robinson's orders. No more flairs for the press."

"Bet you didn't know *Rosemary's Baby* was filmed here."

"No, I didn't," Levitt answered dismissively. "You ever been inside?" she asked as they walked into a large courtyard, around which four nine-story apartment towers loomed. Balustrades, multiple pitched roofs and dormers gave the building the look of a basilica.

Broaden shook his head. "No, my social circle doesn't extend to people who live here."

He pointed at a large, brilliantly-lighted Christmas tree at the far end of the courtyard. "The kind who can afford a Christmas tree that rivals the one at Rockefeller Center. We're more a single strand of lights in the shrubs kind of people. With most of the bulbs missing."

"Yeah," Levitt said, "but are they really happy?" She nodded at the nearest entrance.

"I wouldn't object to living here and finding out."

Their footsteps echoed as they stepped across marble floors toward the concierge station.

Arriving at the waist high desk, Broaden turned in a slow circle staring up at the oak ceilings as

Levitt identified herself. She elbowed Broaden. "Show the man your credentials," she said with a smile. "They're 'credentials' when you're in a place like this." She turned back to the concierge.

"Fiona Davis. Apartment number?"

The man in full livery, complete with epaulets, looked stricken; eyes wide, skin clammy.

"A bunch of you, uh...of your people are already here." He pointed at a bank of elevators. "East side, second floor. The elevator takes you to the foyer in the apartment." As Levitt and Broaden turned away, he asked, "Is she dead?"

Broaden took the few steps back to the desk and nodded solemnly. "Yes, she is. No one outside this building knows that and if anyone gets the word before we release the details, you and I will be having a very serious conversation about need for confidentiality."

"Well, you scared him quiet, tough guy," Levitt said as they walked to the elevators.

"That should keep things sane for an hour before word gets out and every paparazzi within a 50-mile radius shows up. The longer we can do our job without those maggots dogging us, the better."

The elevator gleamed polished mahogany with a brass railing and red carpeting. Broaden leaned in and whispered, "I could live in this fucking elevator."

"Why are you whispering?"

Broaden, surprised he had been whispering, shrugged.

The doors opened to a domed foyer. A huge Empire chandelier extended over a round, marble-topped table supported by three intricately carved spiral legs. Standing on the far side of the table, a patrolman reached into a box and handed Levitt and Broaden PPEs, head coverings, masks and booties.

Half-in the ill-fitting coveralls, the odd couple shuffled down a parquet floor set with mahogany, rose and cherry slats. The walls were wainscoted in colonial style trim molding. Royal purple wall paper extended to the ceiling, which was decorative stamped tin.

A woman met them at the first door. "Same old, same old," she said, nodding toward the naked body lying face up on a large bed in the center of the room. "Ligature marks. Appears to have been raped."

"You can already tell that?" Levitt questioned.

She pointed at the woman's pelvic region. "Blood on the sheets."

"That's different," Broaden said.

"These guys escalate," the woman answered. "Looks like it was rougher with her than with the others or she resisted more than they did. Won't know until the ME gets her on the slab for a closer look."

"Were any of the windows in the living room open?"

"A balcony door," the woman answered. "Forensics will have anything left behind, if it was."

Thick red cord sashes held blackout curtains away from a bank of windows overlooking Central Park. The room showed no signs of disturbance. A vanity positioned on the wall opposite the end of the bed held an array of hair brushes, a row of perfume bottles and a jewelry case.

The CSI noticed Levitt's attention going to the vanity. "Lots of very expensive stuff still there. I suppose something could have been taken but there's no evidence of that, or of forced entry."

Levitt asked, "Is the rest of the place undisturbed."

"Like someone had it sterilized," the woman answered.

Broaden stood at the mirrored, double-doored entrance to a walk-in closet and studied a wall of shoes to his left arranged neatly by color. "More shoes than Florsheim."

"She wouldn't have been caught dead in Florsheim," the woman said. Realizing the context, she raised both arms, surrendering. "My bad."

Broaden walked into the closet between two rows of clothes extending twelve feet on either side. Formal clothes. Business attire. Casual dresses and suit pants. Like the shoes, all arranged by color. Standing over an ottoman in front of a trifold, full-length mirror, he said, "I can't imagine anyone wearing all these clothes, even in a lifetime."

"There's a kid," the CSI said, jabbing a thumb toward the door. "In his bedroom with someone from Child Services."

"Who found the...?" Levitt started.

"The kid found his mother and went across the hall to a neighbor. He's in the living room. Name's Zane Brown."

"Okay," Levitt said to Broaden as he reappeared in the bedroom. "Now we call."

***

Prado and Fisher stood with Broaden at the foot of the bed. "Looks like it's the same unsub," Fisher said.

The CSI approached. "It has same earmarks as the other two with the exception of blood underneath her."

Prado bent over the body.

"Escalation maybe," the investigator said.

"Who found her?" Prado asked.

"Her son. He went to a neighbor for help, and he called it in."

"Is he here?" Fisher asked.

Broaden lowered his head toward the door. "In the living room."

"You talked to him?"

"Nope. Leaving that to you."

"His name?"

"Zane Brown."

"And the child?" Prado asked.

Broaden turned to the CSI who answered. "He's in his room with Child Services. Asked her to stay until you had a chance to talk to him. I'd suggest talking to Brown first. He's on the brink and could go into shock like right now. Want it fresh? Get him quick."

"The boy's name," Prado asked.

"Devon."

Prado and Fisher walked into the hallway. A line of photographs along the walls showed mother and son every year from his birth to a boy about seven years old. Fiona Davis had been a very attractive woman. Dark hair. Large brown eyes. Prominent cheekbones and full lips. The boy looked like his mother.

The living room was bright. Windows lined the far wall and a set of sliding doors led to a balcony. A knotted red and beige rug covered the floor leaving a narrow border revealing the parquet flooring. The wall to the right of the room entrance was mirrored and a grand piano occupied the space to the left. Two navy blue couches faced each other, one full size, the other smaller; a coffee table between. A fireplace filled the fourth wall. Large dark wood sculptures dotted the room.

A man seated on the larger couch looked up as Prado and Fisher walked into the room. He stood, wobbled, holding his arms out for balance, and appeared unsure whether to offer his hand and introduce himself.

Prado took the initiative and held out her hand. "I'm FBI Special Agent Eileen Prado and this is Special Agent Ira Fisher." She nodded toward the couch from which Brown had risen and, with Fisher, took the smaller one.

Brown was balding and had not shaved. He sat stoop-shouldered. His sweat pants and top fit tightly on a soft body, stomach pressing against the shirt, legs straining against the pants.

His round face appeared to have plumped from what once might have been a strong jawline. His eyes were deep set and dark rings underneath added age to his face.

Prado said, "We understand that Devon came to you this morning and you called 911."

Brown opened his mouth to answer. A sound came out. Not words. He coughed, clearing his throat. "Sorry, yes, he did." A pause. "I called 911 after seeing...." Another throat clearing cough. "After finding her."

"Would you run through the sequence of events starting with Devon coming to your door?"

"Sure," Brown said, and stared at the top of the table. "I heard a knock on my door at about 6:30 which surprised me given how early it was. I hadn't even had my first cup of coffee, or shaved." Brown winced. "Is this too much detail? Is this what you want?"

"It's perfect" Prado said. "Go on."

"I was doubly surprised to see Devon. I didn't know him or his mother well. We passed each other in the hall occasionally and said hello. That was about it. He said his mother needed help and I followed him into the apartment." Brown stared sightlessly.

Prado prodded him. "And you found the body."

Brown nodded, his eyes blank.

"You called 911."

"Yes."

"You said you didn't know Ms. Davis well."

"Not at all really."

"Did you ever see her with friends?"

Brown shook his head.

"And never talked to her except here in the building."

"No."

Prado let a moment pass. "Do you know what she did for a living? Any idea where she worked?"

A look of confusion clouded Brown's eyes. "Like I said...."

"We're trying to get a better sense of who Ms. Davis was," Prado said. "I'm hoping some of these questions, even if they seem to be repetitive, will jog something that can help us."

"Graphic artist, maybe," Brown said. He pointed toward the hallway. "I noticed what I think is a drafting table in one of the rooms I passed."

Fisher got up and walked into the hallway.

Prado continued. "Did you ever see her with other people?"

Brown shook his head. "I did see her in the lobby sometimes. When we picked up mail, but she was always alone."

Fisher returned. "There is a drafting table. It looks like she did some kind of commercial artwork. Book covers. Some ads."

Prado nodded and returned her attention to Brown. "What exactly did Devon say when he came to you?"

"He was nervous...uh, maybe scared is a better way to put it. He said he couldn't wake his mother up. Would I please come and help him wake her up. I knew right away, as soon as I saw her...." Brown took a deep breath. "Her lips were blue, or were turning blue. And I saw the red marks on her neck."

"Did Devon say if he had heard anything, seen anyone?"

"No, he only talked about his mother. Nothing else."

"Did you touch anything in the room?"

"No, absolutely not," Brown answered firmly "I know not to do that. I called 911 and have been sitting here the whole time. I was with Devon for part of that time until someone came to take care of him. Where is he anyway? Is he alright?"

"He's in his room. We appreciate your talking to us." Prado leaned toward Brown. "We understand how upsetting this is and if you'd like to talk some more, or can think of anything else later, anything at all, please call me." She slid a business card across the table, which Brown considered a moment before he picked it up.

Fisher suggested: "Why don't you let the EMTs take a look at you."

After walking Brown to the kitchen, where the EMTs had set up, Fisher led Prado into the room where a drafting table occupied the center of the space. "I doubt she used that much," Fisher said. He pointed at a computer. "Probably uses one of those fancy digital art software programs."

"Probably," Prado agreed.

"And look at this," Fisher said, gesturing to the computer screen. "That looks like a book cover and" – he sidestepped to a printer – "she printed it out."

Prado looked closely at the document. "Fuck. Did you see this?" Before Fisher could answer, she ran out of the room to the entrance of the apartment, where had she left her purse on the floor, and retrieved her phone. She ran back into the room, took a few pictures of the page in the computer then shouted toward the hallway, "Someone come in here and bag the page in the printer."

***

"Look at the name of the author," Prado said. Robinson, Levitt and Broaden leaned close to Prado's phone.

"Regina Wozniak," Robinson said, falling hard against the back of her chair.

"Son-of-a-bitch," came from Levitt.

I don't think it's a coincidence that Provine is in the publishing business," Prado said.

"Ten-to-one Davis was designing covers for Provine."

"We found the link," Robinson said. "We found the damn link."

"It fits. Like pieces to a puzzle," Fisher said. "And they all had kids."

"All boys," Levitt added.

"All single mothers," from Broaden. "They lived in upscale buildings in the same neighborhood. Their kids attended private schools."

"Do we know that?" Levitt asked. "That their kids attended private schools?"

"The first one for sure," Broaden said. "We wondered how she could afford it. The second one had a car service pick up her kid to go to school. I can't imagine her doing that and then sending him to the local public school." He shrugged. "I don't even know if there is a public school around there."

"So, what do we have?" Robinson asked. "How does this help us?"

"For starters," Fisher said, "we can say we definitely have a serial killer. Officially, I mean." He signaled quote marks with his fingers as he said: 'A person who murders three or more people with a cooling down time between murders. The separate events are usually driven by a psychological thrill or pleasure.'"

"We have to establish what psychology drives *this* guy," Robinson said.

Prado offered, "Usually these offenders choose their victims based on availability, vulnerability and desirability."

"Our victims qualify," Levitt said. "Single mothers who were alone and vulnerable, although getting into the secure buildings where they lived had to be a challenge."

"Desirability," Fisher continued, "is a little harder to pinpoint. Motivation is a key and it's related to race, ethnicity, gender, age. They fulfill a fantasy the killer has. We already talked about Bundy liking brunettes and Son of Sam had a thing for couples. We have to find out what's driving our guy to go after his victims. Is it related to the kids, or what about the physical characteristics of the mothers? Tall? Short? Petite. Curvy. Blonde? Brunette."

Levitt said, "Wozniak was petite. Provine not so much. Davis was tall. Other than all being brunettes, I'm not seeing a lot of physical similarities here."

"Yeah, well," Prado replied, "we have to go beyond physical similarities. The horrible truth is these sickos want to kill. They like it. That's what drives them. They can be triggered by someone's appearance, or even what someone says to them. We hear about sexual sadists and psychopaths, but they are rare, or rarer than the others who simply have an 'itch' to kill. It's that basic."

"So maybe we should focus tightly on the way our guy operates," Broaden said. "His MO. How he does what he does. I'm hearing that doing what he does is what gets him off; not so much who but how."

"Those ViCAP files I gave you," Prado directed to Broaden and Levitt, "were you able to draw anything useful from them?"

Levitt said, "There's something there. The persons of interest in a few of the sexual assaults, and two of the murders" – she looked at Broaden – "I think it was two, right"

"Yeah," Broaden took up the thread. "Two of the crime scenes in New Jersey were exactly like what we're dealing with. MO the same. A kid at home in both."

"Any other details," Prado probed. "Anything on what he looked like, or anything from CCTV?"

Broaden shook his head. "Nothing."

"Braddock," came from Robinson. "His name is James Braddock."

Levitt and Broaden stiffened.

"What?" Prado asked.

Chapter 10

One Butterfly at a Time

"What the hell?" Willow Briggs exclaimed, staring down at the steep decline. "You want

me to hike down The Exorcist Stairs?" She backed away from the edge and turned toward Prado. "There's a reason anyone who saw *The Exorcist* stays away from here." Briggs pointed at a building to their right. "That's where Father Damien was hurled out the window and plummeted down these stairs. Sorry, but that haunts me. Not happening."

"I might have to rethink my choice of psychologists," Prado said, hands on her hips, voice in mock annoyance. "I never would have taken you for someone who would let a movie prevent her from doing anything, much less walking down a flight of stairs."

"A flight?" Briggs said, pointing at the long line of stone steps. "That's like a hundred steps. More, I think." She bent forward and patted her thighs. "These are short and fat. Not long and strong like yours. All you 'in shape' types have no clue how the rest of us live."

"I don't even know what that means," Prado said. "Okay, back to Wisconsin and Compass Coffee. On me."

Walking past the red brick row houses that dominated the architecture of Georgetown, Briggs had had enough of the small talk and asked, "What do you really want to talk about? It isn't about getting me out of the house 'for my health,' or 'to enjoy a crisp morning walk.'" She looked at Prado, a smile emerging. "Right."

"Right," Prado said as she opened the door to the coffee shop and gestured toward two leather-backed chairs near the entrance. "A latte to fuel the conversation?"

"Vanilla latte."

"Coming up," Prado said.

Briggs leafed through a copy of *The Washington Post* getting as far as the editorial Page when Prado placed a cup on the low table in front of her. "As requested," she said.

"So, what's up?" Briggs asked, lifting the cup to her mouth and recoiling. "Shit, hot."

Prado repositioned her chair turning it toward the front window. "Fisher, my partner, had to drive home for his wedding rehearsal so I hitched a ride."

"That doesn't explain why I got a call at 6:30 this morning insisting that we take a walk." She swallowed a gulp of coffee. "For my health."

"I need to catch you up on what's going on in New York. Where'd I leave off?"

"You told me about a potential conflict between what you needed to do and what you had been asked to do by your friend from Suriname. The CIA guy."

"My 'friend?'" Prado said, shaking her head. "Hardly."

Briggs placed the cup on the table. "So, what's the deal?"

Prado sipped her Chai tea and stared at Briggs over the top of the cup, taking a moment before resuming. "This is a doozy. That's official language when describing a fucked up situation. Okay, here's the deal. Three women have been killed. There are links among the three. One was a writer, another designed the cover of her book, and the third was the publisher. We've established those details."

"I'm guessing that all were victims of the same person."

"The MO and history of the person-of-interest says so, but here's where it gets really fucked up. The cops we're working with knew the identity of the person-of-interest all along."

"Wait," Briggs said, raising her eyebrows in question. "They knew but didn't tell you?"

Prado nodded. "They knew and didn't share it." She leaned forward. "They held back because they're protecting politicians who years ago supported reducing spending on mental health and that resulted in releasing damaged people, like our perp, from mental health facilities, dumping them onto the street. Our suspect, along with God knows how many others, then robbed, raped, and killed people." Prado raised a hand. "I'm not saying that all mentally challenged people...."

"Stop, for Christ's sake. You don't have to do that with me."

"I felt the need."

"All of this is documented? It's more than just people talking to each other. People speculating. It's fact that some of those let out committed serious crimes?"

Prado nodded. "I saw the files on our guy."

Briggs stared hard at Prado. "We're talking about people in office right now who would be fucked if any of this got out. Right?"

"Right."

"How?" Briggs asked, her voice quacking. "How could something like this happen?"

"The detective in charge of investigating the first murders punted."

"What do you mean 'punted'?"

"Didn't pursue the guy once he ID'ed him. He took the information that led him to identify a person-of-interest to the people in charge and made his case. In the process, the information on how the perp ended up on the street came out. A little digging also found out that Braddock, that's the perp's name, wasn't the only one. He was one of many tossed out of facilities when the funding was stopped, or shifted to other programs. Braddock's name was redacted from the files and the detective was asked to find a way to put him away, but without tagging him for murder because that would attract too much attention. The fact that Braddock was released from a mental institution would become the focus. The media, rival politicians, mental health advocates, and who knows who else, would be all over it. In fact, rival politicos *were* smelling blood in the water and the issue had to be erased."

"And?"

"Braddock was put away for sexual assault, and charges for previous crimes were piled on top to keep him locked away. With his name redacted from the case files, the politicians were out of the line of fire."

Briggs raised her shoulders in question. "But he must have gotten out. He's back on the street."

"Yeah," Prado said. "Prison crowding got him out. From what we can tell, he was a model prisoner and when a list was made of who could be released to make room for more bad guys, he was on that list."

"Jesus Christ," Briggs said, raising her hands to her face. "This is awful."

"Awful doesn't even begin to describe it. Three women in New York and at least two others in New Jersey and one in Pennsylvania are dead because politicians wanted to protect their asses."

"What are you going to do?"

"I can't really claim the high ground. I have my own baggage what with the whole CIA thing. If I was to go public, the blowback would make our job finding this guy impossible. The spectacle, the media storm would overwhelm everything."

"The cover-up was years ago, right?"

"Yeah, it was years ago. The assholes who engineered this are now sitting in the Senate and Governor's mansion."

"My God! In New York?"

Prado nodded. "In New York, which means the political backbone of the entire state would shatter if this got out."

"This is not on you, Eileen."

"I keep thinking that if we, me and Ira, and the NYPD had been on the same page to begin with, we might've saved at least one of the women. After the first two, they knew who we're looking for." Prado lowered her head. "Meantime, we were playing our own game. I have to come to terms with this so I can work with these people."

"You want my thoughts." She leaned toward Prado. "As a friend?"

"I do."

"You're putting a huge burden on your shoulders. You have to stop that shit. As far as working with people who withheld information, that's bad, but you know now. They told you. I'm guessing you let them know what you thought of the...."

"Oh, yeah, I did. It's one of the reasons I had to give myself a breather. I needed some space. Some time. I wasn't very understanding. And that's an understatement. I threatened to blow it all up."

"That's where you left it? With them thinking you might blow it up?"

Prado nodded. "But I can't. As I said, it would make it impossible to do our job. And there's also my baggage."

"I have enough common sense, and distance from what you're doing to see that you have your end under control. You never would have allowed anything to get in the way of doing the right thing." Briggs leaned forward and put her hand on Prado's knee. "Can't you see that? Give yourself a damn break. Your instincts and character are sound."

Prado stared at the traffic along Wisconsin Avenue.

"You've always done your job."

The women sat in silence a moment before Briggs repeated, "You've always done your job. That's who you are."

Prado took a deep breath and brought her attention back to Briggs. "Yeah, we're doing our job, but now I know we're working a dirty case."

"The case might be dirty but you had nothing to do with that. Square one, where you began, is clean. Move ahead. Catch this bastard and then you can revisit all this other shit and make some decisions on how you want to move forward. Or not."

"Or not," Prado said. "We have a tendency to bargain with ourselves and the 'or nots' usually win."

"Did I ever tell you the butterfly story?"

Prado shook her head.

"A young boy was staring at a thick book and looking very concerned. His father approached and asked what was wrong. The boy leafs through the book and says 'I have to memorize the names of all these butterflies.' The father sits down next to his son and says 'You can do it. One butterfly at a time.'" Briggs tapped her index finger on the table between them. "One butterfly at a time."

Prado smiled. "Kid still has lots of names to memorize."

"You're good people, Eileen, and good people do the right thing."

"Gotta wonder sometimes if 'good people' make a difference anymore. We got dragged into a real fucked up deal. The victims are almost a sideshow, something to be managed; their situation resolved without upsetting any apple carts."

"If I remember correctly, you held a United States Senator responsible for covering up his wife's fatal hit-and-run. Chased him out of office. So, yeah, good people still make a difference." Briggs lifted her coffee cup into a toast position. "Go forth and do good."

Chapter 11

Uptown Savage

"A fucking press conference," Robinson said angrily. "The commissioner's foisting it off on me."

"He's not going to say anything?" Broaden asked.

"Oh, he'll give a rundown on what we're dealing with and then throw me to the wolves. He wants to cover his ass, but I have to do the covering. Convince the good people of this great city that we're on the job protecting them from the Uptown Savage." She shook her head. "I told you they'd come up with something that would top 'Apartment House Murders.'"

"Whatever shocks and sells the most newspapers," Levitt said.

"Not newspapers," Broaden objected. "Screens, phones and TVs. Newspapers are an afterthought."

Robinson slumped in her chair. "I have no idea what I'm going to say. We got nothing, which is why I'm the face of this thing. Wouldn't be able to pry his fingers off the podium if we had good news. Right now we don't have DNA. We don't have any useful witness statements. I guess I could trot out the ViCAP information about similar crimes in New Jersey and Pennsylvania and say we have an interstate task force or" – she waved her hand in a circle –"whatever."

"That's not a bad idea," Broaden said. "A task force. The illusion of movement without any real motion."

"Of course, I'd have to actually form a task force."

"We" – Prado nodded at Fisher – "used the ViCAP data and put together a profile on Braddock. We included everything we could find on his background. Family. School records. Medical history. Might be presser worthy."

"How'd you find all that?" Levitt asked.

"People are happy to help," Prado said, "when you're the FBI and ask politely for their cooperation. It also helps that he has a long criminal history from which we could pull a lot of detail on his life during his stops through the system. Plus, there are those elves I told you about banging away on computers in the basement of Bureau headquarters in D.C. who know how to ferret out all kinds of stuff."

"That's a vivid and disturbing image," Levitt said.

"What we've been able to find and assemble validates him as a person-of-interest. We used the same approach to confirm our suspect in the Olatha Monster case."

"God," Robinson said disgustedly. "These fucking names. 'Savage'. 'Monster'."

Prado held the pages up. "This creates a profile and aligns that profile with our suspect."

Robinson leafed through the document. "What? This is going to be enough to nail Braddock?"

"Nail him?" Prado said. "No, like I said, it's a profile, not evidence, but it's solid enough to justify holding a press conference to alert 'the good people of this great city' that we have someone in our crosshairs. Someone they should be on the lookout for. Most importantly, something to feed the media."

"I'm not quite sure what you're telling us," Robinson said. "Is this real or just a distraction to keep the noise makers at bay?"

"Yes," Prado said.

Robinson squeezed her face into a look of consternation. "Yes?"

"It's real. It squares with what we know about Braddock. Is it foolproof? Is it absolute proof that we have the right person?" Prado raised her hands, palms out. "We'll know when we have him sitting in front of us and we can question him. But it works as a valid tool identifying Braddock as someone who's dangerous and someone we need to find."

***

"Thank you, Commissioner Kinney," Robinson said as she placed her note cards on the podium and looked out at the overcrowded media room. There was not an inch between bodies. The fire code was being flaunted in 1 Police Plaza. A large overflow was piled into a nearby conference room and tuned in via a remote connection.

"The commissioner has provided the basic facts of the crimes, the victim's names and where we stand with our investigation. I'll now add that we have a person-of-interest."

"Who is it?" came a shout from the back of the room near the platform set up for television cameras. Robinson recognized the questioner as the pancake makeup queen of the top rated television morning show.

"If you'll let me finish, Vera, I'll get to that," Robinson said. "We have fact sheets" – she lifted pages from the podium, waving them – "summarizing what the commissioner just shared. They will be made available at the conclusion of this briefing."

Robinson turned to a 72-inch flat screen behind her and stepped aside, bringing the portable microphone with her. "This is our person-of-interest." An image with a thousand-mile stare appeared. The blankness of the eyes complemented the lack of any distinctive physical traits. Thin face. Sunken cheeks. Close cropped hair. Thin nose coming to a point over a slice of a mouth. "His name is James Braddock. That photo was taken eight years ago when he was confined at Rikers for aggravated sexual assault and indecent exposure. A complete physical description is included in the handouts that come with the fact sheet I mentioned. Basic information is he's 5'11" and weighs 165 pounds. He has no tattoos. No scars." She stared at the screen. "Mr. Average."

Robinson returned to the podium and began reading from an abridged version of the profile Prado and Fisher developed. "First, and easiest, Braddock is a Caucasian male, obviously," she said with a slight turn toward the screen behind her. "He is 37 years old.

"Most theories on the etiology of serial killers..."

"In English, please."

"I'm referring to the predisposing factors," Robinson said. "You need it plainer than that? How about 'why they kill'. The list includes mental disorders, childhood trauma and sexual, psychological and physical abuse. Braddock had all of that. Unlike many of these people, however, he came from a privileged background. Grew up in Detroit. Good neighborhood.

Good schools. His father was an executive with General Motors. When his father disappeared and his mother fell into alcoholism, his life fell apart."

"Disappeared?" was shouted at Robinson. "Disappeared how?"

"Disappeared as in 'disappeared.' Today, I guess you'd call it going off the grid. Years later he turned up in Key West where he was bartending. No more shouted questions," she said, shutting down a chorus. "We can do a short Q and A when I'm finished."

Robinson shuffled her note cards. "James Braddock was mistreated by his mother, and that's an understatement. Locked in rooms for days, primarily in a closet. There were signs of sexual abuse. It was never traced to his mother, but boyfriends who came and went over the years had a history of such behavior. That was eventually reported and Braddock was removed from his home. He was in and out of foster homes until he was 18. He failed a number of grades and never graduated high school. When in school he was accused by several female classmates of 'unwanted advances.'" Robinson looked up from the text. "He was very aggressive in a few of these instances. He was sentenced to juvenile detention a number of times for voyeurism. He was caught peeking in windows around his neighborhood.

"Before I continue, I want to make it clear that we are presenting this information in the hope that your readers and viewers can help us track down James Braddock."

"You're saying he's the Uptown Savage and he's on the loose?" someone called out.

"I'm saying he's a person-of-interest we want to talk to and we need your help and that of the people of this city."

Robinson raised her hand, again stopping a torrent of questions. "I said I'd take questions when I was done." She waited for the drone of mumbling and shuffling to die down before continuing. "We are laser focused on bringing justice to the victims. Regina Wozniak, Dorothy Provine and Fiona Davis. Let's keep them at the forefront of our thinking. This is about the victims. Make that your ledes."

Robinson scribbled on the back of one of her note cards and waved Levitt over. She handed her the card, and continued. "James Braddock volunteered to go into the service as soon as he was released from juvenile detention. He served with the U.S. Army Special Forces in Afghanistan. No black marks there. We have found that military service is considered a pre-dispositional factor for many serial offenders."

The images of Wozniak, Provine and Davis appeared on the screen behind Robinson. She nodded a 'thank you' to Levitt.

"When Braddock returned from Afghanistan he was in and out of trouble. His arrest record shows time served for robbery, assault, sexual misconduct and resisting arrest. He continued where he left off prior to enlistment. He was confined to a mental health facility for a time, released and went right back to doing what he had been doing. He was eventually arrested and convicted of aggravated sexual assault and rape, with time added for other offenses, and was sentenced to 25 years to life. He served 7 years and was released when overcrowding pushed him and others out to make room for those who were considered at the time to be greater risks to society."

"That ended well didn't it?" was hollered, followed by a blizzard of questions. "Who made that decision? What's the name of his parole officer?" A general din of unintelligible shouting filled the room.

Robinson stared at the rabble a moment before threatening: "I'll end this right now if you don't shut up." She backed away from the podium.

Calls for quiet from within the group restored order.

Robinson stood stiffly, her eyes scanning the room before returning to the podium. "Braddock's PO has not heard from him. In addition to being a person-of-interest here in New York, he is a suspect in two murders. Maybe three. For sure in Cherry Hill, New Jersey, another in Philadelphia. Along the way he has adopted a variety of aliases, including Tommy Loughran and Ernie Schaaf.

"For those of you who aren't familiar with the dangers we are dealing with until we capture the person responsible for the three murders here in New York, I refer you to the words of FBI profiler John Douglas. He wrote that 'Being able to dominate, manipulate and control a victim, to decide whether the victim lives or dies, or how that victim dies, temporarily counteract, for some, their feelings of inadequacy....' In other words, raping and murdering sets the world right with them.

"These are very dangerous people who do what they do to give them the power and control they lack in their daily lives. But don't make the leap to thinking we're talking about people who slink around in the shadows, or who shun human contact because they are socially inadequate. Some are, of course, but they could also be your next door neighbor, or the man who helps you take your groceries into the house. At the same time, they're frustrated by not having the job they think they deserve, or are not in relationships they want. They need to take control of their lives, to assert power. They do that by killing."

Robinson looked out toward the crowded room. "Let me leave you with this." She read slowly from an index card. "Ted Bundy said that killing, '...becomes possession. You're looking into their eyes and basically a person in that situation is God.'

"All of what I have presented today describes James Braddock and validates him as a person-of-interest. We have to get this individual off the streets and into custody where we can decide if he advances from a person-of-interest to one we arrest for the multiple murders. We need your help to do that" – she turned toward the screen – "and to bring them justice and make sure no one else suffers the same fate.

"Before I take your questions, we need to have an understanding on something. As to who made the decision to free Braddock" – Robinson shook her head – "that was not us. I can't comment on that. Now, I'll take a few...."

Before she could complete her thought, a woman in front of the podium popped out of her seat and identified herself as "Sally Marker, *New York Post.* You have no DNA, no witness statements that ID Braddock, and, I'm assuming, no CCTV, or you would have shown it to us. Braddock was using aliases in New Jersey and Pennsylvania, yet, you have identified him as your person-of-interest. Why and how did you land on him?"

"As I said, Braddock is a career criminal which means what he does and how he does it follows him like the slime a slug leaves behind. We found most of what we needed from the FBI's ViCAP data base and put the pieces together."

The pancake makeup queen had shoved her way to the front of the room. She did not bother identifying herself or her outlet, instead shouting her question louder than others around her. "Serial killers always have a 'type.' They also have a distinctive MO and signature. How about the Uptown Savage? What is his type? His MO and signature?"

Robinson thought briefly about ignoring the woman but recognized the point of the briefing was to get word out to the public as quickly and thoroughly as possible and the queen carried the largest audience with her. "All the victims were single mothers of young boys. They were successful, professional women living in similar circumstances and in proximity to each other. That's as far as I'm going to go, but it describes a 'type.'" As far as his MO, we're dealing with a very organized offender. He doesn't want to get caught and leaves very little behind for us to work with. Next question."

"Willis Brown, *Newsday*. FBI data and information on the person-of-interest led you to Braddock. Have you also requested direct Bureau participation in your investigation? Are FBI agents working with you?"

"Yes, we asked for and are receiving direct assistance from the Bureau. Please keep the victims at the forefront of your reporting. They are...*were* mothers, they had families who are devastated by these brutal murders. Thank you. "

***

He studied the image on the screen and ran his fingers down the side of his face. The scar extending from his left cheek to the corner of his mouth was raised. It took thirty-two stitches to close the gash. The scar over his right eye pulled the skin toward his forehead lifting his eyelid which remained open even when he slept. He leaned against the back of the couch to get his reflection in the hall mirror. The extent of the damage to his chin created scar tissue that added bulk to the right side. The pain had paid off. The beatings he provoked with inmates and guards, and his time in the ring against anyone who accepted his challenge – fights fueled by the anger his taunting and disrespect stoked in his opponents– provoked furious beatings. The bridge of his nose was flattened and the destruction to his mouth gave him the look of a harelip.

Purposeful. Painful. Successful.

A different kind of pain came with his name change. He had always been the Cinderella Man. His namesake. The Depression-era fighter

James Braddock. A longshoreman down on his luck, forced onto welfare; nothing more than a journeyman fighter, he shocked the world when he won the heavyweight championship. That's who he was. Taking control. Fighting his way free. But he had to move on. Braddock was then. The Cinderella Man was history. He had a new life.

He paused the program so he could read the news ticker carefully. "Nineteenth Precinct Commanding Officer Nadine Robinson described a person-of interest who was a victim of sexual abuse as a child; locked in rooms, primarily in a closet." *How did they find out?* He barely remembered any of it. It was much worse. That he did remember. Awful things.

He felt the rage beginning to boil. It warmed his chest and would explode up into his head if he did not stop it. The stabbing of hot pokers behind his eyes would take him to his knees, and ringing in his ears would get so loud he would pass out.

He jumped up and ran in place. Hard and fast until his legs ached and he gasped for air. He stopped and bent over, his hands on his knees, sweat pouring down his face and dripping into a puddle forming on the concrete floor. A moment to recover and then into the kitchen. He put his head under the faucet, drinking and running water over his face. He dried himself with the tail of his shirt, returned to the living room, and pressed "Play."

"Oh, my," came unbidden when the photos of Wozniak, Davis and Provine flashed across the screen. He felt insulted for them; that they were being exposed this way. So publicly. They were his. He made them his. He knew where they went, when they went, and who they met, which was mainly each other, though not often. The writer almost never went out; the artist only to take her boy to the park, and meet with the others; the other one did go to an office, but not on a regular schedule. He knew their smell. That came when he was with them. One was roses; one was like the earth, but good, clean, not dirty; the one at the Dakota was like Christmas, cookies and pine.

Walking toward the screen he heard: "Ted Bundy said that killing, '... becomes possession. You're looking into their eyes and basically a person in that situation is God.'"

"Yes," he said excitedly. "That's it." His girls will always be with him. They were part of him. They will never do what his mother had done. He kept them good. He saved them and their sons.

He fell into in his chair and stared sightlessly. There were the others. He hardly remembered them. Would that happen with these? He wanted fresh smells. Clean ones.

He caught the words 'his type' and snapped his attention back to the screen. "All the victims are single mothers of young boys."

How was that going to help? Or that ancient mug shot? Or the discarded name. Or anything that woman was saying? It would not, of course. There was no one to touch. They were chasing a ghost.

"I'm not the person you're looking for," he said, jabbing a finger at the television. "There is no James Braddock."

The others had all been questioned. The supers in the buildings where his girls lived. All his friends. To eliminate them, they were told, so they could move on with their investigation. They were asked if they knew each other. *Yes, of course they did. They played poker together.* They and three to four others who were the envied group in the city's luxury residences. No reason to talk to him. His building was not one of the buildings. It was a miracle; it was fate when he became one of them; that he was led to this path. When it happened, it stood out like it was emblazoned in neon lights.

He could not believe it when he saw that name, Max Baer, on the list of supers who died. Mention in the New York Building Manager's Association newsletter. It was a sign. *The* sign. He shouted when he saw it. Getting Baer's information was easy. Making it his own was simple. The only glitch would have come if the homeowner's board at the Manchester checked with the Building Manager's Association. They did not. He was hired. Baer was hired. It was a golden day.

He loved his job. He was good at his job. He learned about plumbing, electrical work, even about boilers and carpentry in prison. He walked a difficult path to arrive. It brought him into the world where he could help others. Save them.

He pulled his phone from his pocket and jabbed at the face until finding what he wanted. He made certain the volume was a high as it would go and put in his ear buds.

Getting strong now
Won't be long now
Getting strong now
Gonna fly now
Flying high now
Gonna fly, fly

He danced. He raised his arms and swayed. He owned Max Baer.

***

As Robinson left the media room to a barrage of voices asking her to take more questions, Prado fell into step with her. They walked toward a bank of elevators. "That was impressive," Prado said.

"Yeah, well, every once in a while I get inspired. Plus, that information you and Fisher put together gave me a good script to work from."

"I wouldn't have suggested that you go out on a limb and name him if I wasn't sure he is the one."

"Oh, he's the one," Robinson said and pointed at an open conference room. "A word?"

Levitt, who with Broaden and Fisher followed behind the pair, whispered, "Oh, shit, a cage match." They averted their eyes as they passed the glass walled room.

Robinson walked to a small refrigerator next to a low slung faux wood cabinet. "Water?"

"No, thanks," Prado said as she stood behind a chair at the head of a polished oval cherry wood conference table. "If this is about what I said the other day. I should have chosen my words more carefully. You caught me by surprise."

"Sit, please," Robinson said, taking a sip from a small plastic water bottle. "I need to do this."

Prado took a chair opposite Robinson.

"I made a judgment call and it was a bad one. I'm not talking about my decision to keep what we knew hidden. I needed time to process how

I was going to handle it in the long run. In the short term, I knew we could work our case effectively without broadcasting what we found."

"Look...," Prado interjected.

"I'm not finished." Robinson paused and played with the bottle. "I had to consider what it meant. Would I eventually have to pull back the curtain? If I did, the blowback would be incredible. If I didn't, would I be able to live with that?"

Prado nodded. "I work in Washington. I have a feel for all that."

Robinson drummed her fingers on the table. "When you walked in it injected a new dynamic. Now, I had the FBI in the mix. My first reaction was to stay the course. That was wrong for all kinds of reasons. I know that now, but...and here comes my rationalization. I was still turning it over and playing with the 'what ifs'. Long story short, I apologize. I hope you'll talk to me before you make any final decisions on what you feel you have to do."

Prado pointed at the bottle of water. "I do need some."

"Go ahead," Robinson said, nodding toward the refrigerator.

"I'm in no position to be judging," Prado said as she returned to the table and sat.

Robinson laughed freely. "In no position to judge? I spilled some serious shit. Bad shit. It was easy to judge."

"No, not really. Or more to the point, I'm in no position to judge." Prado stared at Robinson. "I have my own situation."

Robinson frowned and turned her head slightly, almost defensively. "Do I even want to know?"

"Probably not, but I owe you."

"No," Robinson replied, holding up her hands. "No, you don't. I needed to explain myself. I had my reasons for doing what I did and thought you should know. We have to work together going forward and we have to trust each other."

"Which is why you need to know, or more to the point, why I have to come clean. I said 'cards on the table' when we met without putting them all on the table."

"I'm not going to like this, am I?"

"No, you're not." Prado took a deep breath.

"That bad is it?" from Robinson.

"A few months ago, Ira and I were investigating a case that took us to Suriname."

"Where?"

"Suriname. It's a small country in South America."

"I thought you guys only worked domestically and weren't allowed to do anything overseas. That's CIA business, isn't it?"

"Yeah, and that's part of my story. The Bureau can investigate in a foreign country under certain circumstances and this was one of those circumstances. While we were in Suriname, we stumbled onto a weapons trafficking operation." Prado shook her head as if disbelieving her own words. "It wasn't related to why we were there." She made a sound that could have been interpreted as a laugh but no humor registered on her face. "It was a CIA operation."

"Jesus."

"Yeah, 'Jesus.' As you can guess, we looked the other way. But that's what brought us into this."

"This, as in *this*?" Robinson said, jabbing the table with her index finger. "This here in New York?"

Prado nodded. "Regina Wozniak is...*was* the daughter of a big shot in Suriname who is the money man for the CIA. He pays off the right people to look the other way and makes sure the weapons move smoothly through the country. When you sent your inquiry about Wozniak to ViCAP, it set off bells and whistles. Ira and I were foisted on you to make sure that no one pierces the veil. We were told to manage the investigation so it wouldn't expose arrangements in Suriname."

Robinson nodded. "Okay, you win. Your hidden card trumps mine."

Prado scoffed. "Interesting perspective."

"I'm guessing you've considered that if anything we just laid on the table – either your stuff or mine – falls off the table, we're fucked. And I'm not talking personally, but there is that too. I'm talking how massively everything could blow up in our faces. Blow the investigation up. Maybe even cause it to be compromised so badly, Braddock could skate. I can't think through right now how that would play out, but with the politics and the international aspects complicating everything, Braddock might become an afterthought."

Prado nodded. "The possibilities of how this could go sideways are endless. Let's see if we can keep it simple and just plow ahead with our investigation. Let's do what we do. If we need any workarounds, we'll talk."

"All my cards are on the table," Robinson said.

"Mine too."

***

Eloise was surprised by a knock on the door. She had not ordered groceries and those were usually delivered after an "Okay to come up?" phone call from the concierge, or, if a small order, came via the dumb waiter. Maybe more questions from the police? Eloise shook her head and mumbled "Lord" as she walked down the hallway. The police had already been through the building interviewing everyone, including her. She could not tell them much. Nothing really. She did not know the poor woman. They had not asked to talk to Warren and she did not volunteer him. Were they back because they found out he lived there? She opened the door, fully prepared to explain that she was authorized to speak on his behalf, and faced a dangerously thin young girl, her skin almost translucent.

In a bold, self-confident voice, belying her appearance, the girl asked, "Can I speak to Warren, please?"

Eloise was struck dumb. This was the first time anyone had come to the door and asked for Warren. And this tiny figure, who looked too fragile to be standing, was doing so with an energy that belied her appearance.

"Maddy?" came from Warren, who appeared at Eloise's shoulder. "I thought I recognized your voice."

A tall woman in a light blue uniform stepped into view from the right side of the doorway. Seeing Eloise's eyes shift to the woman, Maddy explained, "This is Nancy. She's my day nurse."

"I don't understand," was all Eloise could muster.

"This is Maddy," Warren explained, carefully avoiding the rectangle of light that sliced in from the corridor and framed Eloise. "She lives in the building."

Eloise turned toward Warren, her face contorted in concern and question. "What?"

"Please," Warren said to Maddy and her nurse, gently pulling Eloise away from the door. "Come in."

"Have you been watching TV?" Maddy asked excitedly, turning toward Warren and walking backward in front of him as they made their way down the hallway. "About the Uptown Savage?"

"No," Warren said. "Who's the Uptown Savage?"

Maddy stopped. "Seriously?" The parade stopped with her.

"Why don't we go into the living room?" Warren suggested, gesturing ahead.

The group started forward and everyone entered a darkened room.

Maddy turned toward her minder. "I told you about that XP thing he has. He has to keep out of the light."

Eloise glanced up at Warren. "That *thing* you have?"

Recessed lighting built into the floorboards outlined the dimensions of the large room.

Maddy asked, "You can't have any lights on at all?"

Warren nodded at Eloise who went to the opposite side of the room and tapped her foot on a floor switch lighting a lamp on an end table flanking a couch. "Better?" he asked.

Maddy nodded.

Eloise clicked on a pole lamp on the other side of the couch revealing a dark brown leather ottoman the same color and material as the couch. Three matching leather chairs arranged in a semi-circle faced the couch. A dining room table was visible in the shadows of a space beyond the living room. A large china cabinet and wet bar completed the layout.

"Could we talk in private?" Maddy asked. "In your room, maybe?"

"I don't think that's appropriate," Eloise said, standing stiffly and looking very uncomfortable.

Maddy laughed. "Believe me, he's safe." She lifted her arms away from her side. "Do I look like I'm in any condition to do anything? Plus," she said, with a quick glance at Warren, "he's old. And I'm underage. Only 17."

"Well...," Eloise started.

"There was a time," Maddy said, "when this" – she posed with her hands on her hips – "was not so bad. Like 40 pounds ago. My boobs alone weighed about five pounds each."

Warren snorted a laugh. He avoided making eye contact with Eloise.

Maddy pulled off her skull cap revealing a very white scalp showing through wispy, thinning tufts of hair. "I had really pretty red hair too. More blond than red really, but there was a lot of it."

"That's nice," Eloise said hesitantly.

Maddy grabbed Warren's elbow. "Come on."

"Why don't you take Nancy into the kitchen?" Warren said to Eloise as Maddy pulled at him. "Offer her something to drink."

Before he could get a response, Maddy yanked him into the darkened hallway. "I said bedroom because I figured she'd freak." She kept her hand on his elbow. "I can't see a thing."

"This way," he said, walking slowly and deliberately, leading them to a doorway. "Wait right there." After a moment of shuffling sounds, a subdued light filtered through lace cloth draped over a lawyer's lamp on a desk at the back of a small room. Warren stood behind the desk. "Can you see okay?"

"Good enough to keep from banging into anything," Maddy answered, walking toward a chair in front of the desk. "This room smells musty, like no one has been in it for years."

"Maybe months," Warren said and pointed to the chair. He sat behind the desk. "It was my father's office. My mother used it too."

Maddy started laughing.

"What?"

"That's like an antique," she said, eyes on a large, bubble-backed computer. "I've never seen one in person. Only in books and old movies."

"Yeah, well, I don't use it. I have a PC." He scooted close to the desk. "So, why are you here?"

"I'd almost think you weren't glad to see me," Maddy said teasingly.

"It's not that. I'm just surprised."

"I could tell from the look I got from that woman...."

"Eloise."

"When was the last time anyone came to see you?"

"Months ago. My doctor comes every...." Warren waved off his words. "You said something about seeing a 'what'? A savage?"

"No," Maddy said with a laugh. "I didn't see a savage. I was talking about what was on TV. What the police are saying. You really don't know about the Uptown Savage?"

Warren shook his head.

"The guy who's been killing people? One in this building. Don't tell me you don't know about that."

"I know about that, of course, but didn't know about the name."

"You didn't watch the press conference about him? It was just on television."

Warren shook his head. "No."

"Those places you said you saw a man dancing around the buildings, including the one we saw at the place where your Beatle guy was killed," Maddy said rapidly, her head and shoulders straining forward, "that's where the people were killed."

Warren considered what she said for a moment before responding hesitantly, "Here, then at the Gramercy and..."

"No," Maddy interrupted, "the first one was at the Gramercy about two weeks ago. Then the others."

"Okay, the Gramercy, then here," Warren said thoughtfully, "and then the Dakota. The same man we saw there was..."

Maddy jumped in. "The dancing man is the Uptown Savage. Can you believe it?"

"Whoa, that's a long leap to a conclusion." Warren raised his hand to stop Maddy, who was leaning into what he knew would be an objection. "I realize it's probably not a coincidence that...."

Maddy barged ahead. "A coincidence? Really? One time it's weird. Twice, you gotta wonder. You saw him here and we saw him at the Dakota."

"I said '*not* a coincidence' and I think you should tell your father what we saw. He's a policeman. Let him deal with it. It's what he does."

"What would I tell him?" Maddy folded her hands together and held them in front of her. "Oh, Dad, we saw a man dancing in the street" – she sing-songed, bobbing her head side-to-side – "and think he's the Uptown Savage."

"There's more you can say."

Maddy shook her head. "That isn't going to do anything except get him asking me a lot of questions I don't want to answer." She talked over another attempt by Warren to interrupt her. "He doesn't say much about what he does. Says he wants to leave his job at the door but I've heard enough to know it takes a lot to get the cops to go after someone. Dancing in the streets isn't going to do that. Let's say he takes me seriously, which he won't. A lot of things would happen, and not good things. First, I'd get yelled at for sneaking out in the middle of the night, and get reminded how sick I am. How weak. How I could catch something and die." She laughed. "The doctors have really said that.

"Next, people will be crawling all over *you*." She stabbed a finger at him. "Not just cops. The word is gonna get out that you and I saw something. That's gonna attract attention. Press people will be everywhere. Surrounding us. Trying to get into the building to talk to us." She sat up stiffly, her eyes wide. "Everyone who knows me will be asked stuff. And you," she said, again stabbing her finger. "No one knows anything about you so they'll make up all kinds of stuff. Everywhere around here will be crawling with cops. Every street corner. Every alley. Not just cops. Reporters. Those magazines like *People* and other ones that have those stories about crime and stuff. It'll be a circus with you in the center ring."

"How will word get out? You're only telling your father?"

"You know," Maddy said, cocking her head, "you really do live in the dark. Nothing's a secret anymore. My father's not gonna say anything if I tell him, but with all the attention on this, and the number of cops who would be looking out for the dancing man, if my Dad believed me, someone would say something. It'll get out, I promise, and in a big way. These days people write about what they have for breakfast on social media. Facebook. Tik Tok. Instagram. Twitter. They post all kinds of shit. We'd be right there in the middle of it all. I promise. Okay, so maybe not our names, although I bet they'd get our names."

"We don't tell your father what we saw? We don't say anything? I don't think that's an option."

"Wait a minute. So you *do* think we're on to something."

Warren held up his hand. "Just wait a minute. I've read about these guys and...."

"Of course you have."

"These serial killers, they don't stop until someone stops them. They have a desire to kill. They *need* to kill. They don't have any empathy. No conscience. You think *we're* equipped to deal with that? What is it you want us to do exactly? Where are you going with this? You think we're going to find out who this person is and make some kind of citizen's arrest?"

"No, of course not. We find out more and *then* take it to my Dad. What do we have now? We saw a figure in the dark. We didn't see his face. Can you tell me how tall he is? What color his hair is? Or even if it's a 'he', for sure."

"That's what the police do. They're trained for that. And there are more of them" He stared at Maddy. "There are two of us and we don't know what we're doing when it comes to something like this. He could be dangerous." Warren paused a beat. "So yeah, this could be the guy who's killing people and you don't want to tell your father about him?"

"Back to the part about people, lots of them, being in your face."

"That's extortion."

"No," she answered forcefully, "it's what's gonna happen." Maddy sat up straight, squaring her shoulders. "I'm gonna find this guy." She shrugged. "Okay, that's an exaggeration. And, yes, I'm being selfish. Maybe totally irresponsible, but really, how much more could the cops do? Two people like us on the street are more likely to see something than a bunch of cops who will scare the guy away."

"A week," Warren said. "Seven nights."

"Okay."

"If we haven't seen anything in a week, you tell your father."

"Deal," Maddy said, a smile and excitement added color to her face.

"I've never gone out seven nights in a row," Warren said thoughtfully. "Two, three nights, at most. I always get some exposure. Street lights, even when I'm careful. There's always some. The exposure is cumulative." Warren shook his head. "Eloise is going to freak. If we need to, we skip a night. Or two."

"But a total of seven, right?"

"Okay, but isn't this bad for you? I mean, I know it's bad for you. Your immune system has to be compromised and you could catch something."

"I've already 'caught' something. I'm dying and these people want to keep me imprisoned. It's not like staying cooped up is going to save me."

"If you feel weak or whatever, we rest."

"If being close to those guys in the park didn't give me something, nothing will. One of them was wearing a filthy rug for God's sake."

Warren repeated, "If you feel *anything*, we rest, okay?"

"Fine," Maddy agreed reluctantly. She scooted forward in her chair and put her forearms on the desk. "Mind if I ask you a few things?"

"Like what?"

"You ever had sex?"

Warren was at a loss. He had no idea how to respond. All that came out was a weak, "What?"

"I tried asking some of my girlfriends, but none of them has had sex. I want to know what it's like, and" – she made a face – "given where I am now, It's not going to...you know...happen to me."

"No, I haven't had sex."

"Really, why not? You could do it in the dark. Hell, you'd have to do it in the dark."

"There are a lot things I've written off as not attainable and I don't even think about them at all."

"Why rule out sex? That's like low hanging fruit. You could hire a nice looking call girl. A classy escort, or something. You could even develop a relationship so it's not like hiring her for just sex. I can see giving up on visiting Europe, or climbing a mountain, but sex is easy."

"Okay, that's all the questions you get tonight."

"I've got more."

"One per night."

"That's only seven questions. I got a lot."

"I don't know why you want to ask me about anything." Warren raised his arms and looked around the room. "It's not like I get out much."

"There's a lot of stuff I can't ask my parents. Like the sex thing."

"I wasn't much help there."

"I'll stick to what I think you can answer."

"Good idea."

Chapter 12

A Place to Meet

Fisher read the name inscribed on a green awning above the entrance, "'Pasion del Cielo'. I got the 'pasion' part."

"Literally," Prado said, "'passion of the skies'"

"Meaning?"

"What does 'Starbucks' mean?"

Fisher leaned back and eyed the twenty-story building filling the sky above the shop. "The Manchester. Another rabbit warren. People packed into hutches."

"Very expensive hutches and no one we've visited is 'packed in.' More space in those apartments than in most homes."

"They feel claustrophobic to me. From the lobby to an elevator to a hallway to an apartment. A lot of walls," Fisher said, his attention on the tower overhead. "How many people do you think live there?"

"Lots," Prado answered her attention returning to the coffee shop. "Provine's boss said the three of them met here once or twice a month."

"He couldn't tell us much about what they discussed. Said they were just a routine 'check the boxes' meetings to make sure everything was running on schedule. Artwork, editing and pending publication dates."

"I'm thinking they probably used the time together for more than just business."

Fisher pulled a face. "Like what?"

"Three single mothers. Juggling lots of balls. Personal and professional. Getting together provided time to trade war stories. Commiserate." Prado waved her hand. "The point is Provine didn't feel the need to share what they talked about with her boss. The bottom line is we don't have anything useful about any of them. Wozniak had her strings pulled by

VandenHeuval. Never went anywhere. Worked from home. According to Fiona Davis's parents, she was practically agoraphobic."

"She did manage to spend enough time with someone to make a baby."

After a side-eyed glare at Fisher, Prado said, "Small town girl comes to the big city. Maybe lonely. Makes a mistake and she crawls into a hole. Couldn't go home with the kid, or didn't want to. Mom said she had to come see her."

"No one knows who the father is. No mention of anyone who fits that bill on her social media accounts; all used for business. Nothing 'social' about them. She's basically a cypher."

"We're lucky Provine wasn't totally cocooned. Not much there either, but we got this," Prado said, nodding at the storefront. "The Gramercy is right next door," she said as she pushed the car door open. "That's interesting."

Prado and Fisher walked into the quiet shop. A single barista behind the counter was focused on his phone. The sound effects from the game he was occupied with pinged loudly enough to be heard in the hush. Brown button-tufted vinyl booths lined the windows; five tables occupied the floor space, single occupants at two of them.

"Excuse me," Fisher said, standing at the counter unnoticed.

"Sorry," the barista responded, slipping the phone into the pocket of his black apron. "What can I get for you?"

"Two medium Americanos," Fisher answered and raised his ID. "But first, we have a couple of questions for you."

The barista approached, his attention on Fisher's ID. "FBI. This is a first. Let me guess, this is about those women? Right?"

"Right," Fisher said.

Prado offered her badge, which the barista also checked, appearing to take delight in doing so.

"I've been waiting for someone to ask about them," the man said as he yanked at levers on a gleaming espresso machine, sending clouds of steam into the air. "Probably should've contacted you guys myself, but I kept thinking the cops would come in."

"Here we are," Fisher said. "Tell us what you know."

Placing the cups on the serving counter, he pointed toward a booth in the corner of the room. "They sat over there. The three of them with their kids."

"How often did they come in?" from Prado.

The barista, looking at the booth, made a humming sound before answering. "Not a lot. Maybe every other week, but not steady."

Now Fisher. "Not steady?"

"It would be like every other week or so for a month and then nothing for a while, then back to that. I probably wouldn't have even thought about it, like thought how often they were here, except when I saw they had been killed, it caused me to think about them." The barista began wiping down the counter. "Disturbing. I mean what are the odds of the three of them being killed like that? And they all came in here." He stopped and stood stiffly. "It's really unnerving." He raised his chin toward the seating area. "It's cut into business, too. Regulars must remember them and are creeped out. Like maybe they'd be next." He shook his head and returned to the hissing machine. "Like whoever did it was targeting our customers. Shit, if I didn't own this place, I'da probably been outta here."

Prado laid Braddock's mug shot on the counter. "Ever see this guy before?"

The barista approached slowly and stopped far enough away that he had to lean forward to study the photo. "Is that the Uptown Savage?"

"A person-of-interest," Prado said.

The barista reached out gingerly and turned the image toward him. He shook his head. "Never seen him before."

"Take a good look," Fisher said. "Maybe he was wearing a hat or had a moustache. A beard. Longer hair. Gray hair. No hair."

The barista bent closer to the photo. "No, he doesn't look familiar."

Fisher pointed toward the upper corners of room. "CCTV, right?"

"Right."

"Do you record over the tapes?"

Shaking his head, the barista said, "I keep them."

Fisher put both hands on the counter and spoke slowly. "Keep them? As in you have copies of everything that's ever been recorded?"

The barista nodded. "Should probably reuse'em but I figured there might be a time when they would be useful. I'm a true crime guy," he said with a hint of pride.

"Can you show us where you keep the recorder and tapes?" Fisher asked.

"'Course. Bert," he directed to one of the customers. "If anyone comes in tell'em I'll be right back." The man nodded and waved.

The barista went to the end of the counter and directed Prado and Fisher to follow him into a hallway that extended from the shop, through a swinging door, and on to the end of the building. Another door, another hallway running along the rear of the building, and into a small storage room smelling of coffee. Boxes were piled around the perimeter of the space.

"This is it," he said, standing behind an office chair and desk on which sat a video recorder and a monitor. He pointed at chrome wire shelving above the monitor. "Those are videos from the past two years."

"Okay," Fisher said, considering the collection. "We'll send some officers to pick them up."

As they walked out of the office, Prado turned toward the balance of the hallway extending along the back of the building. "Where does that lead?"

"To a service elevator for the apartments."

She turned back in the direction they had come toward the swinging door. "Is that always unlocked?"

"Not supposed to be, but we have a pick-up counter in the lobby" – he pointed above his head – "and since the pandemic and the murders, it's been real busy. I'm always going up to deliver orders. It's what's kept me in business. Without the lobby business, I'd be long gone. Locking and unlocking the door to get to the elevator would be a real pain."

Prado turned and gestured in front of her. "We're going to take a look down that way. You can go ahead. Thanks for the cooperation."

"Sure," the barista said with a nod.

Ceiling lights were activated as they walked down the corridor. The elevator was visible at the far end.

Fisher asked, "What're you thinking?"

"Let's see," she said, flagging her arm in front of her, "if this leads to the Gramercy."

"And if it does?"

Prado glanced over her shoulder as they walked. "The three women spent time together in the coffee shop." She turned and lowered her head toward the corridor. "This is an open hall leading to the building where one of them was killed. Worth a look-see."

They stood in front of the freight elevator, a door to their left. Prado leaned into the door which opened to an alley. Fisher followed behind and held the door ajar as he searched for something to keep it from locking behind them. He used a loose brick as a wedge.

Prado looked up and down the alley. She gestured back toward the Manchester. "Seen here, killed there" – a nod at the Gramercy – "and the Plaza is up the block. The Dakota a few blocks away. We're in his comfort zone."

She kicked the brick aside and stepped into the Manchester. The hall lit up. Prado stopped in front of a door across from the freight elevator. M. Baer-Manchester Apartment Superintendent was inscribed on a blue nameplate. "Missed that before." She knocked on the metal door. An echo relayed down the corridor. "Maybe Mr. Baer can help us."

"Sorry to interrupt your lunch," Prado said to the man who opened the door, sandwich in his hand. She displayed her ID. "Mr. Baer?"

"I am."

"Do you have a minute?"

"Sure, please, come in."

Prado and Fisher stepped into a small, windowless living area. Table lamps, the stems extending from garishly painted art deco designed bases, sat unlit on round side tables flanking a beige couch. The flickering flat screen television gave the dark room a movie theater vibe. A plate and glass were centered on a length of roughhewn wood sitting atop cinder blocks.

"Give me a minute," Baer said, placed his half eaten sandwich on the plate, and hurried out of the room, returning with two folding chairs.

"Here you go," he said, erecting them.

"Thanks," Prado said, "but you didn't have to bother." She handed him the photo of Braddock. "Have you ever seen this man before?"

"In the building?" Baer asked as he studied the photo.

"Yeah," Fisher said, "or in the coffee shop. Anywhere actually. Does he look familiar?"

"No" Baer answered slowly, his attention on the photo. "Sorry, I haven't seen him. May I ask what this is about?"

"He's a person-of-interest in a case we're working on."

"The Uptown Savage, I'll bet. Awful, awful thing. Three young women from right around here."

"Did you know the one from next door at the Gramercy? Regina Wozniak."

"No," Baer answered with a shake of his head.

"What about the others? Did you know any of them? Maybe see them in the coffee shop? We understand they met there sometimes."

Baer shook his head again. "Sorry."

Prado shuffled in her purse and lifted out a card holder. "If you can think of anything at all that might be useful" – she handed him a card – "please give me a call."

"Of course, of course," Baer said. He held up the photo of Braddock. "Would you mind if I kept this? As a reference."

"All yours," Prado said and turned toward the door.

"Do you know the superintendents in the buildings where the women were murdered?" Fisher asked as they stepped into the hallway.

Baer nodded. "Sure, we all know each other around here."

"Have they shared anything with you about what happened?"

"Just that they're in shock like everyone else. I think the police questioned them."

"I'm sure they did," Fisher responded. "I was just curious if you all had any conversations, you know, personal stuff you think would be useful to us. Maybe something that you've thought about that raised a red flag. Maybe strange people hanging around the buildings."

"Strange people?"

"Strangers," Prado explained. "Not people who live in the building or regulars in the neighborhood."

Baer lowered his head and stroked the side of his face, his eyebrows knotted. "No, nothing that I can think of."

As they walked away from the door, Fisher said to Prado, "There was a boxer a long time ago named Baer. Max Baer. Heavyweight champion, Wonder if he was named after him?"

"It looks like he went a few rounds with someone," Prado said, "and lost badly."

***

Baer listened at the door as the footsteps receded. He bent backward slightly and raised his arms over his head, mouth open, mimicking a yell of jubilation. He grabbed his cell from the couch, put in his ear buds, turned up the volume and began dancing around the room lip syncing to his favorite tune:

> *Getting strong now*
> *Won't be long now*
> *Getting strong now*
> *Gonna fly now*
> *Flying high now*
> *Gonna fly, fly*

He bounced over to a full length mirror in the corner of the room and held up the photo of Braddock next to his face. He smiled at the reflection and began shadow boxing. A left jab. A right jab. A right uppercut. A left uppercut. A roundhouse right. A roundhouse left.

Chapter 13

Who Are You? Nancy Drew?

"So, why this wall?" Maddy asked, turning toward a section of the stone wall surrounding Central Park that she and Warren were leaning against. "It wasn't built to keep people out of the park and the slanted top isn't good for sitting on. Gotta be some arcane history you know about this."

Warren raised his eyebrows. "Arcane?"

"I was being kind. 'Weird' or 'obscure' stuff no one else cares about."

Warren turned and faced the barrier. "There are various theories."

Maddy began to laugh. "I was kidding. You really know something about it?"

"I do. The designers built the wall with the slant so the snow and leaves would fall off. And they didn't want people sitting on it. Also wanted to discourage vagrants from sleeping on it. They were called vagrants then, not homeless."

Maddy shook her head. "Amazing. You know the history of a wall."

"Not finished yet. Originally the park was supposed to be surrounded by an iron fence."

"Glad they didn't do that," Maddy said, readjusting her position against the wall. "Woulda made this a lot more uncomfortable."

"Speaking of which," Warren said, joining her in staring ahead at the twin pinnacles of the San Remo apartments, "we've been up and down Central Park West for three nights. We haven't seen a thing."

"That means we head back to our side. The Plaza. Manchester. Gramercy. But first we need a 'meet up' place."

"A what?"

"Somewhere we can 'meet up' if we get separated, or if we need to go in different directions for some reason."

Warren turned toward Maddy. "What reason?"

"I don't know." She shrugged. "Maybe we want to split up to head him off."

"Head him off? What are you talking about?"

"The Uptown Savage. For when we see him and follow him. We might have to separate. You go one way, I go the other to cover as much ground as possible. Or we're following him and he slips into an alley. You go around one side of the block while I continue behind him." Hitting her stride, Maddy added excitedly, "Or if we need to split up so he won't know we're following him. All those things. We'd need someplace to meet up." She paused before adding, "Someplace inside the park would probably be best."

"Who are you? Nancy Drew?"

"Who's Nancy Drew?"

Warren waved his hand dismissively. "I guess I hadn't thought this through, or seen it through your crazy eyes. What happened to we're just going to try and get a look at him? Now, we're going to follow him? To find out what exactly? Where he lives?"

"Maybe that. Maybe follow him to see if he does that dance thing in front of another building. He did it other times where he killed people."

"Whoa," Warren said, holding his hands up. "Dancing in front of a building doesn't mean he killed someone in that building."

"That's what we're trying to figure out."

"We're trying to figure that out? This is ridiculous. That's your plan?"

"*Our* plan. *Our* plan. Not *my* plan," Maddy said with a hint of frustration. "If you have a better idea, please share."

Warren shuffled his feet and stared at the ground.

Maddy filled the silence. "Let's see if he does anything weird."

"Weird?"

"Like stalking someone. Or looking for ways to get into a building."

Another extended silence from Warren.

"That might mean we have to separate so he doesn't see us. Where would we meet up?"

Warren sighed deeply. A note of surrender. He nodded toward Columbus Circle a few hundred yards away. "Why not where we meet up every night?"

"It's out in the open. We need someplace we can hide."

"*Hide*? Hide from this guy? You're saying we're going to have a reason to hide?"

"Just in case," Maddy said and pulled Warren toward a gap in the wall leading into the park. "Better safe than sorry."

"I should have known you'd go from 'we'll find out a little more' to 'following' to 'splitting up' to 'hiding.'"

"It's not going to come to that, but...."

"Okay, okay," Warren said. "You're not going to stop until we have a 'meet up place.' Jesus, you must drive your parents nuts."

"I do," she answered proudly.

"I know a place. The Loch. There's a stream there. Some trees and a bridge."

"A bridge," Maddy said excitedly. "I like that. We can hide under the bridge."

"I'm really hoping we never have to hide from anything."

"Do your friends ever go to that part of the park?" Maddy asked.

"My friends?"

"The rug guy and his gang."

"Not really my friends. And they're not a gang. I see them every once in a while when I come to the park. We've talked occasionally. Mostly when I first started coming here. They wanted to know what I was doing."

"What's their deal? Are they the reason everyone says the park is dangerous at night."

Warren answered through a laugh. "Yeah, probably, but they aren't like that. They see the park as theirs. Their place to be. Might get a little territorial sometimes but they're not dangerous. They feel comfortable here. It's the only place they can go without getting hassled."

"They're scary looking. You have to admit that. And they stink."

"They do," Warren agreed, "but, and I'm not saying this because I've had long conversations with any of them, I think a lot of them have mental problems, or they're scared of the rest of us. I'm going by stuff I've read and some that I've seen. I'm oversimplifying, but my point is, they're here because they have nowhere else they can be and it gives them some sense of control to police the park. Make it their own."

Warren stopped and pointed toward a stone arch. "Can't see it too well but that's it. This is the Loch. There's a stream that runs alongside the path."

"Okay," Maddy said approvingly. "That tunnel under the arch will be a good place to hide."

"There you go with the 'hiding' thing, again. Not real comforting," Warren said. "Besides, it's not really a tunnel. It supports a road overhead. Not very deep."

"Seriously," Maddy said, gesturing at the structure. "Cars go over that?"

She took a step toward the arch and was yanked backward. Warren put his hand over her mouth and pointed at the path near the arch while he pulled her toward a stand of trees. A figure was walking on the path toward them, head down, bouncing on the balls of his feet. He bobbed his head, his focus on the ground immediately in front of him.

Warren and Maddy crawled deeper into the underbrush and laid flat. They looked at each other, eyes wide. "That's him," she mouthed.

The man passed them going from their right to their left. He stopped and removed white ear buds, his trance broken. He turned in a tight circle, his eyes scanning trees, the archway, the stream, and back in the direction from which he had come. A moment of stillness before the buds were back in his ears and he was again transfixed and moving, dancing ahead.

Maddy tried to push herself upright. Warren's hand in the middle of her back kept her flat. He pressed a finger to his lips before slowly lifting his hand away.

They stood and keeping low, knees bent, shuffled toward the walkway. Before stepping onto the asphalt surface, Warren stopped Maddy, took a few steps ahead of her, leaned away from the cover of the trees, and stared up the path. He caught sight of the man disappearing around a bend. "Okay," he whispered and motioned Maddy to him.

The two hugged the curve in the path, obscuring their line-of-sight to the way ahead. Warren, in the lead, his hand extended behind him, his fingers on Maddy's arm. They slowly rounded the bend and caught sight of the man in full dance mode heading toward the entrance near Columbus Circle.

"Holy shit," Maddy hissed and inhaled jaggedly. "It's *really* him."

They stopped and watched the man prance through a break in the wall. As soon as he disappeared around the far side of Columbus Circle, they quick-stepped to the base of the statue.

"He's walking toward the Plaza," Warren said, peeking quickly and pulling his head back.

Maddy leaned forward. "He stopped in front of the Manchester. He's just standing there." She flattened against the stone base.

Warren turtled his head forward. "He's walking toward the alley between the Gramercy and the Manchester."

Maddy, who had scooted to the other side of the foundation, said, "I don't see him anymore. What do we do?"

Warren turned toward Maddy, her back to him. "Follow, maybe?"

Maddy jumped up and was five yards away, in a crouch, running toward the Manchester, before Warren moved.

"What're you doing?" he said when he reached her side. She was sitting in the gutter behind a post box.

"What you said we should do. Following." She peeked around the edge of the post box at the empty sidewalk and shot toward the Manchester. Warren hustled after her. They crouched on the sidewalk and leaned against the front door of a darkened coffee shop.

"We can't just walk into that alley," Warren said. "What if he's standing there?"

Maddy jiggled her arms and hands nervously as she hummed in thought. "Fuck it," she said. "We're gonna lose him." She darted around the corner of the building and toward the entrance to the alley.

Warren raced to catch up. "This is nuts."

They stood a few feet from the alley entrance, their backs pressed to the wall of the Manchester. Maddy peeked around the corner.

"What?" Warren whispered.

"I don't see anything," she said and took a few steps into the alley. Warren at her side.

A door opened ahead and a sliver of light sliced a piece out of the dark, then was gone with the closing door. Maddy and Warren sidestepped behind a dumpster.

"We can't stay here," Warren said. "It stinks. I might be sick. And this has got to be bad for you. It's like an incubator for germs."

The door opened and a figure emerged, stood a moment, and walked toward the opposite end of the alley. The door crept toward its jamb and held. A thin ribbon of light escaped into the dark.

Maddy peeked across the top of the foul smelling dumpster. "I'm going to go see what I can find."

"Go where?"

"Where he came out of."

"Are you crazy?" Warren hissed angrily.

Maddy scooted out from behind the dumpster. "You follow him and call me if he's coming back." She played with her phone. "I'm putting it on vibrate. We'll meet here" – she eyed the dumpster – "or at the meeting place."

"Why don't I go in and you follow him?" Warren said as he trailed behind her.

Maddy was at the door, which had caught on a brick pushed onto a step leading into the building. "Very noble, but there's probably a lot of light in there." She gestured for him to move away from the door before opening it enough to let herself through. "Go," she said and disappeared inside.

A few steps inside and across from a freight elevator was a door with an M. Baer/Superintendent nameplate. Maddy walked past and into a darkened corridor that lit up as she went. The passageway led to another door, which she opened. To the left she could see the silhouettes of chairs balanced on tabletops. Coffee shop she thought, stepped back into the corridor and walked toward the freight elevator as the lights went on in front of her and then off behind.

She stood in front of the door marked with the nameplate. Her phone vibrated. She peeked out the doorway into the alley. It was clear. She ran toward the dumpster, swung behind, slamming into Warren, who was crouched in the dark. "Goddammit," came out of her. Warren was trying to bring his breathing under control.

"Where'd he go?" Maddy forced out between gulps for air.

"A bodega around the corner. What'd you see?"

"It's the basement. There's only one apartment. It's the super's. It's gotta be his. Why else would he have gone in that way? His last name is Baer."

As if on cue, the figure appeared around the far corner of the alley.

"What now?" Maddy asked.

"Let's have this discussion away from here," Warren answered, his faced pinched as he watched the man.

***

A new deck of cards. Host always has a new deck. A rule. He stopped and stared at the alley door entrance to the Gramercy. *The other times I stayed inside after the game. Found a spot and waited. How am I going to work it this time?* He walked ahead. *Rosnick will be at the game. Gotta do something with that.* He stared at the ground, slowing almost to a stop, then raised his arms and jigged a few steps. *Got it. The boiler. We need a new boiler. I'll ask Rosnick to show me his after the game. He shows me the boiler. We talk about it a little. I tell him I know the way out and find a place to wait. Same one as last time maybe.*

He looked up along ledges above the first floor at the CCTV systems bolted to both buildings. *A little dab of black paint took them out.* He squinted. *Still blacked out. No one will see me coming or going.*

He danced up to the threshold. *What the hell?* The door was closed. *Shit! Now I have to walk around to the front.* He toed the brick. *Must've kicked it away when I came out.* He made a face at the jagged end of a broken key in the lock. He started toward the alley exit.

Maddy and Warren stiffened, flattened against the wall and closed their eyes. Like ostriches, if they could not see him, he could not see them.

Need to get that lock fixed. He laughed. *Sounds like a job for the super. Hafta learn how to be a locksmith. I could make a fortune with all these dumbos always losing their keys.*

***

"Holy shit," Maddy said as they raced from the alley to the sidewalk bordering 59th street. "My heart's going a mile a minute." She held her hand flat to her chest.

"This can't be good for you."

"Yeah, it can. Sitting in a chair absorbing chemo or waiting for the doctors to decide what's next are bad for me."

Warren opened his mouth to respond but found he had nothing. He glanced at a smiling Maddy as he shook out his arms and legs to control his nerves. "In hindsight, and not a lot of hindsight, that was really, really stupid."

"You want to hear 'stupid'? I was thinking about going into the apartment."

Warren stopped dead in his tracks. "What?"

"You had an eye on him. If it was open maybe I could've found something."

Warren stared at Maddy.

"I know, I know," she said, her voice a whine. "But in that moment it made sense."

Warren nudged her forward. "We have to reach some kind of understanding on what we're doing. 'Hiding' and 'meeting places,' and going into apartments are...uh...." He lost his words to frustration, paused, and found them. "Really dangerous."

Maddy nodded. "Yeah, that was stupid. My boundaries have gotten really confused lately."

"You call sneaking into the apartment of someone who could be killing people 'a problem with boundaries'? That's what that was?"

"I don't know what else to call it," Maddy answered shakily. "I told a teacher to go to hell the other day. She was trying to be nice and wanted me to leave class and go to the nurse's room and lie down. I guess I looked like I needed it. It pissed me off. And I told the driver Leopold sends for me after school that I was gonna walk home from now on. I did. It's like five miles. I was dead when I got home." She paused a beat. "Probably not the best choice of words considering. So, yeah, I'm doing crazy stuff."

They walked the rest of the way to the Plaza in silence. Warren pointed them toward the Oak Room, ushered Maddy to an alcove and arranged two facing chairs.

"I think it's time to call this off and tell your father what we found," he said when they were seated.

"What've we found?"

"The dancing man," he replied forcefully. "The Uptown Savage."

"How do you know that?"

Warren gave Maddy a look.

"We don't know what we've found and if I started to tell him about tonight, I wouldn't get past saying we were out in the middle of the night. He'd ground me for the rest of my life, which, granted, is no longer really a threat, but still." She poked Warren on the knee. "You'd be in trouble too."

Warren tapped his toes and ran his hands up and down his thighs. "All right, I get it, but no more of what you did tonight." He stared at Maddy. "We keep an eye on him, from a distance. Okay?"

Maddy nodded. "Okay."

Warren lowered his head and leaned slightly toward Maddy. "I'm serious. Just keep an eye on him and see if we can come up with something that way."

"Yeah, sure," Maddy said energetically. "I'm in. Meantime, I'm going to Google this guy Baer and see what I can find."

Chapter 14

Déjà vu All Over Again, All Over Again

Prado sat down, looked around the conference room and declared: "Déjà vu all over again."

"Actually, this is déjà vu all over again, all over again," Fisher responded and searched for a coffee station. Not finding one, he sat down next to Prado. "How much worse can it be than the last time? What can he do? Ask us to take Wozniak out of the rotation? She wasn't killed because she was never there?"

"Don't even joke like that. Having to cover Chandon's ass is bad enough."

"It never seems to be 'bad enough'. The bottom just keeps dropping."

"We really don't know what the people in the upstairs suites at the Bureau know about any of this." Prado side-eyed the door of the room. "The SAC keeps his distance like we're contagious. Maybe that's the way everyone is dealing with this. With us. Hear nothing, Say nothing. See Nothing."

"Someone must know something or we wouldn't be having these conversations here in the Manhattan office."

"All I got was a phone call from AD Cicero's office telling us to be here. It wasn't even from him. It was that skinny little assistant of his with a face like a ferret."

"Karen?"

"What a perfect name for her. She said we needed to be here this morning. No explanation." Prado spread her arms in front of her. "Here we are again and this time without anyone else. No ATF. Whatever this is...it's all about us."

"So, you think an assistant to the assistant director of the FBI might be running this operation?" Fisher asked teasingly.

"I'm saying I'm beginning to wonder if anyone who should know what's going on does know."

"Ah," Fisher said with a wry smile. "The real question is 'Does anyone *want* to know what's going on'?"

Fisher raised his chin at the large flat screen on the wall at the head of the conference table as it was coming alive. "Good morning" greeted Prado and Fisher before a clear image materialized. Slowly, Chandon's face filled the frame. No insincere smile as had been his habit. He was grave, solemn. Dark circles under his eyes and a few day's growth of beard.

Fisher let his head drop. Prado expelled a long sigh. Their displeasure obvious.

If Chandon noticed, it had no effect. He launched ahead, his intensity palpable. "There have been some developments you need to be aware of."

Prado interrupted. "Hold on. There are a few things we need to get straight."

Chandon narrowed his eyes. "Really?"

"Really," Prado answered defiantly. "First, who at the Bureau are you dealing with? Who okayed this arrangement?" She pointed at Chandon and back at herself. "Us? You?"

Chandon shook his head. "Irrelevant."

"Not to us it isn't. We haven't heard anything directly from Cicero, and no one here" – Prado gestured at the surroundings – "appears to have any idea what's going on. We're in their city and not a single resident agent has asked us what we're doing. That's not only odd, but wrong." She jabbed a finger at the flat screen. "So, I want to know who you're dealing with at the Bureau. Who knows what you're asking us to do?"

Chandon took a deep breath. "Think about what you're asking."

"And there it is," Fisher said with a nod to Prado. "No one wants to know."

Chandon folded his arms across his chest. "You and Mr. Fisher have been assigned to work with me. No formalities needed."

"Who agreed there wouldn't be any formalities?"

Chandon shook his head slowly. "There will be no papers signed. No details recorded on what you are doing to assist a fellow law enforcement agency. This arrangement is accepted within our community. It enables us to cooperate on exigent assignments without the delay that comes with red tape."

"'Exigent assignments'," Fisher said. "That's the euphemism for 'plausible deniability'."

Chandon let a moment pass. "Do you really want me to formalize this? I don't think your people would appreciate that. It would leave a paper trail. Require briefings. Budget considerations. Congressional notifications. Is that what you are asking me to do?"

"Just so we're clear," Prado said. "Cicero is fully aware of what you've asked us to do and he's okay with it?"

"He knows you are doing your job," Chandon said flatly.

Prado glanced at Fisher, who shrugged. "We're off the books, then. He doesn't know what we're doing."

"I did not say that. You are very much 'on the books' with your investigation of the murders."

"Stop with the double talk. I'm asking if he knows that we're working with you on this case? If he knows *how* we're working this case?"

Chandon stared ahead.

Prado got up and approached the flat screen. "He doesn't know. We're on our own. You aren't going to take any responsibility for what you've asked us to do. If this goes south, we go with it."

"Do your job," Chandon replied, annoyance in his voice. "Find the person who killed those women."

"But do it *your* way," Prado said. "What happens if you decide to duck out of the picture, or are called on to do something else? What if something gets leaked about who Regina Wozniak is and about what we've" – she turned toward Fisher – "been doing? You'll be long gone and the Bureau knows nothing about the nature of our involvement."

Chandon allowed himself a stiff smile. "Very good, Ms. Prado. "If I'm 'called on to do something else'. If I'm 'out of the picture'." He stroked his stubble. "You're obviously aware that VandenHeuval made a ham-handed attempt to remove me from, as you put it, 'the picture'. He failed." Chandon's smile disappeared. "What exactly do you know about that?"

Prado took her time returning to her chair, which she stood behind. "We know enough to suspect that he was lying to us when he said he was interested in cleaning things up given the economic changes in Suriname.

Now, you tell us. What the hell is going on?"

"First I want to thank you for letting me know you had a conversation with VandenHeuval about all of this," Chandon said sneeringly. "A call from you would have been appreciated."

"We don't owe you shit," Fisher shot back.

Prado laid a calming hand on his shoulder. "We weren't about to get caught up in your meat grinder. We told him as much and said we were going to proceed with our job no matter how it played out."

"You owe *us* on this one," Fisher said. "He tried to enlist us."

"Really?" Chandon answered, his curiosity piqued. "How?"

"He wanted us to back his play. Say we couldn't work with you anymore. That you were hindering our investigation." Fisher leaned forward. "So, fuck you and any thoughts you might have about us owing you anything."

"Back to 'what the hell is going on'?" Prado said.

"Mr. VandenHeuval appointed himself liaison between the industry and his government. It's an unofficial position, of course, but he believes it gives him influence. "

Prado sat. "Where do things stand?"

"Mr. VandenHeuval has much broader ambitions than rooting out corruption; establishing 'clean government', which he has no intention of doing. He wants to use his perceived power base with the industry to persuade a kingmaker like Panday to align with him, and then he will move into the driver's seat."

"You're talking about a coup?"

"Effectively," Chandon said. "He thinks he can succeed because he has the support of the industry." Chandon's face lit up in a genuine smile. "He overplayed his hand. Those people could not care less about what we are doing. We had the foresight some time ago to make our peace with them. They have no hard and fast allegiances, but if asked to choose between VandenHeuval and the CIA, who do you think they would align with?

"As for cleaning house in Paramaribo, not something they care about in the least. They would never say that publicly, which is why they did not dismiss VandenHeuval's charade out-of-hand. Optics."

"Does that mean things are on hold? VandenHeuval thinks they're listening?"

"In one ear, out the other, but not on the record. I know because I've been told not to worry. They are solely interested in stability no matter how that stability comes about. These are global companies. Pragmatic business people. They are sophisticated enough to understand that a culture like that which exists in Suriname, and has for generations, is imbedded. We have promised to respect that culture. Maintain stability. VandenHeuval wants to be 'King of the Mountain.' No one believes his appeals for reform. He's way out of his depth."

"He doesn't have any leverage then?" Fisher said. "He's dead in the water."

"Not quite, and that's where you come in."

"I'm already not liking this," Prado said.

"VandenHeuval has Panday's grandson."

"What do you mean 'has'?" Prado asked.

"Kidnapped. He has not made any threats or attempted to use the boy as a bargaining chip, but the message is clear. He is here in Suriname and has met with Geoffrey Panday. We've been told the discussion touched on the boy though there was not any overt quid pro quo mentioned."

"As in 'you align with me because I have your grandson'?" Prado asked.

"Yes."

"I don't see how having the kid is much of a bargaining chip," Fisher said. "What? He's going to kill the boy unless Panday comes around and supports whatever harebrained scheme he has to take over the government?"

"The threat is not about taking the boy's life. It's about the opposite. Exposing the boy. VandenHeuval is in control of a secret Panday wants to keep secret. He does not want any of the details of his daughter's pregnancy, the birth of the illegitimate child, or the identity of the father to be revealed. VandenHeuval is holding 'disgrace' over Panday's head. A sharp sword that could cut him deeply."

"That explains why we got that sociology lesson from VandenHeuval," Fisher said under his breath.

"He doesn't need the boy for that," Prado said.

"Again, you're missing the point. VandenHeuval is demonstrating his complete control of the situation. He not only controls the narrative, he controls the proof for that narrative. He might not need to prove anything, but he can."

"Bottom-line, this is the ol' 'my dick's bigger than your dick' routine," Fisher said.

"Very well put," Chandon said showing his teeth in a poor attempt at a smile.

Prado said, "I don't see how we tie into any of this."

"Oh, but you do, in a very important way. I need you to find the boy and send him to Panday. Actually, you don't have to find him. We know he is with VandenHeuval's niece in his apartment in New York."

Prado and Fisher sat in complete silence. Neither twitched a muscle.

"Absolutely not," Prado finally blurted. "We are not kidnapping a child. That's a hard 'no.'"

"The child is kidnapped and you are freeing him" Chandon countered.

"No," Prado said. "VandenHeuval has legitimate custody. Child Services handed him over to VandenHeuval. We take that child and we're the kidnappers. It is not happening. No way, no how."

Chandon sat a moment, running his hands over his stubble. "Back to the conversation about interagency cooperation."

"You mean the cooperation that no one knows anything about," Prado spit back.

"Yes, that cooperation. I could make it formal. I could formally request that you assist a person who is critical to our relationship with a nation that is a growing presence in the petroleum producing marketplace." He paused. "We've gone over this. That would require official notifications and acknowledgements and the need to expose details. Or you can go ahead and do what the FBI is known to do. Locating and freeing kidnapping victims is one of the agency's primary responsibilities."

"Arresting the kidnapper is also one of our responsibilities." Prado said. "That would be terribly inconvenient."

"Find the child and send him to Suriname. That's all I need from you. Do it while VandenHeuval is here in Suriname. I'll handle things at this end."

"This is way worse than déjà vu," Fisher said.

"Pardon?" from Chandon.

"Nothing," Prado said. "If you know where the kid is that means you've done some work on this. Some surveillance. Why not just go ahead and finish the job?"

"Do I really have to answer that?"

"Yeah," Prado responded insistently. "A lot of things can go wrong with this." Her face reddened. "Starting with it's not a sanctioned operation. We're going to have to break into a secure building for Christ's sake. It's not like we can make an announcement that we're there to rescue a kidnapped kid, who isn't kidnapped, and who we have no authority to rescue. Then, we're going to have to break into a private residence. And… ." Prado took a breath and placed her hands flat on the table. "We're going to scare a woman and a child half to death and try to keep them calm enough not to attract attention from their neighbors." She stared ahead. "This is a shit show waiting to happen."

Fisher added, "If this goes sideways, no one is going to be there to take the heat. How're we going to deal with the many ways this can bite us in the ass?"

"What do we do with the kid and…?" Prado stopped mid-sentence. "Did you say niece or is that a euphemism?"

"No," Chandon answered with a toothy smile. "She is his niece. We will have a plane at the Marine Terminal at La Guardia ready to bring them to Suriname. The details will be sent via an encrypted message that you can pick up there at the Bureau office."

Prado buried her face in her hands through which she asked, "When?"

"The sooner the better. As I said, VandenHeuval is in Paramaribo. He will not be there to interfere. We will deal with him."

"In the meantime," Fisher said, "we're trying to track down a serial killer while working with a set of conditions strapped to our backs."

Prado said, "This seems like a good time to tell you that I briefed the commanding officer of the precinct about our situation."

"Our situation?" Chandon asked, caution in his voice. "You told him about our involvement?"

"It's a 'she'" Prado said. "And, yeah, I told her."

Chandon tucked his chin into his chest and tensed. A deep breath, then: "You trust this person?"

"I do now."

Chandon lifted his head. "Now?"

"Two things," Prado said, raising a finger. "We have to stop this murdering piece of shit. He's killed three women and will keep at it until he's stopped. We can't do that without working effectively with the cops. To do that we need full trust and confidence. We start in a hole every time we step into an investigation. Whenever the FBI shows up the locals become defensive. Like we're there because they can't do their job."

"That's even when they ask for our help," Fisher added. "It's knee jerk stuff."

Prado continued, "It takes time to win that trust. We don't have time."

"You had to tell her everything?" Chandon asked, skepticism in his voice.

"Yes, and I wish we had done it sooner."

"Really?" Chandon asked aggressively.

"Here's the second thing. If we don't find this guy soon, the pressure from local politicians and the press will become more and more intense. Serial killers fascinate everyone. They are assigned names like 'BTK,' 'The Night Stalker,' and 'The Green River Killer.'"

"'The Uptown Savage,'" Fisher said.

"Cable news has 24/7 schedule to fill. Reporters will begin digging deeper, and the longer it goes on chances increase that someone could stumble onto who Regina Wozniak is."

Chandon nodded. "Okay, I get it." He moved forward, filling the screen. "Whoever you told has every reason to keep their mouth shut. If it ever leaks that they cooperated with us to protect what we're doing, they would be run out of town."

"Leave it to a paranoid to go there," Fisher said.

Chapter 15

Cinderella Man

"We're on our way to Philly to talk to a surviving victim," Broaden said to Robinson. "We sent the ViCAP files we got from Prado and Fisher to homicide there and a detective got back to us. He handled a few cases with MOs like Braddock's. There's a surviving victim and he arranged an interview."

"The MO tied Braddock to a victim in Philly?"

"Right," Broaden said. "He wasn't calling himself Braddock back then. According to the guy we're meeting, he used Tom Loughran and Ernie Schaaf interchangeably. The details in the ViCAP reports caught this guy's attention. Not Braddock's name. A Detective Mike Wilson."

"A surviving victim," Robinson said thoughtfully. "Hope you can get a more complete physical description that we can match with Braddock. Maybe the victim can also add some detail to the MO."

"Yeah, and there is someone else Wilson is going to take us to talk to. This one goes back a ways. Predates Wilson. It's probably a long shot, but he has someone who filed a sexual assault charge and says the description of the crime has similarities to our guy."

"Goes back how far?"

Broaden leafed through a notebook. "Before he went to prison."

"The more recent one is after he got out but before he started here?" Robinson asked.

"Yeah."

"Okay, if you get back before say, uh…," Robinson paused a moment before completing her thought. "If you get back before seven, check in."

"Will do. Rolling up to our interview now."

"Good luck," Robinson said and disconnected.

Broaden laid his phone on the dashboard "Into the breach."

"Is Wilson meeting us here?" Levitt asked, releasing her seatbelt.

"Must be him at the door," Broaden answered as he stepped from the passenger side of the car and waved at a man standing on the porch.

"Detective Wilson?" Broaden called as he approached a glass-walled, modern, two-story, white, flat-roofed home. A pool area to the right of the entrance fronted a large stone grill.

"That's me."

"Thanks for arranging this," Broaden said and offered his hand. "Jim Broaden."

Wilson, a tall man, thickening around the middle, nodded. "That would make you Jane Levitt," he said congenially, a smile fighting the appearance of sadness that came from eyes that drooped like a basset hound's. His jowls added to the look of a melting face.

"I am," Levitt responded.

"Detective Broaden told me he worked with a better half."

"Surprised he'd admit that."

Wilson showed an accordion file in his hand. "After I looked over what you sent, I dug into some of my reports on Schaaf and..."

"Schaaf is the name of the perp on this one?" Levitt asked casting a glance at the house.

"Yes, on this one," Wilson answered and knocked on the door. "Loughran in the other visit we're going to make. This victim, Lorna Miley, was living in Society Hill at the time. We're in Bryn Mawr now."

"Come in," a voice called. Wilson pushed the door open and pointed Broaden and Levitt ahead.

"Come on up," a white-haired man in a blue cardigan and tan chinos invited from the top of stairs facing the door. "Welcome," he said as they made their way up the slatted wood steps extending from the wall. No banister.

"Mitch Miley," he said, offering his hand to each as they reached the top of the stairs leading to a large open room.

An attractive woman in a navy blue silk pantsuit walked toward them. Minimal makeup and short hair framed a gracefully aging face. Her smile generated laugh lines around full lips turned up at the corners into an inviting smile.

"Thank you for seeing us," Detective Wilson said, offering a polite bow to the woman. He turned to Broaden and Levitt. "These are the detectives I told you about who are working on a case similar to yours in New York, Mrs. Miley."

The woman stepped forward and shook hands with Broaden and Levitt. "Please," she said, turning toward a couch facing two light blue swivel barrel chairs, the color and design matching the couch. "Can I get you some water, or perhaps something else? Juice, maybe?"

"No, thank you," Levitt said, sliding between a coffee table and the couch, where she sat. Wilson and Broaden also demurred and joined her.

"Thanks for taking the time to meet with us," Broaden said, nodding at the couple seated across from them. "As Detective Wilson explained, we're dealing with a case similar to yours, Mrs. Miley."

"Lorna," the woman said. "Please, call me Lorna."

"Yes, ma'am," Broaden acknowledged. "A case similar to yours, Lorna."

"We've read about it," the man responded, his voice deep and tinged with a New England accent. "Awful." He reached out, taking the woman's hand. "We'd like to help in any way we can."

Levitt sat forward. "We realize this might be unpleasant, but in order to find out if we're dealing with the same person who attacked you, and to get any information that could help us with our investigation, please tell us in as much detail as possible what happened to you."

"I understand." Miley glanced at her husband, who offered a smile of encouragement. She took a deep breath and closed her eyes. "I woke up to a man standing over my bed." She opened her eyes and focused on the middle distance. "It was dark and I could only make out his silhouette initially. I started to jump up and he jammed a tie into my mouth. Actually, more like he forced it between my teeth lengthwise. I later found out it was my son's school tie that he must have gotten from his room. Fortunately, he wasn't home. He was with Mitch," she said with a nod in her husband's direction. "We were separated at the time and Mitch had Ron for the weekend. The man said he'd come back and kill Ron if I didn't cooperate." She stared into her lap. "The rest gets very hazy for me. Mitch can fill in the rest."

"Yes, well, I was bringing Ron home. I was very late."

"He always is," she said, a smile working at the corners of her mouth.

"But you were expecting your husband and son that night," Levitt clarified.

"Yes."

"How did you know it wasn't your husband in your room when you woke?" Broaden asked.

"This person was taller than Mitch and he didn't stand like him."

Levitt leaned in. "Stand like him?"

"Yes, this man hovered. He had a menace about him." She raised her shoulders. "That probably sounds ridiculous. Of course he had bad intentions, he broke in to my apartment, but it's the way he stood that told me it wasn't Mitch. He was poised to strike. I don't know how else to describe it. Mitch wouldn't stand over my bed looking at me like that."

Levitt returned her attention to the husband. "Please, continue."

"The apartment was freezing cold. I noticed the sliding door to the porch was wide open and went to shut it when a man ran past me, knocking Ron to the ground as he went out the front door. I was confused and froze in place trying to understand what happened when Lorna screamed."

"When Mitch came into the room I was scared it was the man coming back," she said. "I didn't know why he ran out. I didn't know Mitch and Ron had come into the apartment. I was completely bewildered."

"She was already in shock, I think. She couldn't explain what had happened. Actually, she couldn't talk at all."

"Did you get medical attention?" Levitt asked.

"Yes," Mitch answered. "Our doctor met us at the hospital. He insisted on doing all kinds of tests and fortunately there was nothing physically wrong with her."

"You were not sexually assaulted?" Levitt asked.

"No, thank God," she said, her voice quavering. She leaned into her husband who put his arm around her. "There was nothing physically wrong with me. It did take years of therapy to keep me from going around the bend though."

Broaden handed her a photograph. "Is that him?"

She began shaking her head immediately. "No, the man was scarred. It looked like his nose had been broken many times and not repaired correctly. He had lumps of scar tissue above and below his eyes, and his upper lip was terribly disfigured."

"What about him?" Wilson said, passing her another photo.

"Oh, God, yes," she said, shoving it back at Wilson. She covered her face with her hands and began to sob, her shoulders heaving. Mitch got up and disappeared into an open doorway, returning with a glass of water and a box of tissues.

Wilson gave the photo to Levitt who stared intently before passing it to Broaden.

"I have a few more questions, if you don't mind," Levitt said after giving the woman time to compose herself.

She wiped her cheeks, blew her nose and squared her shoulders. "I'm fine," she said hoarsely.

"You said you found out the man used your son's school tie. Did he leave it behind?"

"No, he took it. We found one missing from Ron's closet later. That's how we knew what he used. Ron went to St. Peter's. We were living in Society Hill at the time and the school was nearby."

"We moved fairly soon after that," Mitch added.

"One final question," Levitt promised. "Did you notice anything out of the ordinary about your apartment after the attack?"

"Like what?"

"That answers my question, Mrs. Miley," Levitt said and stood. "Thanks for your time.

"Was I any help at all?" she asked.

"There are similarities between what happened to you and the way the man we're after is attacking the women in New York."

"But the photos?" Lorna said. "They're different."

"That's something we have to reconcile," Broaden responded.

***

Wilson, Broaden and Levitt stood together in the gray pea gravel driveway. "This is the person who attacked her?" Levitt asked, studying the mug shot Wilson had shown Lorna Miley.

Wilson tapped the photo. "Ernie Schaaf, the man we liked for it. Looks nothing like Braddock."

Levitt nodded and then shook her head. "Confusing."

"Was she really helpful? Wilson directed at Levitt. "Do you really think there's some kind of connection or was that a 'pity reassurance'?"

Levitt cocked her head. "Pity reassurance?"

"You know," Wilson responded, "the 'you've been very helpful' thing."

"We don't do 'pity reassurances' in New York. There's something there. The tie. The window being open. She fits the victimology. But...." Levitt shook her head as she studied the photo of Schaaf. "There's this."

"There are also some discrepancies with the victimology and MO," Broaden said. "She was married and her kid wasn't home."

"She was separated with a kid," Levitt countered. "He probably saw her alone with the boy a few times and thought she was a single mother. Plus, her kid was going to a private school, like the others. The threat he made to harm the boy unless she cooperated also matches. And, he was trying to strangle her with his school tie. That all fits."

"You're sure your guy is using a tie as a ligature?" Wilson asked.

"No," Levitt said, "actually we're not. But all the vics were strangled. A tie fits the ligature marks and we now know what to look for in the kids' closets."

"You didn't get anything from your scene?" Broaden asked with a look back toward the house. He waved at the Mileys who were standing at the bank of windows. "DNA? Fingerprints?"

"If we had, you'd know. Hell, if we had we'd probably have the guy and you wouldn't be here." Wilson shook his head. "The scene was compromised by the husband and the kid. They were all over the bedroom and the husband closed the sliding door to the porch, covering up any prints we might have found. Other people contaminated the scene before we could secure it; EMTs, building concierge. It was a mess. You haven't gotten anything from yours?"

Levitt shook her head. "The question I had about whether she noticed anything unusual in her apartment afterwards is because our guy is cleaning up after himself."

"Cleaning the entire apartment," Broaden added.

"Didn't you say he was threatening to hurt the kids?" Wilson asked. "There are kids in these apartments, right? How does he...?"

"I know," Levitt said resignedly. "How's he not waking the kids when he's cleaning? It's not like he's vacuuming or anything. It's more like 'tidying up'. Wiping down surfaces."

"But it's noticeable," Broaden said. "He's doing a really good job."

Levitt asked Wilson, "Without DNA or anything else, how'd you settle on Schaaf as a person-of-interest?"

"He'd been spotted hanging around Miley's building. Dancing, if you can believe it, on the sidewalk in front. Plus, he had some minor stuff going on at the time, like threatening some people in the neighborhood. Society Hill area is upscale. The complaints got immediate attention."

"Threatening people?"

"Being a nuisance. Following women. Threatening to expose himself. Pretending to masturbate. Scaring them. A real scumbag."

"Where to next?"

"South Philly. You can follow me, but in case we get separated, the address is 1519 S. Bouvier Street. Don't be looking for anything like this," Wilson said lowering his head in the direction of the house. "Another world entirely."

***

Broaden stared at his GPS app as they exited 95 and drove into South Philadelphia. "We are definitely not in Kansas anymore," he said shifting attention from his phone to rows of pitted brick brownstones. Uneven sidewalks extended from pothole ridden black asphalt to the foundations of the buildings. Not a lawn in sight. Telephone wires strung from leaning wooden poles crisscrossed above the streets. The wires were strewn with shoes, pieces of clothing and the occasional kite.

Levitt eyed the surroundings. "You ever been to Kansas?"

"No," Broaden answered, "never been, but I'm guessing I'd like it better than this."

"Could be the Bronx, Yonkers, Brooklyn."

"Yeah, my point exactly."

Broaden nodded at a three-story, red brick building. "We're here." Rusted, dented, peeling tin siding fronted the second and third levels. A Police Benevolent Association sticker adorned one of two first floor windows to the right of the front door. The two window pattern extended to the second and third floors.

"There's Wilson," Levitt said as she pulled to the curb, pointing in the direction of the detective walking up the sidewalk toward them.

Standing in front of the address, Wilson said as Broaden and Levitt approached, "Annie Real. Her relationship with Loughran was...."

"Not Schaaf?" Levitt asked. "Loughran?"

Wilson nodded. "The incident we're looking at here was like 12-years ago. Loughran was the name he used with her and with the cops who interviewed him."

"You didn't work this one?"

"No, I was in robbery then. What I know about this is from...." He raised a manila folder.

They climbed cement stairs. Wilson searched for a doorbell and not finding one, used a fist-shaped door knocker. Remnants of green paint were visible in fissures scarring a red door where the wood was beginning to rot. Once, twice and after the third hammering, a middle-aged woman yanked open the door, a scowl plumped full cheeks. "What?"

"I'm Detective Mike Wilson, Philadelphia Police. We talked yesterday."

"Okay, yeah, right," the woman said attempting to comb her fingers through a nest of unnaturally dark black hair. White roots haloed her forehead. A puffy face gave signs of once being pleasant, even pretty. Large green eyes and a hint of high cheekbones made for an attractive profile.

The smell of tobacco wafted out the door. "You're gonna hafta give me a second. I got two sick kids home from school." She waved them inside and ushered the pack down a narrow hallway past a kitchen where cereal boxes and glasses filled with purple liquid were scattered across a bare wood table. A few photos dotted the walls. Square patches of bright red wallpaper revealed where others had hung.

"In there," she said, walking past a doorway. "I'll be right back."

The three stood in a staggered line at the entrance to a small room. Ahead a Barcalounger, pleather armrests flaking, and a couch were positioned in front of a huge flat screen. A threadbare rug covered the floor in front of the furniture. The linoleum floor behind was bare. A small end table and lamp sided the couch. Against the wall to the right was a cabinet filled with ceramic frogs of all shapes, colors and sizes. To the left a fireplace and mantel. A coating of black soot covered the underside of the mantel and licked up both sides of the white brick fireplace. The walls were yellowed but might have been a dark green at one time.

The sounds of very unhappy children funneled down the hallway from the back of the home. The woman's voice dominated the clatter demanding that "You'd better do what I tell you or your father's gonna hear 'bout it." Pushback from little voices were muffled behind a slammed door.

Wilson and Levitt had taken up positions near the couch, which was covered with magazines and toys. Broaden stood in front of the Barcalounger.

"Sorry 'bout that," the woman said and dropped her shoulders dramatically, dangling her arms. "Some days they take it all out of you." She straightened. "Sit. Oh, wait a minute." She disappeared out the door; her exit soon followed by clatter in the hall. The woman reappeared with two straight back wood chairs. She pointed at Wilson and Levitt. "You two take the couch. Toss all that on the floor," she said of the magazines and toys littering the cushions. She handed Broaden a chair and motioned for him to place it in front of the couch, where she settled.

After everyone was seated, Wilson made the formal introductions. "Detectives Jane Levitt and Jim Broaden. These are the detectives from New York I told you about."

The woman held out her hand first to Broaden and then Levitt. "Annie Real."

Wilson continued, "I told you they're working on a case that has a lot in common with what happened to you."

"With Tommy Loughran," the woman said.

"Yes," Wilson replied. "Would you please tell them what you told me about that?"

"Sure," she said and stood, plumbing the pockets of her jeans which strained unsuccessfully to contain a protruding line of pink stomach peeking from under a yellow pullover. Gazing around the room, she located what she had not found in her pockets. She walked to the mantle returning with a pack of cigarettes. "Mind if I smoke?" She did not wait for an answer and sent a gray cloud toward the ceiling, then sat.

"Please," Broaden said, "tell us about Mr. Loughran."

"Mister? Ha," the woman said with a burst. "He's not a mister. More like a weirdo. A really scary one." She drew hard on the cigarette creating a long ash. "We had a coupla dates, maybe more, things goin' pretty normal. So, this one night he comes to my house." She tugged at the cigarette again and leaned her head back releasing the fog. The ash fell into her lap and she brushed it away. "Wasn't living here then. Wasn't married, of course." She laughed. "He comes to pick me up. I think we were gonna go to a movie or somethin'. He comes inside. First time inside my place. We always went back to his but my roommate was outta town. Anyway, he comes inside and starts in on how dirty it is. Sayin' really nasty things and how his mother taught him to be clean. To keep things tidy. Said she was a nut about that. Then, he goes into the kitchen and grabs a bucket and wants to know where my cleaning stuff is." She smiled and made an attempt at a laugh. A shiver shook her shoulders. "Can you believe that? He begins cleaning the whole damn house and when he finishes like two hours later, he rapes the shit outta me."

She stabbed the nub of the cigarette in an overflowing ashtray and coughed, clearing her throat. "I mean, we had sex before. It's not like he had to force me, but he did." She tipped the pack of cigarettes, sliding another out and lit it. "He was really rough and wants to go in the back door. I say 'no', he does it anyway. Then, he gets up, goes to my closet and comes back with a...uh, sash I guess you'd call it, from a robe I had. Chinese one. Red and black silk. Fancy. Never forget that." Her eyes widened. "The fucker tries to kill me. Strangle me." Real stood and raised her arms sending the pullover to the middle of her ribs. "Hey, like I'm not a small woman and I was in a lot better shape back then. None of this," she said of her stomach as she yanked down the pullover. "I'm fighting with everything I got and he gives up. Just gets up and walks out. Never saw him again. Wouldn't've wanted to."

Wilson says, "You reported the incident."

"Fuck, yes, I did, but I made a mistake. I took a shower as soon as he left. Then, it was just a 'he said, she said' thing. No evidence that he raped me, not that if I had left him inside me it woulda made a lot of difference. We had consensual sex before, so I had nothing really solid to go on to get the guy. It's not like the cops made much of an effort to prove what I said. They made me write it all up and sign it."

"What about when he tried to strangle you?" Levitt asked. "That must have left some bruises and marks on your throat. You fought him."

"I had all kinds of bruises and scratches. They took pictures of everything. Even made me take off my clothes for a full scan."

"And?" Broaden asked.

"He said we had rough sex. I couldn't prove any different."

Broaden handed her the photo of Braddock. "Is this the man?"

"Older but that's him." Real stood and walked to the mantel. She turned away from Wilson, Broaden and Levitt, lit another cigarette, fighting to steady her shaking hands.

Levitt allowed a moment to pass before asking, "Do you remember if he said anything during the rape, or anything at all while you were seeing him that could give us a better idea of who this man is?"

Real flicked the cigarette ash into the fireplace. "He told me he was an orphan then changed that to he was given away by his mother 'cause she didn't want to raise him. How she was mean to him, locked him in a closet or somethin' like that and...uh, I think he said she drank a lot. Said he wanted to be another person. Change his life. That kinda shit."

"Anything else?" Levitt probed.

"While he was trying to...." Real put a hand up to her throat. "While he was on top of me with that sash, he said I should never have kids because I wouldn't be able to raise them right. That I was dirty and couldn't teach them how to be good people." Her eyes narrowed and she spit out, "That really pissed me off and" – she pushed her hands out in front of her – "gave me the strength to get him off." She laughed. "Like you hear about those mothers who can lift up cars and stuff to save their kids."

"Anything else? Anything at all?"

Real stared at a spot on the floor in front of her. "About his mother making him clean stuff. He said she would make him clean the floors in the house with a toothbrush." She jerked her head up. "No, a wire brush on the kitchen floor and a toothbrush in the bathroom."

Levitt shook her head and raised her shoulders in question.

"She told him he was a dirty boy 'cause he'd complain about the men she brought home. He'd say he saw her doing bad things with them. 'Cleaning up' – is what she called it he said – was his punishment. To make him clean away his dirty thoughts."

"Also, he did the weirdest thing when he finished cleaning my place. He danced around."

"Danced around?" came simultaneously from Levitt and Broaden.

"Like those things we did in high school gym class," Real said and pranced cross-legged in front of the fireplace. "He said he was dancing on her grave." She stopped and put her hands on her hips. "I forgot all about that and the wire brush and toothbrush thing until right now. Haven't thought about it for all these years."

Broaden asked Wilson to "Show Ms. Real the photo of Schaaf," which he did. Real shook her head. "Never seen this person."

***

Wilson, Levitt and Broaden sat in the Flying Monkey Bakery in the Reading Terminal Market. "This is called a Whoopie Pie?" Broaden asked, wiping vanilla frosting from the side of his mouth.

"A local delicacy," Wilson answered. "A thick layer of vanilla icing sandwiched between two pieces of moist chocolate cake."

Levitt bit into a fist-sized brownie and managed to mumble, "Annie Real was definitely attacked by the same person we're looking for." She paused to swallow. "She ID'ed the photo, the MO matches, and what she said about him fits the profile Prado gave us."

"You have a profile?" Wilson asked, studying his oatmeal raisin, macadamia nut cookie.

Levitt nodded. "Braddock was abused as a kid by his mother. She used to lock him away. She farmed him out to the foster system when she didn't want to deal with him anymore, but we think he was taken from her. Either way it was a shit life and the details were mostly confirmed by Real. The abuse, the pillar-to-post years in the system...all of it a recipe for disaster."

"That cleaning thing she talked about is also consistent with our guy," Broaden said. "Plus, I think I'm seeing some psycho-sexual connection between that and raping and killing the women."

"Psycho-sexual connection?" Levitt said, smiling broadly. "What? You a psychiatrist now?"

"You two have been partners for a long time," Wilson observed.

"Too long," said Levitt. To Broaden, "Where are you going with this psycho-sexual business?"

"Not sure," he admitted, "but it isn't a leap to think that cleaning triggers thoughts of his mother and that leads to the rape and murder."

"Well, it's a helluva leap for me," Levitt said, licking her fingers. "So, we can forget about victimology? It's about cleaning. He's selecting women because of their messy apartments?" She winked at Wilson.

Broaden made a face. "Of course not. We've identified why he selects his victims. They're single mothers with kids. Like him with his mother. He cleans because of a compulsion that goes back to his abuse, and it triggers a rage. Seems plausible."

Levitt shook her head. "It doesn't track with the idea that he's cleaning the scene *afterwards* to get rid of any sign of himself."

"Okay, so he's cleaning after. Either way, before or after, I think he's doing it for reasons other than just to cover his tracks."

"Let's not overthink this," Levitt said. "We're looking for rational explanations of things an irrational, very disturbed person is doing. Unless we're as fucked up as he is, we're never going to understand him, and I don't want to try. I want to find him and make sure he's gone forever. Good, old-fashioned police work is what's going to catch this guy, not theories about psycho-sexual behavior."

Broaden shrugged and cleaned his hands with a Wet-nap. "Bottom line is we now know for certain that the person who beat and raped Real is the person we're after. That raises him from a person-of-interest to 'the' person."

"Which helps us how, exactly?" Levitt asked.

"He isn't going to stop. He started a lot of years ago and is still at it. If we agree that Braddock and Schaaf are the same person...."

"And Loughran," Wilson said. "Braddock, Schaaf and Loughran."

"Okay," Broaden agreed. "Putting aside the difference in appearance that we still have to figure out, it looks like he has refined his MO. Granted, there was a hitch with Miley, no cleaning, but that's easily explained. He was interrupted. He has been polishing his MO."

"We knew this creep wasn't going to stop so we can't chalk that up as a new piece of information," Levitt said. "His appearance? That's a question. And, for sure, he isn't calling himself Braddock anymore."

"He was also using Schaaf in Cherry Hill," Wilson added.

"Where?" from both Broaden and Levitt.

"Your ViCAP files included details on B and E's and an assault in Cherry Hill. He was hauled in for questioning. Using Schaaf there. They never could pin anything on him."

"Okay," Levitt said, "so we know he used Braddock when he got to New York. That's the name he was convicted under and it's his given name. Went back to Schaaf after getting out and" – she nodded at Wilson – "that's what you know him as."

"On the names," Wilson said, "my experience is these guys try out all kinds before they go permanently to a new one. It takes work to change an identity; get a Social Security number, driver's license and the rest of it. He went into prison under his real name, James Braddock, because he hadn't done the work to get a new one. But I'm betting he has a new one now."

"Safe bet," Levitt said, dipping her napkin in a glass of water and cleaning her mouth and hands. "How come you never picked up that he was using an alias when you were looking at him for Miley?"

"He told us his name was Schaaf. I had no reason to think it wasn't. He claimed not to have any ID, no driver's license. He was a day labor guy when I was onto him and didn't need any ID for that. If I'd been able to pin anything on him, I could have gotten his DNA and fingerprints. Since he was in the system that would've given me Braddock. Never got that far so he was Schaaf to me."

"How did you connect him to the attack on Real?" Levitt asked. "He was calling himself Loughran."

"Like I said, from the FBI files you sent to me. I searched what we had on similar MOs and came up with the attack on Real."

"The detective who handled Real must've checked in with ViCAP," Levitt said. "That would explain how the FBI got the info in the first place."

Wilson nodded. "He did go to ViCAP. Notes in our files say the detective who was working on some other cases he had Loughran good for wanted more information, but nothing came back from ViCAP. At least nothing that I could find. I'm guessing Loughran hadn't built up enough of a pattern yet to establish a recognizable MO."

Broaden nodded, "That makes sense. He was still a work in progress."

"I got something else you should look in to," Wilson said, taking a final bite of his cookie and washing it down with a swig of lemonade. "My father was a dedicated boxing fan. Not today's boxing, but the old days of Dempsey, Joe Louis, Gene Tunney and those guys. James Braddock was the name of a heavyweight champion. Made a movie about him a few years ago called 'Cinderella Man.' A Rocky type story. Braddock fought two guys named Tommy Loughran and Ernie Schaaf." Wilson smiled. "See the pattern? Your guy has probably adopted another boxer name."

***

"Whatcha got?" Robinson directed at Levitt and Broaden, sitting across the desk from her. Prado and Fisher on either side of the detectives.

"We met with Lorna Miley the survivor of an attempted rape by Ernie Schaaf," Levitt said. "Schaaf is an alias Braddock used in Philadelphia."

"A step back," Prado said. "You're working from ViCAP information, right?"

Levitt nodded. "Wilson made the connection to Miley and an older case after seeing the ViCAP reports we sent him. Bottom line is what we found in Philly matches what we have going on here. Miley said her assailant threatened her kid and tried to strangle her. As it turned out the kid wasn't there. Her husband, who she was separated from at the time, had the kid and he showed up in time to scare off the assailant."

"There is a fly in the ointment," Broaden said, "Miley couldn't ID Braddock from the photo I showed her. She did ID her assailant in a photo Wilson showed her. It was a mug shot of Ernie Schaaf. Braddock and Schaaf look nothing alike."

"That's a huge hole," Robinson said. "I'm assuming the Miley case went nowhere or Schaaf..." She shook her head. "Or whoever would've been off the streets before he ended up back here."

"Right," Levitt said. "Forensics on the Miley scene came up empty. It was badly compromised."

"We had better luck with another person who claims Braddock raped her." Broaden said. "She ID'ed him from the photo we showed her, but knew him as Tommy Loughran. Her name is Annie Real. She said they had a consensual relationship but..."

"'Consensual' as in they had a sexual relationship?" Fisher asked.

Prado pulled back her head, surprise on her face. "C'mon, Ira. You're not going there are you? A woman can't be raped if she's in a relationship?"

"I'm not saying that but I can see where complications could come up."

"And they did," Broaden said. "But before we get there, Real said Loughran raped her after – wait for it – 'cleaning her house.'"

"What?" Robinson said, eyes wide.

"He came to pick her up for a date and was upset by the mess he found at her place. He cleaned it up and...."

"Like really cleaned it according to Real," Levitt interjected. "Scrubbed the place down for hours."

"Then raped and sodomized her," Broaden continued. "Tried to strangle her."

"He cleaned the place *before* he attacked her?" Prado asked.

"Yeah, I know," Broaden said. "Doesn't fit with what we got going. The prospect that he's covering his tracks."

Prado shrugged. "What he did with Real was a reaction to seeing what her place looked like, not a premeditated act."

Broaden glanced at Levitt before offering, "This might be 'out there', but I'm thinking this cleaning thing might have some psycho-sexual elements. Like he gets his kicks combining cleaning and sex."

Levitt shook her head and looked around the room for a cue to continue.

"With these people," Prado said, "never dismiss anything. Control is a big factor for many of them. They have to orchestrate everything so, yes, the cleaning part probably plays some role."

"Armchair stuff," Robinson said. "I'm not dismissing it but we have to deal with facts. What else you got?"

"Real did confirm some things we already know," Levitt said. "Like his mother kept him locked in a closet and he ended up being passed around in the system."

"Did she file an assault charge against Braddock?" Robinson asked.

"Loughran," Broaden interrupted. "Sorry, I'm not trying be an asshole, but it's important to be clear about the different names. I'll get to 'why' in a second."

Levitt directed herself to Robinson. "Real did report the assault but right afterwards she did the exact wrong thing. She showered." Nodding at Fisher, Levitt said, "Loughran claimed it was consensual and that made it a 'He said, she said' thing."

"But he tried to strangle her," Fisher said. "Did she fight back?"

Levitt nodded. "She did. There were scratches and ligature marks, but Loughran said it was from rough sex. Back to 'he said, she said.'"

Robinson stood and began pacing behind her desk. "The attempted rape and the rape both have MOs similar to what we're dealing with. There are enough similarities to suspect they were committed by the same person." She stopped behind her chair and focused on Levitt and Broaden. "Right?"

"Right," came back to Robinson, who resumed her pacing. "What does that get us?"

Broaden answered, "You already said it. It confirms most of what we know about the Uptown Savage."

Robinson screwed up her face into a look of disgust. "Don't call him that, but, yes, it does."

"There's one more thing," Broaden said. "This is about the different names. About the importance of these names. Braddock. Loughran. Schaaf."

Robinson leaned her arms along the top of her chair. "Go ahead."

"James Braddock was the name of a heavyweight boxer years ago. He was an underdog type of guy." Broaden reached into his suit coat pocket and removed a piece of paper, which he unfolded. "I've done a little research."

Robinson looked at him quizzically.

Broaden read from the page: "'Braddock lost several bouts due to chronic hand injuries and was forced to work on the docks and collect social assistance to feed his family during the Great Depression. He made a comeback and won the heavyweight championship as a huge underdog. Two people he fought were Tommy Loughran and Ernie Schaaf." Broaden folded the page and returned it to his pocket. "*Our* Braddock has a thing for fighters. Sees himself in the *real* James Braddock. He's probably using an alias that is the name of a boxer from that period."

"Max Baer," blurted Fisher.

Prado followed with, "Holy shit."

"Who?" Robinson asked and sat down.

"Max Baer was the fighter Braddock beat to win the championship," Fisher said. "I saw a movie called...."

"The Cinderella Man," Levitt and Broaden blurted simultaneously.

"Yeah," Fisher responded, eyeing Levitt and Broaden. "It was about Braddock and his fight against Baer."

"And?" Robinson asked impatiently. "Where are you going with this?"

"The superintendent of the Manchester apartment building's name is Max Baer," Fisher said excitedly.

"Fuck," from Broaden.

Robinson opened her mouth to say something but only squeaked a sound. She cleared her throat and asked, "How do you know about this person?"

Fisher answered, "We were talking to the owner of the coffee shop in the Manchester and...."

Prado interjected, "It's where the three victims met sometimes."

"The place has a CCTV security system. The recorder is in a room in the basement of the Manchester."

"Which is next door to the Gramercy," Prado said.

"Where the first victim was found," Fisher followed. "We went to the room and decided to take a look around while we were there. The building superintendent's apartment is in the basement."

"We met him," Prado said. "His name is Max Baer. It didn't mean anything to me."

"And?" Robinson asked, her impatience bubbling to the surface. "Did you talk to him?"

Prado nodded. "We asked the expected questions. We showed him a photo of Braddock and asked if he had seen him. The photo looks nothing like him. Baer is a wreck. Nose all messed up. Scars on his lip, cheek and chin."

"Oh," came out in a low groan from Levitt. "That's Schaaf." She explained. "The mug shot Wilson had of Schaaf. He's all beat up like you just described."

Broaden reminded everyone, "That's the guy Miley ID'ed."

"Okay," Robinson said, "some of the pieces are coming together. What about the coffee shop guy? Did you show him the photo of Braddock?"

Fisher nodded. "Yeah, nothing."

"Did you get a photo of Schaaf from the detective in Philadelphia?"

Broaden shook his head. "But I can have him email a copy."

"Like right fucking now," Robinson said, shooing him toward her door. "Wait," she said, stopping Broaden. "Braddock's PO," she said, drumming her fingers on the desk. "Can't think of his name."

"Mel Carp," Broaden said.

"Get in touch with him too. He should have prison intake and exit shots of Braddock."

Robinson returned her attention to Prado who was nodding in thought. "The owner of the coffee shop told us that the door between the basement of the Manchester and the shop was always open. That could explain how Baer found those three. He was watching them."

"And it tells me we're not going to find him on the shop CCTV," Fisher said. "I'm betting he stood at the back entrance, away from the cameras. Never went into the shop. He must've followed them to find out where they lived."

"We need to get Baer in here," Levitt said. "I don't care if he looks like Frankenstein. We have to get a read on him."

As if on cue, Broaden walked into the office holding up two mug shots. "From Carp. This is James Braddock." He wiggled the photo in his right hand. "And this is James Braddock," he said wiggling the photo in his left hand.

"How the hell is that possible?" Levitt said. She stood and studied the two images. "That's him and that's Schaaf."

"That's Braddock after he got the shit beat out of him," Broaden said. "Like over and over again according to Carp." He sat down and laid the photos on Robinson's desk. "Carp said Braddock sparred in prison obsessively and..." He put his hand on the photos. "Was also on the losing end of other fights. Not in the ring. He was a punching bag according to the records Carp has on him. He said that might be one of the reasons he was released early. Prison officials might've been afraid he was going to get killed in there. And, like we know, Braddock was otherwise a model prisoner. His problems were with other inmates, not the administration, so he was an ideal candidate for release."

"We got him," Levitt said excitedly. "We have a reason to haul his ass in. He's been violating his parole. Never checked in with Carp."

"We could do that," agreed Robinson. "We could arrest him for violating his parole and then press him. Try to get a confession." She bobbed her head in thought. "But if he doesn't give us a solid reason to hold him, we'd have to let him go."

"We could hold him on the parole violations," Levitt countered.

"Not for long. He'd agree to meet with his PO. Might have to do some kind of community service." Robinson sighed in frustration. "But he'd be back on the street."

"I have a suggestion?" Prado offered.

Robinson nodded. "Go ahead."

To Levitt, "You and Jim go talk to him informally. Say you heard he was cooperative when we came by and you're following up with a few more questions."

Levitt objected. "I say we bring him in. It's more effective than a 'few follow up questions.' It's intimidating. He might not confess, but we can put the fear of God into him. Then we could surveil him 24/7. Keep the pressure on until he cracks."

"These people don't crack," Prado said. "They have no conscience. If you put him on a lie detector, he'll pass. He can lie without feeling one bit of guilt."

Fisher said, "While an informal conversation with you is not likely to cause him much concern it lets him know we're interested. It also gives us eyes on him. You can get a read. Maybe his reaction will give us some hint on how to follow up."

Prado added. "With you two, it's routine. Having the FBI show up on his doorstep again could cause him to run."

Robinson leaned over eyeing her cell phone in the center of her leather desk pad. "It's seven-thirty. If we really want to give the impression that we're only interested in a conversation, save this for tomorrow morning." She let her eyes run down the line from Prado to Broaden to Levitt to Fisher. "Agreed?"

Nods all around.

Chapter 16

Instinct

Levitt and Broaden stood in front of the door, both studying the M. Baer name plate. Broaden glanced at Levitt before knocking. Once. Twice.

"Mr. Baer?" Broaden asked the man standing in front of them.

Levitt felt a hollowness in her stomach. Instinctively she moved her hand to the holster and thumbed the snap securing her weapon.

Baer smiled broadly. "Yes."

"I'm Detective Jim Broaden and this is Jane Levitt," he said, pulling his suit coat away from the shield attached to his belt. "Do you have a minute?"

"Always," Baer responded pleasantly and stood aside. "Come in."

Broaden and Levitt took a few steps inside the small apartment waiting as Baer preceded them past a kitchenette to the right of the door. "Please," Baer said pointing to a cloth-covered beige couch. As they moved to sit down, Baer lifted a remote from a side table and turned off the flat screen. He sat in a folding chair opposite them.

"We're following up on a conversation you had a few days ago with some of our colleagues," Broaden said.

"First time I've ever talked to FBI agents," Baer said, his eyes going from Broaden to Levitt. "Kinda neat."

"Right, well, they showed you a photo...."

Baer leapt from his chair causing Broaden and Levitt to recoil in surprise, tinged with alarm.

"Ah, here it is." Baer's voice came from a room beyond. He returned waving a page in front of him. "This one," he said and handed it to Broaden.

"Yes, this one," Broaden said with a quick glance at the photo. "You don't recognize this man, correct?"

"No, I don't, but I've been on the look-out for him. I even made copies and gave them to a few of the other supers around here. I asked them to let me know if they see him. Or call 911."

"Thanks for that," Levitt said. "Did you know any of the victims? Ever see any of them?"

"No, which is what I told the FBI agents."

"Yes, like I said" – Levitt heard a tremor in her voice, which surprised her – "we're following up on your conversation with them. Double-checking because we've been told they met with each other at the coffee shop in this building." Levitt raised her arm. "Just down the hallway from you."

Baer smiled, one side of his lip pulled higher than the other by scar tissue. "Yeah, the FBI agents mentioned that too. I'm not a coffee drinker. I prefer tea. So, nope, didn't know any of them. Never saw'em. But I do know the supers in the buildings, where they were killed."

"The ones you gave copies of the photos to," Broaden said.

"More than just them, but, yes, to them also. We talk all the time." He nodded at a card table resting against the wall next to the flat screen. "We have a kinda club. You know, the 'best of the best' kinda thing. Best supers in the best buildings. I know it's silly, but we take pride in what we do. A fraternity. We play poker with each other once a week. Tonight's my night to host. We talk about these things." He leaned toward them. "All this is unnerving. We care about the people who live in our buildings."

"You'll let us know if you hear anything that might interest us," Levitt said.

"Of course," Baer said adamantly.

Broaden asked, "You've never seen anything or anyone that seemed odd, or caught your attention for any reason?" He raised a cautioning hand. "I know you've probably been asked this already, but maybe something has come to mind since. Maybe someone looking out-of-place. Hanging around with no apparent reason to be here. Showing up more than once, at odd hours. Anything like that?"

"I keep pretty regular hours," Baer answered. "Early to bed, early to rise. Busy days spent mostly inside the building. If I had seen anything, I would've reported it right away." He lowered his head and rested his arms on his thighs, bringing him closer to Levitt and Broaden. "I know from reading about these things that you withhold certain details about the crimes so you can catch a suspect talking about something only the guilty person would know. Have you got anything like that I can share with the other supers tonight at our poker game? I know it's privileged, but if you have one small thing" – he raised his hand and brought his index finger and thumb close together – "that isn't *too* privileged, maybe I could find out something for you. Not saying I suspect any of these guys, but...well, who knows, right?"

"There is something," Levitt said and made a point of surveying the room. "All of the apartments where the women were killed have been immaculate, like the person who murdered them cleaned up." She lowered her voice, adding, "We think it's to remove any incriminating evidence and also because the person has some sort of compulsion they can't control."

"Compulsion? What do you mean?"

"In previous cases, when we got profiles done, there are usually references to trauma the killer suffered when he was growing up that leads to the development of compulsions they can't control. Like Ted Bundy killed women with brown hair parted down the middle because his only serious girlfriend had hair like that and she broke up with him. Ed Kemper killed women because he hated his mother."

"Really?" Baer said. "Fascinating. I'm not familiar with Kemper but I've heard of Bundy, of course. I'm going to tell the supers what you just told me. About the cleaning thing. You're okay with that, right?"

"Sure. Hope it rings a bell with one of them." Levitt stood, prompting Broaden to his feet. "Thanks for your time."

"My pleasure," Baer responded, ushering them to the door.

Levitt stopped in the hallway. "Who knows? Maybe one of them knows someone who is compulsively clean."

***

Baer sat down heavily on the couch, his attention going to the room. He turned and studied the kitchen.

Were they fishing? Compulsively clean? And that stuff about trauma. Was that supposed to get me going? Make me nervous? Morons.

He probed the couch cushions, found the remote and turned it over in his hand. He placed it on the side table where it belonged. He must have left it on the couch when he went to the door. He retrieved his phone and ear buds.

It had to be done. I had to do it. Can't ignore the consequences. It might be a drop in the ocean, but first a drop, then a puddle, and then who knows?

Baer slipped in the ear buds, found his song and notched it to full volume.

Getting strong now
Won't be long now
Getting strong now

Gonna fly now
Flying high now
Gonna fly, fly

He pushed himself off the couch and moved the chair to one side of the room. He rolled the octagonal-shaped table to the space between the flat screen and the couch, clicked the legs into place, and brought the single chair to the table. He surveyed the setting. *Perfect.* He would retrieve six more chairs from the recreation room on the mezzanine of the Manchester and arrange them around the table.

They had to be saved from themselves. Stopped before it was too late. They might have left them. Or sent them away. Or worse. It was already beginning. Farming them to schools where they paid people to herd them around all day. Coming home to four walls. I saw them sitting like lumps, being ignored while the three entertained themselves. Nothing more than accessories. Afterthoughts.

"I was the relief."

Bundy. Kemper. Maybe that fat slob of a detective was expecting a reaction. She is not very clever.

He raised his arms and jigged around the table, the rhythm carried him into his room. He opened the door to a rosewood chifforobe, pulled out a drawer and removed a cardboard box. He lifted out three neckties wrapped in tissue paper, replaced the box, and closed the door. He carefully pulled back the edges of the tissue paper and laid the ties side-by-side on his bed, and took a step back.

It was a good deed.

He took a deep breath and closed his eyes.

The first one had not fought at all. She closed her eyes and did not make a sound. Didn't have to warn her. Like she understood. Not the second one. Had to hit her, then she went quietly. The third? Baer stared at the line of ties. He pursed his lips. *I don't remember much about her. Must have been another quiet one. Maybe they all knew deep inside that I was doing them a favor. Doing their sons a favor. Like an avenging angel.*

Baer lifted his arms, moved his feet and began snapping his fingers.

This is the last one for now. After tonight Max Baer is done.

***

"What the hell was that?" Broaden said as they stood at the barista station.

"Call it instinct."

"Instinct? What was your thinking?"

Levitt gave him a look. "I said 'instinct,' which means I didn't give it a lot of thought."

"No shit."

"The guy was creeping me out. I guess I wanted to push him into saying something he shouldn't."

"I agree he's a creep, but he didn't say anything we can use. Truth is, other than looking like he walked into a moving plane propeller, if I didn't know he was a creep, nothing he said was really that unusual. He said what I would expect. I've interviewed and listened to hundreds of people. He would fit with most of the normies."

"That guy seemed normal to you?" Levitt asked incredulously.

"Set aside what we know about him and think about it. It was a pretty standard conversation as these conversations go. His answers made sense. He didn't hesitate or contradict himself. That's what we usually get from these guys."

Levitt thanked the barista for her cappuccino and asked, "But you think he's the guy, too, right?"

"Oh, he's the guy," Broaden agreed emphatically. He raised his eyebrows and looked around the near empty shop. "I can't believe you braced him with that stuff. 'He cleans up to get rid of evidence?' 'He's driven by a compulsion.' I mean, holy shit, Jane. He might bolt."

"Prado said these guys aren't bothered by that kind of stuff. No conscience."

"They aren't bothered by *normal, expected* conversation. You went way past that."

"What then? We go back and arrest him for the parole violations. Tell Robinson we suspected he was gonna run so we brought him in?"

"No, that would make her very unhappy and I hate making her unhappy." Broaden tried for a smile but failed.

"We need surveillance on him."

"We know where he'll be tonight."

"We believe him? That he's playing poker?"

"Shit," Broaden said, "now you've got me worried. I *did* believe it. There is that card table."

"But you said you think he's gonna do a runner."

"I know what I said, but let's go with he's playing poker and we need surveillance."

"We go back, we tell Robinson what we think."

"So, you're going to tell her everything? Tell her what you said?"

"She'd throw me out of her office. I'll give it some context and then tell her we were setting the stage for surveillance. Maybe....uh, getting him a little nervous so we could see how he'd react."

"Dropping in that 'trauma' business was a bit much."

Levitt bowed her head. "I think I'd better just come clean with Robinson. She's not gonna like it but I really think if what I said makes him sweat he might make a mistake."

"Like?"

"I don't know," she answered impatiently.

***

"Bob McCay here," came through the teleconference device on Robinson's desk.

"Bob, it's Eileen Prado."

"Good to hear your voice. So, you're after another one."

"We are and thanks for taking time out of your busy day to talk to us."

"Always have time for you."

"I'm here with the Commanding Officer of Precinct 19 in New York City, Nadine Robinson, detectives Jim Broaden and Jane Levitt, and Ira Fisher."

"Mr. Fisher," McCay said with a smile in his voice. "Good to reconnect."

"Back at you, and one of these days we have to get together under less fucked up circumstances."

"I've told them about our time together in Olatha," Prado said. "Bob was our guide and mentor there. He's with the FBI's Behavioral Analysis Unit. A senior profiler. I thought it made sense to dial him in to help us out now that we have concrete evidence identifying our offender. About that, we have a situation we need some guidance on. I'm turning you over to Detective Jane Levitt."

Levitt reviewed her conversation with Baer concluding, "I was acting on instinct. I hope I haven't screwed this up."

"That was a very interesting approach," McCay said.

"Do we have a problem?" Prado asked, then corrected herself. "That was stupid. Of course, we have a problem. What I meant was...."

"I know what you meant," McCay responded. "You want to know how Detective Levitt's approach might influence his next move."

"If I was out of line...," Levitt started.

"No," McCay interrupted, "that's not really the issue. This person" – the sound of papers rustling – "Baer. He will act as his compulsions force him to act. He's motivated by a desire to kill. He's not going anywhere until he feeds his urges. That said, for certain he is going over what you shared with him. He likely understands that if you haven't focused on him exclusively as the offender, you have a profile that fits him. He also realizes that sooner rather than later he'll be in your crosshairs."

"I attached a file with my email," Prado said. "About 20 pages. I assume you have it all."

"Right in front of me, including your profile of Baer. I'm impressed."

"Coming from you," Prado responded, "that's high praise."

"You learned well, grasshopper."

Prado laughed. "An obscure reference to your taste in classic television."

"You know it," McCay said teasingly.

"My father watched *Kung Fu* religiously."

"A soulmate."

Robinson's eyes went from Prado to the phone device. An unspoken "get on with it."

"Okay then," Prado prompted.

"From the information Eileen sent to me, I would say Baer is a mission-oriented offender. I think he might be a little different from most who believe they have a calling to get rid of people who are immoral and burdens on society. I'll get to the differences in a moment. Big picture is this type takes their warped version responsibility very seriously. They see themselves as righteous; as delivering justice.

"Only he really knows why he selected the three victims you're dealing with, but a rough guess would be that they were single mothers like his and he thought they would mistreat their children the way he thinks he was mistreated. Don't hold me to that. It's a quick and dirty opinion.

"Mission-oriented killers are generally organized and can be difficult to identify, but Eileen has done an excellent job. Her profile is sound and lands squarely on Baer."

Prado said, "We confirmed that it is Baer based on conversations Detectives Broaden and Levitt had with surviving victims, and after we bridged the confusion over the differing photos."

"That was a twist I've never experienced before," McCay said. "I'm looking at the photos."

"And there was also the blizzard of aliases," Levitt added.

"Another twist," McCay said. "None of the offenders I've dealt with have physically altered their appearance. Some, like Bundy, grew beards or changed their hair color, but none permanently changed what they looked like. The aliases are something else I haven't come across. Most are so arrogant and convinced they can out think the police that they don't bother. Others are too mentally challenged to manage."

"Do we have a unique offender on our hands?" Prado asked.

"In some ways, but Baer is cookie cutter in others. Like many, he has a criminal history. None of them goes from zero victims to multiple ones. Your guy is a prime example of someone who started with petty crimes, graduated to sexual assault and eventually began killing. He shares other basic characteristics. He's male; he has abandonment issues; was in the service; he's employed in a blue collar job.

"But there are differences, as I mentioned earlier. Most of these types want to rid the world of what they consider evil, immoral people. They rarely show their victims any mercy and the kills can be messy. Not your guy. Other than the ligature marks, the victims don't show signs of being beaten or abused. No overkill."

"There are the rapes," Prado said.

"Of course, I didn't mean to dismiss the violence. I'm simply pointing out that Baer sees himself as a benevolent killer. He's saving these women from the fate his mother suffered, and also saving their children from the fate he had to endure. Violence for the sake of violence as we see in serial sadists or revenge killers as a means of satisfaction is not a driver for Baer."

"What about the victim we talked to?" Broaden said. "Annie Real was brutally raped and beaten."

"That wasn't premeditated like his future acts. As I said, he still acts because of a compulsion and he still wants to kill these women. He's giving himself a reason. It's part of his evolution. He's been evolving through the years, not only his technique, but also his approach psychologically.

"There are no absolutes. I do believe the man you're after is sane. He is not irrational or psychotic. That said, Herbert Mullins, one of the most well-known mission-oriented serial offenders killed thirteen people claiming he did it to prevent earthquakes. In simple terms, he was 'barking mad.' Again, no absolutes.

"What I'd like to leave you with is. Baer is a very dangerous person. I think he has probably killed many more people than we know about. He's in the manic phase of his addiction. He is losing control. The defined 'cool down' period between his recent killings is getting narrower. There have been three; one following the other in quick succession. I'm certain he has already targeted his next victim. "

"Jesus," Levitt blurted.

"Be very careful," McCay continued. "He leaves nothing to chance and would have absolutely no compunction about killing any of you. In fact, as keepers of what he considers laws that protect people he thinks should be erased, you are as bad, or worse, than they are. On that happy note, I'll leave you unless you have any questions."

"No," Prado said. "We're good. Again, thank you for your time."

"My pleasure. Let me know how things go."

Prado hit the 'off' button. "We have to keep an eye on Baer starting tonight. Ira and I will sit on him from nine to two. You" – she directed herself to Broaden and Levitt – "take him from two to seven." She looked at Robinson. "That should give you time to work out a 24/7 surveillance schedule with your patrol people. I know it's going to dip into overtime and...."

"I got this," Robinson said flatly. "Your guy just scared the shit outta me. I mean, I knew we are dealing with a really bad guy, but..... Wow!"

***

"This is perfect," Prado said as she and Fisher left Robinson's office.

"What's perfect?"

"The set up. We can get the kid tonight."

Fisher put his hand on her arm, stopping them as they stepped into the hallway outside the squad room. He took a quick look around before asking, "You arranged that? Set us up to get the kid?"

'Of course not," she replied, and pulled him forward toward the exit of the building. "It just fell into place. We're going to be watching the alley between the Manchester and Gramercy. That's where Baer is most likely to come out if he makes a move tonight. He's not going to leave through the lobby. We'll be right there ready to go once we're relieved."

"Assuming we're not called away to follow a serial killer."

Prado gave Fisher a look. "Don't play that card with me. I've said all along that we're going to do our job, but if the opportunity is there to get the kid, we'll take it. Okay?"

"How is this going to work?"

"When we were in the alley after talking to Baer, I noticed a back entrance to the Gramercy. It's almost directly across from the Manchester. We'll go in about ten minutes before Broaden and Levitt show. We can keep an eye out from inside the Gramercy until they're in place. Then we head for VandenHeuval's apartment."

"What if he goes tonight and they need backup? What're we going to say? 'Sorry we're in the middle of kidnapping someone?'"

"I'm not going to play hypotheticals with you. When we're relieved tonight, we go."

"How do you plan on getting into the building? That isn't a hypothetical."

"I have my ways," Prado said with a wink. "Bring a hoodie and gloves."

"Burglar tools. Great, I feel like we're planning to rob a bank or something."

"It's an 'or something.'"

Chapter 17

Gonna Fly Now

Warren walked around the base of the statue in Columbus Circle. Maddy sat facing away from the Plaza. "How do you get out without your nurse hearing anything?" he asked.

She stood on her tiptoes and walked slowly toward him. "By being very, very quiet," she whispered dramatically.

"You're not worried she might get up and see that you're gone?" he asked as they started across 5th Avenue toward the Gramercy.

Maddy shrugged. "I used to worry about a lot of things that I don't worry about anymore. Kinda adopted a 'whatever' attitude. She gets up and sees I'm not there. She calls my Dad and Mom. They freak out. I tell'em I had to get out. I felt claustrophobic and was wandering around the building." She raised a finger. "*Inside* the building. They tell me never to do that again. I agree. End of that story."

"That would be the last time we ever did this," Warren said, turning off of 5th Avenue and walking into the alley between the Manchester and Gramercy.

"Who says?"

"I says. They'd have you under lock and key."

"You worry too much. Let's concentrate on where we are now. Be in the moment. There might be only one like it your whole life."

Maddy froze and grabbed Warren's hand squeezing it in a vise grip.

A figure was walking toward them from the other end of the alley. They shuffled to the wall, where they flattened themselves in the shadows. They crabbed sideways and squeezed behind a dumpster.

"Again?" Maddy hissed. "A dumpster?"

"Do you see anywhere else we can hide?"

The outline of a man coalesced as he neared the steel door entrance to the Manchester.

"Not the dancing man," Maddy whispered.

The man pulled the door open and disappeared. As he did, two other figures entered the opposite end of the alley and walked past Warren and Maddy, who turned their faces away and held their breath. Another pull on the door, two more disappearances.

Maddy held her nose and made a face. Warren raised his eyebrows in alarm. Light from an opening door fell across the front of the dumpster. A man walked from the Gramercy into the alley, stood three feet away from the where they were shoehorned, lit a cigarette and walked away from them toward the end of the alley, returned in their direction, stubbed out the butt with a heel of his shoe and disappeared into the Manchester.

Warren surveyed the alley to his right; Maddy to her left. The sounds of traffic were fading. Lights winked off in windows above them. The only sounds that increased were the squeaks of rats now scuttling to and from small openings in the foundations of the buildings. The scratching of their tiny feet probed the contents of the dumpster hemming Warren and Maddy.

"I'm not particularly scared of rats," Maddy said, kicking her feet, "but this is really, really icky. I felt one run across my foot just now."

"This smell is making me sick," Warren said.

"You said that last time and you were fine."

"I wasn't 'fine.'"

"Got any suggestions?"

"The door that man came out of...."

"Across the alley in front of us?"

Warren nodded. "I didn't hear it click shut. Let's try it. If it's open, we can hang inside and keep an eye on what's going on from there." Warren raised his chin toward the door to the Manchester. "We really need to get away from here."

"Good idea. I can't take another second of this," Maddy said, the words trailing behind her as she dashed for the door.

Warren was wedged in place and had to push the dumpster to loosen himself. That set off the rats inside. Dozens of panicked, screeching rodents scuttled from rust holes along the bottom. Others wiggled free from under the lid and jumped out, bouncing on the alley floor. Warren ran with a pack as he hurried for the door, which Maddy held open. She kicked at a few trying to follow Warren into the darkened hall sending them sprawling back into the alley.

Warren shook his arms and legs wildly and stomped his feet. He shivered with a chill that ran up his spin. "I've heard the stories about rats in the city. There being more than then are people. I only half believed them until now." He continued stomping his feet and shaking his arms and legs. "I'm glad we live way up and away from the street."

"Hate to burst your bubble," Maddy said, peeking into the alley, "but those suckers can climb. You might be safe from the hoards but you're not safe from the ambitious ones."

"Thanks for that," Warren said.

"What was that parade into the door over there?"

"We're not talking about the rats, right?"

"Maybe human ones," Maddy said, then waved off her words. "I'll never call anyone a rat again." She held her eyes on the alley. "Whaddya think's going on over there?"

Warren eyed the back door to the Manchester. "It's not closed. There's light."

"What're you saying? That we should take a peek?"

Warren shrugged. "I wasn't, but maybe a quick peek."

"We walk outta here and over there like normal people would. Calmly and slowly. We take a quick look inside and walk back here. Calmly and slowly."

"But not right now. Maybe in an hour or so. Maybe they'll all leave. Let's give it some time."

Maddy turned and walked into the darkened hallway. Fifteen yards in she stopped. "There's a laundry room. We can wait in here."

Warren studied his cell phone screen. "I'm setting an alarm for an hour."

"No," Maddy said emphatically. "No alarms." She nodded at the phone. "It's 11:30. We go at 12:30. Make that 1:00. Safer. And turn off the ringer.

***

"Who the hell is that?" Fisher said, pointing toward the alley. He moved closer to the passenger window of the car they parked at the head of the alley.

Prado leaned forward. "Two people going for a walk."

"At" – Fisher eyed the digital clock above the car radio – "1:00 in the morning?"

"We're in the city that never sleeps."

"They left the Gramercy and are walking straight across toward the Manchester." Fisher lowered the window to get a clearer view. "One of them went inside."

Prado turned in her seat, facing the alley. "Is the person outside keeping watch?"

"The one who went inside came back out and they're heading back to the Gramercy."

Prado reached into her purse searching for her phone. Finding it, she brought up a number, hit 'call' and then 'speaker.'

"We're almost there," Levitt said.

"We have a situation here," Prado said.

"What's going on?" Levitt responded, concern in her voice. "Did he leave?"

"That's not it. A couple walked out of the back of the Gramercy into the alley and went over to the Manchester. One went inside right where Baer's apartment is, then the two of them went back to the Gramercy."

"And?"

"It's strange, no? I thought you should know."

"You could have told us that when we got there."

Fisher raised his eyebrows in concern.

"We're going to take a look for ourselves and won't be here when you arrive. Oh, shit."

"What?" Levitt asked on the verge of a shout.

"There's a stream of people coming out of the Manchester."

"Oh, yeah," Levitt said. "My bad. I should've told you that Baer said he was having a poker game tonight. Must be over. Those are the supers from neighboring buildings."

"Shit, yeah, you should have told us," Fisher bellowed.

"Baer is walking out with them." Prado said, now leaning so far forward she was almost in Fisher's lap. "He's going into the Gramercy with someone."

***

"Holy shit," Maddy said, tugging at Warren's sleeve. "Two of 'em are coming this way."

They ran from the door toward the laundry room entrance, sliding inside as two men stepped into the hallway, one saying to the other, "We've had the Weil-McLain SlimFit Commercial Condensing Boiler for a couple of years. It's lightweight, got a compact design, weighs less than 500 pounds and is only about 18 inches wide."

A door shut, cutting off the conversation.

Maddy and Warren were crouching between a row of dryers and a wall. He pointed at the door. "Let's get out of here."

A door opened. The conversation continued. "That's amazing."

Maddy grabbed Warren's arm, holding him in place.

"It's new technology. Don't need those big units any more. Saves space, money and my time 'cause it never breaks down. Had it three years and I haven't had a single call from anyone in the building about not having hot water or the pressure being bad, or anything."

"Thanks, Paul. That's gonna be our new boiler." The man laughed. "I'm not even sure you can call what you got a boiler. Anyway, it looks like what you got is the way to go. Could you email me the name and information for the people you got yours from to MBaer@themanchester.com?'

"Got it. Thanks for the game, Max."

***

"Baer came back out of the Gramercy, but he's standing at the door, looking back inside," Prado said.

"We're almost there," Levitt replied.

"He's lighting a cigarette and leaning against the wall."

"He's not going back to his place?"

190

"No."

"I see you," Levitt said.

Prado and Fisher watched Levitt park behind them. She turned off the headlights well before stopping at the curb.

"He's going back into the Gramercy," Prado said, disconnected and pushed open the passenger door. She rested her arms on the top of the car and stared into the alley. Broaden and Levitt approached, their attention also on the alley.

Prado came around the front of the car followed by Fisher, Broaden and Levitt. "We're going to find Baer. You two," she indicated Broaden and Levitt, "go to his apartment."

"*To* his apartment?" Broaden asked.

"*Into* his apartment," Prado answered. "Toss it."

"Without a warrant?" Broaden asked as they started in opposite directions.

"Yes," Prado said. "We have the right guy. No one is going to gig us on a warrant to protect this asshole."

***

Warren and Maddy crawled out from the space next to the dryers as the voices faded. They were lifting themselves from the floor when a figure whisked past the door. They froze a moment and listened. A door opened and slammed closed. Cautiously, they walked to the doorway and after a shared glance, leaned forward. It was very still and very dark.

Warren put a hand on Maddy's forearm keeping them in contact as they walked away from the laundry room toward the only door along the corridor. He opened it slowly and listened to footsteps padding up a staircase. He waited until they began to fade and started up the stairs, Maddy on his heels.

***

Prado and Fisher sprinted to the alley door leading into the Gramercy where they stopped. The door was ajar. She leaned forward and eyed pitch dark. She removed her weapon, lifted it in front of her and shouldered through the door, pushing it open enough to allow light from the alley to create shadows. She studied the hallway carefully before moving ahead, staying to the right side, her shoulder in contact with the wall. Fisher followed, sliding along the wall to the left.

Prado motioned Fisher forward toward an open room on her side of the corridor. He crouched low, inching to a spot opposite the black hole. He took a penny from his pocket and tossed it into the room. It hit a washer and stopped. Fisher waited a moment before mouthing "Clear" and moving ahead. Prado scurried past the opening.

Fisher raised his chin indicating a door on his side at the end of the corridor. Prado nodded and crossed over into a position behind him. He duck-stepped across the front of the closed door and nodded, reached for the lever-style handle and pushed the door open. Prado darted inside, pointing her weapon up the darkened staircase; the only light a pinprick of red came from a wall-mounted fire alarm station on the next landing.

Her adrenaline already on boil, she felt herself jerk involuntarily at the sound of footsteps above.

Fisher mouthed, "More than one person."

Prado, keeping her hips against the inside railing so she was not a target in the middle of the staircase, crossed one leg over the other, testing each footfall for traction and silence.

***

Maddy took off her shoes and signaled Warren to do the same. They shared a nod and moved ahead.

Warren kept his attention on the shuffling above him; timing his climb to keep up while maintaining a distance that felt safe. With eight floors behind them, Maddy was feeling a heaviness in her legs and had to slow. As Warren disappeared ahead of her, she caught sounds coming up the stairwell. This motivated her to catch Warren. She pointed down the stairwell. "Someone's following," she whispered.

Warren kept his attention ahead. "What?"

"Someone's following us."

Warren tensed, one leg on the step ahead. "Following us?"

"Yes."

Warren shook his head and took the next step. "It's just someone using the stairs."

Maddy followed him to the next landing. Her legs were jelly. She felt pressure on her chest. "I'm done." She leaned against the door. "I'll yell if someone is following you."

Warren hesitated momentarily, suddenly feeling vulnerable. He had not allowed himself to think even seconds ahead. They had reacted. They had no plan.

"Fucking go," she whispered.

***

Prado held up her hand and listened. She turned to Fisher, who nodded his understanding that they both heard something. Prado leaned forward and peered up the spiral staircase. Whatever it was, stopped.

Prado pushed herself away from the railing and started ahead. Comfortable with her muscle memory of the staircase, and driven by urgency and adrenaline, she moved quickly, Fisher close behind. They climbed rapidly, silently and determinedly, a flow interrupted when Prado stopped short. Fisher – concentrating on the steps – almost ran up her back. She pointed at two pairs of shoes and craned her neck to see up the staircase. Fisher moved to her side. She gestured toward the next landing.

Prado held up her hand and raised one finger, then two, then three and darted up the stairs to face a small girl, on her haunches, hands raised, staring at them, her eyes wide with terror. Prado leaned forward and her badge tethered to a lanyard fell in front of her. "He's going upstairs," the girl said frantically. "My friend is following him."

"You okay?" Prado asked.

"I'm fine," Maddy answered, urgency in her voice. "Go."

Prado had lots of questions that would have to wait. "We'll come back," she whispered. "Stay right here."

***

Warren could no longer hear anything above him. What he heard was Maddy. He could not make out the words, but the urgency in her voice was clear. He momentarily considered turning around, even took a step down.

Nope. Maddy would've screamed if she was in trouble.

Warren continued his climb, stopping at the 12th floor landing where the stairwell door was slowly closing. Security lights in the apartment corridor were clicking off from the far end of the hallway to his right; the darkness working down to the elevator to his left. He put his shoulder against the door and listened. Nothing.

Warren pulled the string of his hoodie tight. He reached into the front pocket and thanked Eloise for slipping in his sunglasses. He put them on, took a deep breath and opened the door. The hallway began lighting from the elevator toward him as soon as he opened the door causing him to flinch and squint so tightly he could barely see. Making things worse, his eyes began to water. He pulled his gloves over his wrists.

Warren walked ahead studying the hallway for a sign of life. A sound. Anything. He walked to the first apartment and pressed his ear against the door. Quiet. He stepped across the hall to a second door. Quiet.

Movement behind him caught his attention. He turned and faced two people, guns raised, then quickly lowered. A woman was in the lead. She held up a lanyard and badge, then put her finger to her lips. A man behind her motioned for him to move out of their way.

Warren backed up against the wall and felt his legs give out. He slid down and bounced on his butt, his legs flopping straight out in front of him.

Prado moved quickly; a stiff-legged jog. She stopped in front of apartment 1209, crouched and studied the lock. She ran her finger along its surface. Standing, she leaned close to Fisher. "I don't fucking believe this. He's here. He forced the lock."

Prado and Fisher backed away from the door. Fisher raised his leg and pounded. Once. Twice. The door sprung open.

"FBI," Prado and Fisher shouted simultaneously. They quick-stepped ahead. Prado waved Fisher past her as she ducked into the first doorway. The kitchen. "Clear," she shouted and heard Fisher screaming, "Stop."

Prado ran into the hall and had taken a few steps toward an open room beyond the kitchen when she was knocked to the ground. The body she collided with bounced off her, slammed into the wall, ricocheted away, ran out an open sliding door and hurtled over the glass and aluminum barrier.

***

Warren raised his hands to cover his face and closed his eyes tightly. His heart was beating so furiously it felt like he was bouncing off the floor. He tried to take a deep breath. All he could manage was a trembling intake. He could not breathe. He was on the verge of panic.

"Come on," Maddy's voice came through. She tugged at his shoulder. "We have to get out of here."

Warren stared up at her. He could not process what she was saying.

"Get up," she implored. "Get your ass up."

"What?"

"You want to deal with this?" she said, looking down the hall at an open door. "Or that?" she added, her eyes on a man standing in a doorway across from them yelling "What the hell is going on?"

Another voice, this one more frightened than angry, announced, "Whoever you are down there, I just called the police."

Maddy had handfuls of Warren's hoodie and was tugging hard. "This is gonna be a circus. Get up, dammit."

Warren pulled his legs toward him and using the wall for stability, pushed himself upright.

"Good," Maddy said and grabbed his hand. She walked toward the exit door. "We need to get out of here before the shit hits the fan. Well, make that more shit."

As they stepped through the door onto the landing, Warren asked, "What happened?"

"Walk and talk," Maddy said insistently. "The two people we saw?" She hesitated a beat. "You saw them too, right?"

Warren offered a weak, "Yes."

"They're cops and they busted down the door of one of the apartments. The one where the dancing man went, I'm guessing."

Warren felt his breathing slow and his legs were working. "They got him?"

Maddy nodded. "I'm betting 'yes.' Don't know for sure. They seemed real determined to get into that apartment."

Warren stopped. "Why are we leaving?"

Maddy turned her face up to him. "Seriously? You want to spend the next few hours in a police station? You want to spend the next few months, maybe the rest of your life, talking about all this?" She pulled him toward her and continued down the stairs. "I don't. I have an expiration date coming due real soon and I want to do what I want to do until then. They don't need us."

***

Prado tried to push herself off the floor. She could not. A searing pain stabbed into her right collarbone like a hot poker. She took a deep breath, rolled to her left and pulled her legs underneath her. She kneeled and steadied herself by putting her left hand on the wall. Another deep breath and she pushed herself upright.

Fisher ran past. "In there," he shouted pointing behind at the room from which the man had come.

Prado, unable to stand fully erect, leaned forward, cradled her right arm, holding it still with her left hand. She walked slowly and deliberately into the room toward a bed. A woman was lying on her back staring at the ceiling. Nude from the waist down, tears were streaming down her cheeks. A boy brushed past Prado, bumping her; her right arm fell forward. The shock wave of pain almost sent her to her knees. She resettled her arm against her side and straightened very gradually. The boy laid his head on the woman's shoulder. "Pris, please be okay," he pleaded.

Prado's instinct was to pull the boy away to preserve the scene. She did not. She could not. The pain – her own and the boy's – did not allow it.

The woman's eyes came to life. She put her arms around the boy and hugged him. He climbed onto the bed.

Prado felt a presence and turned toward Fisher, who was on his cell. "The cavalry is coming," he said, just then noticing that Prado was curled forward, her eyes slits, her jaw clenched. "Shit."

***

Robinson, Broaden, Levitt, Prado and Fisher stood in a huddle in the living room. "This is VandenHeuval's," Broaden said. "What the hell?"

"What'd you find in Baer's place?" Prado asked.

"He's our guy," Levitt responded. "We found school ties. They're gonna correspond to where the victims' kids went to school. Guaranteed."

"You've already been to his apartment?" Robinson asked, aggression in her voice, which quickly modified when she followed with, "Not that a warrant really matters now."

"There's other stuff," Broaden said. "Could link him to more victims."

"He kept the sash he tried to kill Annie Real with," Levitt said. "Looks like the one she described. Silk. Red and black."

"Also got more confirmation on Baer's 'makeover,'" Broaden crowed. He displayed an evidence bag. "Baer had these. It's like one of those time lapse videos, except with photos. Guess he was proud of himself."

"These guys think they're so fucking smart but end up pointing fingers at themselves," Fisher said.

"Oh, it gets better," Broaden said, holding up a larger plastic bag. "These are pages from the prison newspaper. He has a stack of them."

"I didn't know there were such things," Fisher said.

"There are articles in here about Baer fighting. Ring fighting."

"Not very good at it," Levitt said, "but that wasn't the aim."

Broaden laughed. "Prison version of cosmetic surgery."

"Jesus," Fisher said with a sigh of relief. "Good you got all that. Can you imagine if he wasn't our guy? What a fucking mess this would be." He jerked his head toward the balcony. "He sure can't say anything now. An oil spot on the pavement twelve floors down."

"Control is a factor for most of these guys," Prado said. "They want to control everything, including how they die. We got the right person."

"We know now why the doors were open in the other apartments," Levitt said. "It sure as hell wasn't to preserve the bodies. It was to create another." She let her attention go to the room. "You notice this place isn't spic and span?"

Prado nodded, wincing as she did. "I'm guessing he knew he didn't have time and just went right at it. No tie either. He was using his hands."

"He knew we were following him?" Fisher asked.

"Knew something. Knew it was the end of the line, or sensed it. That's the best I can do as far as an explanation goes. He broke his pattern and had a good reason. Good reason for him. Felt the need to hurry through it."

"That's Wozniak's kid in there," Levitt said. "First his mother. Now this. A lot of therapy in that kid's future."

"I thought VandenHeuval sent him to his relatives," Broaden said.

"Guess he didn't," Levitt said.

Prado tapped Robinson on the arm. She nodded toward the hall and walked them into the kitchen. Robinson sought out a chair, finding one under a white, Formica-topped table in a breakfast nook. "Sit down," she said, turning the chair toward Prado. "You're white as a ghost. Your arm?"

"Think I broke my collarbone. I'll have one of the EMTs check it out." She sat down very carefully. "You must have questions."

"I do. Go ahead and answer them."

"What have you told your people about any of this? Any of what we discussed."

"Nothing. Figured that was a 'no-no.'"

"I don't care what you tell them," Prado said. "I'll leave it up to you on what you think they should know. Or need to know to make sense of this."

"I feel a 'but' coming," Robinson said.

"Not a 'but', well, not a 'but' like you're thinking." Prado raised her eyebrows and took a deep breath. "Baer led us here, but we were coming anyway."

Robinson rested her arms on the table and clasped her hands. "This should be good."

Ten minutes later Prado put a period on the end of her explanation with: "The long and short of it is we would've been here, Baer or not, 'but,'" she said with a sly smile, "it's better if no one knows that."

Robinson sat for a moment. "You want to keep the identity of this victim, and the kid, secret?"

Prado pointed toward the hallway. "I'm putting them on a private plane first thing in the morning. They'll be gone. My suggestion is you go with 'the family has requested respect for their privacy' and leave it there. If you think you have to deal with this straight up, go ahead, but know that no one is going to corroborate anything you say."

"I have to convince the commissioner that we should withhold their names? Use 'privacy' to put a blanket over this?"

"A perfectly legitimate request and I'm guessing the commissioner will accept your suggestion without any hesitation."

"What if he calls your boss to clear it with him? To cover his ass and get sign-off from someone he can point a finger at if he has to? If things unravel. If some enterprising reporter comes knocking with details he pried from a source. What kind of response is he going to get?"

"He'll never get through to him. You'll be doing yourself and the commissioner a solid by letting this go with the 'respect their privacy' approach. Substitute gory details, whatever. Overwhelm them with background on Braddock. These guys always get more ink than the victims. Use that. And, yeah, I know I'm being an ass and this is disgusting, but it is what it is."

Robinson nodded. "I can't think of a better option. But Levitt and Broaden need to know something more than 'respect their privacy.' They are definitely not going to buy that knowing who the kid is and where all this went down" – she raised her arms and gestured at the surroundings – "given what they know about VandenHeuval."

"If it was me, I'd tell them everything. They deserve to know and they'll respect the need for keeping everything quiet. They won't like it. I don't like. You don't like it." Prado shrugged, grimaced, and cradled her arm.

"They're also going to be very pissed off people. I could lose their trust and confidence."

Prado shook her head. "You won't. I put you in an impossible situation. They'll recognize that. They're going to be really pissed at me and Ira. At 'those assholes from the FBI,' but that's okay. We're gone tomorrow."

Prado and Robinson returned to the living room. Prado looked around. "Where are those kids? I want to find out what their story is."

"What kids?" Broaden asked.

"A small girl," Prado answered. "Early teens. Pale, kinda sickly looking. There was also a boy. Could've been a man. We saw her on the way up the stairs and she seemed to know what we were doing. Same with him. He was in the hall outside the apartment. I think they were following Baer. Could have been the two people we saw in the alley when you all arrived. They went into this building."

Broaden raised his hands and shrugged. "Don't know. I didn't see anyone when I came in."

"No one on the way up here either," Levitt added. "We took the stairs figuring if Baer got away from you, he would be coming down that way."

"You didn't see anyone like that in the hallway?" Prado asked. "A girl. Pale. Thin. A man or boy in a hoodie?"

"Nope," Levitt said.

Robinson leaned toward Prado. "A fly in the ointment?"

Chapter 18

We don't compare cases. We solve them.

Robinson, Prado, Broaden and Levitt walked into the media room in 1 Police Plaza and stepped onto an 8-inch riser. A podium in front of them was crowded with microphones, the tangle of cords snaked over the top and across the face of the NYPD coat of arms. The room was teeming with a restless scrum of reporters; the fortunate ones who had made it into the room. The overflow was packed into a smaller space nearby where the proceedings would be broadcast on two 32-inch flat screens mounted on opposite sides of the room.

When Robinson and the others had settled into a line along the back of the riser, a small man in a blue dress uniform adorned with brass buttons and a salad of ribbons grunted himself onto the riser and marched to the podium, hat under his right arm. An almost perfectly round, bald head sat atop narrow shoulders and a figure that widened at the hips giving definition to his nickname "The Pear." He put his hat on a shelf inside the podium and removed a script from an inner pocket.

"I'm Police Commissioner Leonard Kinney."

"Good thing he had that written down," Broaden whispered.

"I'm pleased to inform you and the citizens of New York City that we have identified the man responsible for the murder of three women and an attack on a fourth." He smoothed his script against the reading surface.

"The man has been identified as James Braddock who was using the alias Max Baer. He was the building superintendent at the Manchester

Apartments. He had a long history of criminal activity, including being a person-of-interest in a number of serious incidents in Philadelphia and Cherry Hill, New Jersey."

Kinney paused and studied his remarks before continuing. "He served time in prison for sexual assault and various felonies, some under aliases, including Ernie Schaaf and Tom Loughran. We tracked Baer to the intended victim at the Gramercy two nights ago. This was also the location of the murder of Regina Wozniak some weeks ago.

"Thanks to the diligence of the Commanding Officer of the 19th Precinct, Nadine Robinson, Detectives Jane Levitt and James Broaden as well as FBI Special Agents Eileen Prado and Ira Fisher, New Yorkers are safe from James Braddock."

Kinney turned slightly toward the line-up behind him. "Commanding Officer Robinson" – the cue for her to replace him at the podium – "is available for any questions you might have." Before Kinney could step away from the podium, reporters were leaping from chairs, shouting questions, creating an unintelligible babble. Kinney left abruptly, forgetting his hat.

"Thank you, Commissioner," Robinson said loudly and stared at the chaos. "Sit down, please."

The room quieted slowly as Robinson stood and surveyed the room. "I have a few remarks of my own and then I'll be happy to take your questions. Despite every effort to arrest Mr. Braddock, he took the coward's way out and ended his own life. We are engaged in an ongoing investigation of events and I will be answering your questions under caution.

"We've done this many times and we'll follow our usual protocol. Please raise your hand and I'll recognize you one at a time. Identify yourself and your outlet." She pointed at a woman to her left.

"Marjorie Wendell, CBS2 News. How did you identify Baer as the Uptown Savage?"

"A lot of hard work."

"Specifically," Wendell shot back.

"Detectives Broaden and Levitt followed up on a number of leads, including some that took them to Philadelphia. They interviewed a detective there who worked cases that had Braddock as a person-of-interest, and talked to witnesses. This led us to Max Baer who we already had on a list of suspects."

Broaden gave Levitt a look, his eyebrows raised. "What list?" he whispered.

Wendell, still on her feet, was waved off by Robinson. "One question, one follow-up." She nodded at a man in the center of the room.

"Roger Cox, *Newsday*. If I'm understanding what you just said, you had Max Baer in your sights earlier in your investigation. Why didn't you arrest him then?"

Robinson let her eyes drop to the top of the podium. "Because" – she raised her head and stared hard at Cox – "we didn't have conclusive proof. We kept him on our radar as we gathered information that would move him from a person-of-interest to the status of alleged offender."

"I'm still not clear how Baer was identified as the alleged offender. Did he commit a similar crime in Philadelphia?"

"The focus on Baer was narrowed after a grueling investigation and a lot of leg work."

Broaden leaned toward Levitt. "We 'lucked into it' wouldn't sound very impressive."

"That doesn't answer my question," Cox protested as Robinson called on a woman in the front of the room.

"Connie Fortuna, *Huffington Post*. You've released very little information on the victims and none on the latest assault victim. Why?"

"We have released all the information we've been able to gather on the three murder victims. We'll be passing out press packets as you leave that contain the latest details. As for the assault victim, her family has asked us to respect her privacy."

"'Respect their privacy' as in you won't be providing any information at all? Not even her name? We know she was attacked in the apartment of Daniel VandenHeuval, a former Surinamese ambassador and U.N. envoy. Is the request coming from the family or the government of Suriname? Or maybe our own government?"

"As I said, we agreed to respect her privacy."

Prado moved slightly to get a good look at the reporter. *Bright woman.* She made a mental note of her name and who she reported for and would pass it along to the comms people at the State Department. They would be hearing from her and needed to have the right answers.

Robinson called "Lily Grimes" by name. She identified with Fox News and asked, "How did Baer get into these buildings? Aren't they all secure? Covered by CCTV? And once he got into the building, how'd he get into the apartments?"

"As I said, this is an ongoing investigation and we are still working out a lot of the details. As for getting into the buildings, Baer played poker weekly with a group of supers whose living quarters aren't monitored by CCTV. He avoided those areas around the residences that are monitored. We matched the dates of the murders with those when the poker games were played. Baer likely remained in the building after the games concluded and waited, hiding until he attacked the victims.

"The offender was an experienced criminal who had a history of burglary and breaking and entering. We have determined he used lock picks to get into the apartments." Robinson nodded at Grimes. "That's two. Next," she said gesturing to the far corner of the room.

"Lisa Garcia, *New York Post*. Criminologists have estimated that there are 2,000 serial killers active in the United States today. Given that New York City is one of the largest urban areas in the country, where many of these killers operate, and we have had our fair share of serial killers – Joel Rifkin, David Berkowitz, Richard Cottingham and Rex Heuermann, among them – how many do you think are active in New York right now?"

"That's a question for my colleagues from the FBI," Robinson said and stepped to the side of the podium. Prado put her hand in the center of Fisher's back and pushed him forward.

Fisher gripped the podium and shuffled his feet finding a comfortable stance. "The FBI estimates...."

Garcia interrupted, "Would you please tell us who you are?" Quickly to Robinson: "That's not one my two questions."

"Special Agent Ira Fisher. The FBI estimate on the number of active serial killers is much lower than the figure you quoted. We believe there are 25 to 50 in the United States today. I won't speculate on how many, if any, are active in New York City."

"If I recall, you worked the Olatha Monster case," Garcia said. "How would you compare that to the Uptown Savage case?"

"We don't compare cases. We solve them."

Robinson stepped in front of Fisher. "There's your headline for the *Post*, Ms. Garcia." She selected another questioner.

"Moira Stein, *Village Voice*. "Most serial killers have a type. Why were these four women targeted? What was the distinguishing factor here? Or was it just random?"

Robinson turned to Fisher who retook the podium. "Although there have been a number of studies of serial offenders and theories have been advanced on victimology, there are no absolutes. When the compulsion strikes some of these people they will take anyone. They won't be very selective. Others have a fantasy they want to fulfill. They will wait for a victim who allows them to fulfill that fantasy. But we're dealing with psychopathic individuals who are amoral. There are no hard and fast rules.

"With that caveat, we found that the victims in this case all had young sons. They were single mothers. They lived in upscale buildings. So, it appears this offender had a type." Fisher raised his hand. "Before asking the next obvious question, we are still mining Baer's background and psychology to determine conclusively 'why' this type, or if he definitely had a type."

Stein announced, "My second question. Baer cleaned up the scenes. Is that why you couldn't find any DNA or other forensic evidence?"

Robinson stepped in front of Fisher. "You have good sources, Moira, and as soon as I find out who they are, they will be 'former' sources." She stepped back and gestured Fisher to the podium.

"Yes, cleaning the scenes probably contributed to our not finding the forensics required to ID him early on. That said, like most serial killers, and other types of offenders frankly, he perfected his routine over time and learned how to eliminate leaving anything of himself behind. Baer was what we call an 'organized' offender. Also, the scenes were compromised for various reasons complicating the job of the forensics teams."

"One more question," Robinson said. She picked out a hand waving frantically in the back of the room.

"Ned Devine, *The Guardian*. I'm assuming you had a mug shot of Mr. Braddock. How is it that you missed his resemblance to Baer when you were standing right in front of him and interviewing him?"

Fisher glanced at Robinson, who waved him ahead.

"I'm guessing that most of you are either crime reporters or have been assigned to follow this case from its beginning. That makes you amateur detectives."

"Oh, shit," Prado said, bowing her head to mask a budding smile.

"In *your* world" – Fisher punctuated his words with a jabbing finger – "the steps to solving a crime proceed from A to B to C and so on. That's because *we* lay it out for you after we draw conclusions during the conduct of our investigation. The answers are handed to you so you can follow things in a logical order. But we don't discover things in a logical order. Not A to B but more often A to D back to B then all the way to Y.

"Yes, we had a mug shot of Braddock. The man in the mug shot looked nothing like Baer. It was Braddock before years in prison, before years of what we have discovered was an effort to change his appearance through beatings and, likely in other ways. Perhaps even self-mutilation. We started at A with the photograph, and had to get all the way to Y before we could get back to A and understand what we had.

"Bottom line, the photo of Braddock was useless until we did a lot of digging, hours of investigation, more hours of interviews and so on." Fisher turned to Robinson. "Do you have one of those press packets?" Robinson motioned to a communications staffer who handed a packet to Fisher. He pulled out the photographs and held them up. "This" he said, raising his right hand, "is Braddock. It was shown to you at the previous presser. This," he said, raising his left hand, "is Baer after years in prison." Fisher paused a beat before saying, "Not obvious is it?

"You make your judgments *after* all the facts have been provided to you." He turned toward Levitt and Broaden and Prado. "By them.

"Another thing to keep in mind as you dissect what we did and you write your stories, and make your judgments; we operate on very strict protocols that protect your rights. We can't bust down a door and arrest someone because we *think* they committed a crime. We have to have probable cause just to talk to them." Fisher took a deep breath. "I know

I'm stating the obvious, but it would be nice if the obvious was a bigger part of your reporting."

"And that is a wrap," Robinson said. "Thank you for your attention."

As Fisher walked past Broaden and off the riser, the detective patted him on the back. "Been wanting to say that for a long time, but I'd get fired."

"The day is young," Fisher said. "I'm expecting a phone call from Washington any minute."

***

Robinson ushered Prado into her office. "Well, that was fun," she said, directing Prado to a chair in front of her desk. "Who knew Fisher had that in him?"

"I suspected," Prado answered with a broad smile.

"Obviously, the commissioner was fully onboard with your option."

"I thought he would be. He's not a cop anymore. He's a politician."

"No, more like petty bureaucrat."

"I stand corrected."

Robinson gestured toward a framed proclamation on the wall. "Ever feel like those are handed out to keep us pacified? Like a binky we give babies to keep them quiet."

Prado stood and walked over to the gold-lettered parchment. She read: "To Commanding Officer Nadine Robinson. Medal of Valor for performing an act displaying extreme courage while consciously facing imminent peril." She turned toward Robinson. "I'm impressed. I don't follow the binky reference."

"Like a pacifier. I'm not saying it means nothing or that I'm not grateful for the recognition. It means a lot and I am grateful. Almost got my ass shot off pulling a woman out of a house while her dip shit of a husband uzi-ed the entire place. She died two days later from the beating he gave her. Anyway, what I'm saying is it sometimes feels like it's supposed to be enough. That we're supposed to consider it enough." She tilted her head and looked at Prado intently. "Feel me?"

"I do," Prado said, "but maybe I'm coming from a different place. Getting to the Bureau was not an 'enough' kind of thing. They came to me. Asked me to join them. I gave up a lot of blood, sweat and tears, literally, and it was definitely not a pacifier."

"I know all about that."

"Really?"

"What? You think I don't know how to use Google?"

Prado laughed and sat down. "But I do understand. How can I not? I'm a woman and a minority woman at that."

"Ever think about closing the circle on how you ended up at the Bureau?"

Prado shook her head. "What do you mean?"

"They sought you out. You didn't just earn a shot. You called your shot. It's not like you had to prove anything. That was satisfying, no doubt." Robinson leaned forward and rested her arms on her desk. "There's another step. It's more personal."

"I'm not following."

Robinson opened the top desk drawer, removed a sheaf of papers and laid them in front of her. "We get notices periodically about what's going on within the law enforcement community in the city and state. Newsletters and other communications." Robinson searched through the pile and separated out a few pages which she slid toward Prado. "Take a look at the front of that newsletter toward the bottom of the page under prison transfers." She tapped the section with her index finger. "That should interest you."

Prado turned the document toward her and found a three-sentence reference that brought an involuntary "Shit."

She read: "Ivory Harris was transferred to Rikers Island to alleviate overcrowding in the Huntsville Unit (Texas) prison. A formal inmate exchange arrangement allows prison authorities in New York and Texas to cooperate when housing conditions require adjustment. Harris and 11 other Texas inmates will be in Rikers for 3 months."

Prado searched the masthead for a date.

Robinson said, "Harris just got to Rikers. How would you like to visit him?"

Prado felt a heaviness in her chest and an unpleasant tingling along her jawline. She was aware of her body and pain. Not the sharp pain of torture, or that from months of surgery and rehab, but the dull pain of remembering. She sat back in her chair and stared past Robinson.

"How's the arm?"

"Collarbone. Fractured. Got a pin put in. My collarbone survived the Dooney Boys. One of the few bones they didn't break. Suppose it was destined for this," she said and laid her hand on the sling.

Robinson pulled herself close to the desk. "I'm guessing you'd want to be full strength to see Harris. Show him he had no effect."

"Oh, he had an effect."

"My bad," Robinson said with a nod. "Of course he did. You're stronger and you're free. That cocksucker is in jail." She let a moment pass. "I can help if you're interested in seeing Harris. Actually, you can help yourself." She gestured at the commendation. "We can ask for more than a token. We can play their game and beat them at it."

Prado shifted her attention to Robinson. "What? How?"

Chapter 19

This Is Your Game. You Made the Rules.

Robinson and Prado walked into the lobby of the Ritz Carlton. Their heels clicked on veined marble floors as they approached the concierge desk. "Can you please point us to the Private Club Lounge?" Robinson asked a smiling, perfectly coiffed young woman in a tight-fitting blue blazer who responded with a slight bow of her head and "I'll do better than that. I'll take you." She came around the side of the black and white marble and wood counter and gestured for the women to follow. She escorted Robinson and Prado through the lobby brightened by elegant chandeliers and pinprick strip lighting strung along the floorboards. Floral print couches and chairs were lined against walls tastefully ornamented with intricate crown moldings.

"Busy few days for you," Robinson said to the concierge. "National Governors Association Conference must have everyone on their toes."

"Yes, we're very busy, but it's an honor to be hosting such an important event," the young woman replied and stopped at the entrance to the lounge. She pointed Robinson and Prado ahead. "Have a wonderful day."

"Timing is everything," Robinson said, smiling and waving at two men seated at the far end of the room. "Senator Raymond Sims from our great state is giving the welcoming address and Governor Willis Reasoner is sponsoring the conference. Two birds."

"What did you tell them about why we wanted to meet?" Prado asked.

"I didn't," Robinson answered and offered an enthusiastic, "Thank you for agreeing to meet with us," as they stopped in front of two men standing alertly.

"Ray Sims," the taller of the two said, offering his hand first to Robinson and then Prado. A Hollywood casting call for a United States Senator could not have produced a more likely candidate than the senior

Senator from New York. Over six-feet tall. Broad shouldered. Trim. Strong jaw line. Full head of wavy brown hair. Straight nose. Deep blue eyes.

New York's Governor Willis Reasoner was next with a handshake, his pudgy fingers fitting the rest of his short, stubby stature. He needed only a cigar and pinkie ring to complete the cartoon image of a precinct politician.

The men directed Prado and Robinson to white leather chairs inset with pale blue cloth cushions. A highly polished round table held two amber-colored drinks.

"I don't know if you recall, Ms. Robinson," Reasoner said as they settled, "but we met some years back."

"I do remember. It was an awards banquet."

"Where I had the honor of presenting you with the Medal of Valor."

"I'm impressed," Sims said and gestured to a waiter standing nearby. "What will you two ladies have?"

"Coffee is good for me," Prado said. "Cream and sugar, please."

"Same," agreed Robinson.

Sims smiled graciously and watched the waiter leave before saying, "Always a pleasure to meet with those on the ground level who keep our cities" – a nod to Robinson – "and our country" – a nod to Prado – "safe."

"We're grateful you made time to meet with us," Robinson said.

"Does the commissioner know about this?" Reasoner asked Robinson. She shook her head.

"The director?" Sims asked Prado.

"No."

"Well, then," Sims said, clapping his hands together, "I am very curious. What can we do for you?"

"This is more about what we can do for you," Robinson said, handing each man a file.

Sims hesitated a moment before accepting the material. Reasoner placed his on the cocktail table, saying, "I'm guessing you're going to brief us on" – his eyes went to the file folder in front of him – "this. It looks like it would take a while to read through all that."

The mood changed quickly. Both men stared at Robinson; Sims through a squint, Reasoner raised his chin and looked down his nose at her.

"Yes," Robinson said, "I'll give a quick review and you can digest the details when you have more time." She turned her shoulders slightly toward Prado, keeping her attention focused on Sims and Reasoner. "You've heard, I'm sure, about the serial offender we recently apprehended." She raised her hands. "Not apprehended really. He killed himself before we could make an arrest."

"Yes," Reasoner said, "A hell of a thing."

"I followed developments, of course," Sims added.

"The person responsible for the murders was James Braddock. He was using the alias Max Baer. He was active in the city years ago. Murdering and robbing, among other crimes. A true sociopath who had been a resident of one of the state's mental health institutions."

Sims glanced quickly at Reasoner.

"Braddock was released from that institution when funds were no longer available to house him and others during...."

Sims was now shaking his head. "We're not going to revisit all that are we?"

The four fell silent as the waiter approached. He placed China cups and saucers in front of Robinson and Prado followed by a sterling silver cream dispenser and a small plate with brown rock sugar swizzle sticks and an assortment of Ladyfingers.

Sims watched the man walk away and, waving the file at Robinson, said, "Our reform programs reduced costs at state mental health facilities and redistributed state funds to other more deserving and effective programs. Our policies were not the cause of increased homelessness and crime by patients released from those facilities."

Robinson nodded, acknowledging his remark. "I don't know enough about the issue to comment."

Sims took a sip of his drink, swirled the ice in his cut glass tumbler, leaned forward, placed it on the table and stared intently at Robinson. "Then let me educate you. That nonsense was concocted by political opponents and those in the mental health industry who themselves were responsible for mismanaging and overspending and needed to caste the blame somewhere else."

"We're not here to debate any of that," Robinson said reassuringly. "In fact, we're here to make sure that nothing in there" – she nodded at the files – "reignites that debate. The challenge we face is that years-old police reports have surfaced with Braddock's name redacted. He was a person-of-interest in several murder investigations and a number of assault cases. Mysteriously, his name is blacked out. All kinds of unwanted speculation could grow from that."

Reasoner retrieved his file from the table and began leafing through the pages.

"Those redacted reports all have your signature, Governor Reasoner. Your signature as Commissioner of Police."

"How do you know the redacted name is Braddock?" Reasoner asked.

"A couple of ways. The MO found at each of the crime scenes matches Braddock's to a tee. Plus, he was identified to us by the detective who investigated the crimes. He named Braddock as his prime suspect in those reports."

"Why am I here?" Sims asked. "What has any of this got to do with me?"

"You're absolutely right, Senator, speculation about the programs your administration supported being responsible for a hike in crime and homelessness was largely dismissed as unwarranted, but...." Robinson held up her hand. "A sidebar here. We do have a box full of files on crimes committed by dangerous people like James Braddock who were released from mental health care facilities during your administration. Crimes that were never properly investigated. Actually, they were ignored. We know you and Governor Reasoner discussed the politics of this issue, the negative potential that it could bring, and agreed the best course was to redact Braddock's name, and put a lid on the other investigations."

"That's absurd," Sims objected.

"No, it's not," Robinson retorted. "It's not absurd at all. It's a fact and in those files is proof of that fact."

"You can't tie me to this," Sims said, his voice raised. He leaned over the table. "This is extortion."

"Extortion?" Robinson said, feigning surprise. "We haven't asked for anything."

"Then get on with it," Sims insisted indignantly.

"As a police officer, if any of this ever surfaced, I would be terribly embarrassed and, more importantly, it would reflect badly on the entire NYPD. Details of investigations altered. Prime suspects ignored. The potential for a lot of very, very negative press is right there," she said, pointing at the files being held by both men. "The bottom line...the public would lose faith in law enforcement and in elected officials such as yourselves."

"This is nuts," Reasoner protested.

Robinson directed herself to Reasoner. "Your signature is on the reports." She shifted her focus to Sims. "I doubt the attention would stop at his door. It would likely find its way to yours, especially when the source who told us about the redactions and your role is found and interviewed."

"Let's cut to the chase," Reasoner said. "What do you want?"

"I want you, Governor, to put the word out that you're not happy with Commissioner Kinney. Not officially. Not publicly. Get the message to the mayor and city council."

"You want to be commissioner," Reasoner said, a mix of accusation and relief in his voice.

"And you can make that happen," Robinson said. "As a former police commissioner and current governor, if you tell the right people you've lost confidence in Kinney, he's gone. But we can do it without a lot of strum and drang. Let's keep this low key and let others suggest to Kinney that it's time for him to retire and spend more time with his family."

"What about you?" Reasoner said to Prado. "What's your price?"

"She's not finished," Prado said with a hard look at Reasoner. "When you're responsible for the murder of at least three women, you have to pay a *steep* price."

"Thank you, Agent Prado," Robinson said. To Reasoner: "I'll be calling you one day to ask for your endorsement when I announce my candidacy for mayor and...."

"Oh, for fuck's sake," Reasoner said in disgust.

"Oh, no, no," Robinson said through gritted teeth. "No, no, you don't get to do that. This is *your* game. *You* made the rules. This is *exactly* how you and your friends" – she gave Sims a side eye – "have been running things for years. That's how we got here today. And I'm fine with that, but now it's my turn. I'll be playing right along with you." She took a breath and smoothed the front of her silk blouse. "When I call, I'd appreciate your endorsement." She sat back in her chair and cocked her head at Prado. "Your turn."

"In your file," Prado said to Sims, "you'll find a short article on the murder of a Surinamese diplomat, Daniel VandenHeuval. He held a couple of different positions for his country here in the United States, including as ambassador and as an envoy at the U.N. He was killed at the direction of the current American ambassador to Suriname, Alexander Chandon."

"What?" Sims squeaked. "How do you know this?"

Prado reached into her computer bag and produced a sheaf of papers. "I've put all the details together for you. Short version, I handled a case some time back that took me to Suriname where I first encountered Mr. Chandon. His position was cultural attaché, but I learned it was a cover. He was CIA and running a weapons trafficking operation to supply guns to clientele selected by the agency. He has since expanded that operation. In addition to skimming funds for himself and...."

"Wait," Sims said, waving his hands. "Seriously? The CIA? What the hell do you expect me to do?"

"You're chairman of the Senate Select Committee on Intelligence. You have jurisdiction to look into CIA activities in Suriname; and when you do you're going to uncover unsanctioned assassinations and bribery not only by the CIA, but by international business interests, mostly American owned, pouring into the country to take advantage of oil assets. You should have a field day, and it could mean a lot of favorable coverage for you." She smiled at Sims. "You're welcome."

"What do you get out of this?" Sims asked. "Is this a career move for you? Am I supposed to give you credit for this? Call the director and say nice things?"

"No," Prado said, "I don't want to be mentioned. I don't want to be involved at all. You'll have plenty of people to help you make your case."

She nodded at the material she handed to him. "Everything you need is in there. Names. Who did what to whom? Everything."

"Then, why?"

"Chandon is a scumbag. He has to go." She turned to Reasoner. "I want you to call the warden at Rikers."

Chapter 20

Move Motherfucker

Prado was surprised at her calmness. She was completely serene, totally relaxed.

She walked behind a guard as they passed through areas where the general population was housed. The noise level was deafening. They left the larger units and crossed a green space entering a low slung unattached building. The quiet in this sterile, gray walled space was almost unsettling.

The guard stopped in front of a steel door at the far end of the building. He peered through a small window protected by wire mesh and pulled on an elastic cord attached to his belt holding a ring of keys. He turned to Prado. "This guy is very dangerous."

"Oh, I know."

"I really don't think you should go in without me but the warden said you wanted to meet with him alone. I'll be right here, Miss."

"Thank you. I'll be fine."

The guard hesitated a moment before unlocking the door. He reminded Prado, "I'm two steps away."

A slender African American man stared at her. His orange shirt and pants, two sizes too big, swallowed him. Hair cut short. Shoulders drooped in relaxation. His eyes were wide, welcoming. A shadow of a smile crossed his lips. "Who are you?"

Prado stood a moment, feeling the door close behind her. She walked slowly to the stainless steel interview table where Ivory Harris was handcuffed to a restraint ring. His legs were cuffed together at the ankles.

She felt a rush of adrenaline and the prick of perspiration across her hairline and on the back of her neck. Prado kept her eyes on Harris as she pulled a chair away from the table and sat down opposite him. She stared at him. She tried to put herself back in the warehouse where Harris and others were taking turns beating her. Raping her. Laughing. She could not.

"Who are you?" he asked again.

Prado felt the calm returning. "You don't remember me?"

"I never met you before in my life, lady," Harris said disdainfully. He laughed boisterously. "But it's nice to see a pretty face." He made a point of staring at her breasts.

With the jolt, she was back in that warehouse. In that chair. Sitting in her own blood. The pain numbed. Her nerves destroyed by the beatings. Her eyes were so swollen she could not see. Her eardrums ruptured. She could barely hear. It was the laugh. He would hit her and laugh. He stood in front of her when she was being sodomized and asked "Does that feel good?" and laughed.

"Estrella," she said.

Harris leaned toward her. "Estrella? The undercover cop?"

Prado forced a smile. "Yes, Estrella, the undercover cop."

"Fuck, we thought you were dead."

"Surprise," she said, raising her hands to either side of her face.

He laughed that laugh. Full-throated but with no joy. It was a declaration of his total disregard for joy. A unique statement of the man's deviance and sense of superiority. His intent to inflict pain and joy at violence. It cut through Prado like hot knife.

"Well, shit," he said, his eyes registering recognition. "You were that 'secret witness' at the trial. The one they hid behind a curtain."

Prado bobbed her head. "That was me. I never understood why they needed to do that." She waved a hand in front of her face. "I was all bandaged." She mimicked another smile. "They had to rebuild my face. New teeth. You yanked most of mine out with pliers. Remember?" She wiggled her fingers. "Broke these with a hammer."

"Yeah," Harris said and stared. "You do look different, but a lot the same, you know?"

"Oh, yeah," Prado said. "I know. It took me months to find the old me in the new me."

"I never figured out how they found you."

"I had a tracker in my earring. You cut my ear off, but the tracker still worked even if it was soaking in my blood on the floor." She tweaked her right earlobe. "An original part. They found it on the floor and reattached it."

"Shit." He laughed. "You are one tough bitch. You still a cop?"

Prado smiled. "Better. I'm a special agent with the FBI."

"No, shit," Harris said, true surprise in his voice, then quickly his eyes clouded with suspicion. "You here to try and talk me into being a CI or something? 'Cause that ain't gonna happen. We should've killed you as soon as we figured out you was a cop instead of playing with you."

"You should have, but you couldn't resist having your fun. Must be why they nicknamed you B-Stupid."

"Fuck you. No one ever called me that to my face."

"I hope you're enjoying your time here in Rikers. It must be an adjustment. You don't have your butt-boys around to protect you. Feeling a little vulnerable, maybe?"

"No one is gonna touch one of the Dooney Boys. We have protection everywhere."

Prado smiled. "Do you have any idea how ridiculous you sound?" She raised her arms and looked around the room. "You're in one of the most dangerous prisons in the country. People are killed here in bunches and no one gives a shit. And for sure no one gives a shit about you. No one is going to care if Ivory Harris is shanked and bleeds out in the showers or if the Aryan Brotherhood hangs you in your cell, or sets it on fire with you locked inside. Protection?" She shined with a genuine smile. "You're a big man. A Dooney Boy. What a load of shit."

"Fuck you, bitch. You're a fake person. We fucked you up so bad, they had to put the pieces back together." Harris tapped the side of his head with his index finger. "I'll live in your head for the rest of your life." He laughed. "You're the one in a prison."

"Excuse me for a minute," Prado said and walked to the door and knocked. "Guard."

"Oh, did I hurt your feelings?" Harris said teasingly. "Are you gonna cry about it to the guard?"

"You okay?" the guard asked as she stepped into the corridor. She closed the door and guided him a few feet away from the room. "I need the keys to his cuffs and your baton."

The guard stiffened and stepped away from her. "No, ma'am that would be crazy."

Prado pointed at the man's shoulder mic. "Call your warden. He'll give you the okay. But you know that. You got the word to bring me here and do whatever I asked." She let the words settle before adding, "The warden isn't going to happy to hear from you about something you've already been asked to do. He probably doesn't want to know any more about this than he already does. And neither should you." She held out her hand. "Keys, please, and baton."

Prado returned to the room displaying the keys. "When was the last time you weren't handcuffed and shackled?

Harris closed one eye in question. "What the hell are you talking about?"

Prado walked around the table and told Harris to, "Turn your legs toward me." He did. She released the leg irons, straightened, bent forward and unlocked Harris's handcuffs. "Feel better?"

Harris rubbed his wrists and stared at Prado. "Now, what? We gonna fuck or something?"

Prado reached toward the small of her back, brought the baton forward, snapped it to full length and swung it against the side of Harris's head. He raised his hand to his cheek which was split from his ear to his lower jaw. She hit him again, breaking his hand.

"You had me tied to a fucking chair," Prado screamed at the cowering man. She did not recognize the growling voice that came from deep within. "I couldn't move. You can. I've given you a chance. Move, motherfucker."

Harris spun away and stood. He crouched and ran at Prado, tackling her and driving her to the floor. His blood was pouring into her eyes. She kneed him in the groin and he rolled off of her. She jumped to her feet and brought the baton down on his knee. Harris howled in pain.

Prado wiped her eyes and stared at the blood. She felt violently ill and staggered to the door. The guard was there before she had time to say anything. She handed him the keys and baton and threw up.

Harris was yelling, "You bitch," and screaming with pain. "You broke my fucking leg."

Prado could not help herself. She ran back into the room. "Your leg? Your leg? You coward. You broke both my legs, both arms, my wrists, my hip, my jaw, dislocated my shoulders. You stuck poles inside me. I can't have children. You scalped me. You destroyed my face."

The guard pinned Harris to the ground his knee in the middle of man's back. "You okay?" he asked her.

"This is his blood," Prado answered. "I'm fine."

The guard yanked Harris upright and pushed him toward the chair. "He gets his ass kicked all the time. Must've pissed off the Nazi Low Riders."

"What?" Harris screamed, his shaking hand hovering over his shattered knee. "You gonna lie?"

"You'd prefer I said a lady did this to you," the guard answered. He looked at Prado. "No offense, ma'am."

"None taken. Go ahead and let everyone know a woman did this to him. A small woman alone in a room with him, and his cuffs and shackles were removed."

"I can arrange that."

"Bathroom?" she asked.

"Near the entrance, but wait here. Let me get him to the infirmary and I'll come back for you. I can get you out of here without having to go back through the main building."

"That would be good."

Chapter 21

Never Better

"Who's that banging on my front door?" Willow Briggs called out as she walked down her hall.

Prado stood on the top step holding two cups of coffee. She offered one to Briggs as soon as the door opened. "It isn't a wolf."

"Another last minute call, but always welcome," Briggs said and stood aside. "Coming in?"

"We have to talk."

"You feeling okay?"

"Never better."

Chapter 22

Bucket List

Three Years Later

Warren sat in the dark. His chair near the head of the bed so he could watch her breathe. Make sure she was breathing.

Maddy turned onto her side facing Warren and opened her eyes. She jerked away from the edge of the bed. "Jesus, you scared the hell out of me."

"Sorry."

Maddy yawned and pointed to the tray at the foot of the bed. "Water."

Warren pulled the tray to her, filled a plastic cup and handed it to her. She took a long sip. "Help me sit up. Pile the pillows behind me."

Warren moved her forward gently and arranged the pillows against the headboard. Maddy scooted herself into a sitting position and fell back against the pile.

"Now, I'm tired again," she said with a hoarse laugh. "What's new in your life? Mine's really dull."

"I'm going to go to Philadelphia."

Maddy's eyes lit up. "Really?"

Warren nodded.

"Taking my advice. How're you getting there?"

"Town car."

"Fancy," she said energetically. "Finally after all my prodding. Just wish I wasn't dying and I'd go with you."

"You'll be with me," Warren answered solemnly.

"That was corny, but I appreciate the sentiment. Make sure you get a cheesesteak on South Street." She nodded knowingly. "Gotta do that. Ask your driver to go into one of the shops and get it for you. You'll love it. My Dad took me to see the Yankees play the Phillies once and we had

223

one. It was great."

"I will."

"And Constitution Hall. Gotta see that and the Liberty Bell." Maddy laughed, her eyes crinkling. "Boy, do I sound like a nerd."

Warren nodded. "Those are definitely things I should see."

"Was it our trip to Battery Park that convinced you to go? Couldn't believe you'd never seen the Statue of Liberty or the 9-11 site."

"Eloise pitched a fit. Thought we went in the subway."

"She was even freaked that we might've taken a taxi. Couldn't believe she didn't know about Uber."

"She protects me like a hawk, and I'm not going to say a word about Philadelphia. She'd have me in leg irons and throw away the key."

"This is terrific." Maddy grunted as she shifted her weight. Warren jumped up from his chair and stood over the bed, poised. "Relax, I'm good, just need to reposition my butt. It's falling asleep."

Warren walked to the window and looked down at a parking lot.

"You'd think a hospice would have better views," Maddy said. "I saw one of those 'end of the world' movies once and people in a hospice kinda place were allowed to commit suicide. Before they did, they were shown wonderful videos about what life was like before whatever happened, happened. Anyway, I was thinking they should do something like that in hospices. Give us a choice of what we'd like to see on the way out"

"'Feelies'," Warren said.

"What?"

"The videos were called 'Feelies.' The movie is *Soylent Green*."

"Yeah, we definitely have to get you out more. Anyone who knows that spends way too much time indoors. For my 'Feelie', I'd pick a day at the beach. You?"

"A day at the beach sounds good. Never been to the beach. Maybe a forest. A snow-covered forest."

"You know, you can go to the beach. You can hike through a snow-covered forest."

"At night."

"Sure, at night. It would be an experience a lot of people don't get. Well, maybe they can go to the beach at night, but not many hike in the forest at night. You should do it."

Warren sat down and reached for Maddy's hand. "Maybe I will."

"No maybes. No time for maybes, and I say that from the unique perspective of someone with no time. So, what was your favorite walkabout? One we did together."

"'Walkabout'? I told you I called them that?"

"Must have," Maddy said, squinting in thought. "No, actually, it was Eloise. She talked to Nancy about it. That's how Nancy found out we did them. Freaked her out, but she never said anything to my parents. A good friend. Besides you, she's been my only friend for the past few years. I love her to death but how pathetic is that? My best friend is my nurse."

"She was the one who got me in and out of the hospital before they moved you here. Somehow convinced security and the floor nurses to ignore me sitting in your room in the middle of the night."

"Like I said, a good friend." Maddy took a deep breath, causing her to cough violently. Warren jumped up and offered her the cup of water, which she waved away. Maddy closed her eyes. Warren remained standing until her breathing steadied.

"Now," Maddy said, opening her eyes slowly, "which was your favorite walkabout?"

"I'd say the 'dancing man', but that really wasn't a walkabout."

"No," she agreed. "Whole other thing. Let me guess." She stared ahead. "When we went to Brooklyn. To my house."

"Our first Uber trip," Warren said. "That was a good one."

"I can't believe we broke into my own house."

"You had the keys and security code. Not exactly a break in."

"It kinda was. It would've been a shit storm if we were caught. It was fun doing that and showing you my room." Maddy waved her arms in a circle. "Gave you a peek at a side of me other than all this."

"Oh, I got a pretty good peek other times. You threatening the rug man was a good one."

"You talking about when we first met?"

Warren nodded.

"On this 'favorites' thing, how's that book coming?"

"Slowly."

Maddy slapped her hands on the bed. "C'mon, you promised me you were going to write about the walkabouts; about all the stuff you see and do when you go out at night; the special places and those things you know about them."

"I've got nothing new to add. No unique vision."

"Of course you do. No one sees them like you do. And you get to tell it all from a place no one – well, hardly anyone – sees them from. A vampire's view of New York." Maddy laughed herself into another coughing fit. She raised a cautioning finger keeping Warren in his seat. Coming out of a cough she insisted, "Write the damn book."

"I'm working on it."

Maddy turned her body fully toward Warren. "I'm serious. You have to write that book. If you don't want people to know it's you, use a pen name, or make it a novel. You have no idea how differently you see things. Plus, they don't ever see the rug man and the bird man. They don't know them like you do."

"I don't really know them."

"Yes, you do," Maddy said insistently. "You know them as people." She fell back against the pillows, breathing heavily. Alarmed, Warren stood and leaned over the bed. Maddy waved him back to the chair. "You know what I mean. Until I went with you I never knew people like that existed. I mean I knew there were homeless people, but I didn't know they had lives. Like they exist for a reason." Maddy shook her head in frustration. "I'm not saying this right, but you will.

"And there's the 'dancing man.' To us that's what he was. No one but us knows him that way. It doesn't change that he was a murdering maniac, but it is something else about him."

"I'll always wonder if we did the right thing, leaving like we did."

"That's something you can write about. I think we did the right thing. It's not like we had anything to add to what happened. We couldn't tell them anything they didn't know, or weren't going to find out. We would've been like a sideshow. Hell, we would've been the main show," Maddy added dramatically, "'A dying girl and a man who has a rare skin condition that makes him allergic to light had been following the Uptown Savage for weeks.' Imagine how that would've played out? We would've been put under a microscope. And I'm not talking only about the police, which would've been bad enough. We wouldn't have been able to move without having a trail of people following us around. Forget you ever being able to do your thing. People would be camped outside the Plaza every night waiting for you. We would've been stuck inside."

"Does your father ever talk to you about it?"

"The dancing man?"

Warren nodded.

"No, he never talks about his work. Says 'I love what I do, but if I don't leave it at the office, it would kill me.'"

"The perfect recruiting pitch."

"Hey, I have the perfect title for your book. *Mapping the Night*."

Warren stood and put his hand on her shoulder. "Okay, I will. Now you have to calm down."

Maddy laughed. "Why? So I don't excite myself to death?"

"Yeah, that."

"You need a bucket list."

"A bucket list?"

"Yeah, like with the hike in the forest and the trip to the beach on it. Write down things you want to do before you die."

"Okay, I will."

"Promise?"

"I promise and I'll bring it with me tomorrow night for you to see."

***

Nancy called Warren with the news that Maddy died.

He did not know how long he stood with the phone in his hands. He could not move. It felt like he had been hit in the chest by a sledgehammer and his heart exploded. He had to breathe very shallowly. The pain was too intense otherwise.

Eloise found him standing in the hallway. She knew what it was without asking and walked him into his room. He sat on the bed.

"I'm so, so sorry," Eloise said and left him alone. She knew he was not the type who wanted someone with him.

Warren fell back and the tears came almost one at a time at first, then in a rush, then so many and with such force that he realized he was wailing. But he also realized it was not only for Maddy, it was for himself.

He calmed and went to his computer. He wrote out a bucket list with five items:

Go to Philadelphia
Go to the beach
Hike a snow-covered forest
Finish the book
Hire an escort

The End

About the Author

John David Bethel is the author of award-winning novels, *Unheard of* and *Holding Back the Dark*. Other published novels include *Little Wars*, *Capitol Evil* and *Hotel Hell*. He has also been published in popular consumer magazines and respected political journals.

Mr. Bethel spent 35 years in politics and government. He served in the Federal Senior Executive Service as a political appointee where he was Senior Adviser/Director of Speechwriting for the Secretaries of Commerce and Education; Editorial Director for the U.S. Small Business Administration; and Assistant Administrator for the U.S. General Services Administration's Office of Communications and Citizen Services. Bethel also worked as press secretary/speechwriter to Members of Congress.

Mr. Bethel is a senior consultant for a number of prominent communications management firms, including Burson Marsteller and The Wade Group.

He graduated with Phi Beta Kappa honors from Tulane University and lives in DeLand, Florida.

For sales, editorial information, subsidiary rights information
or a catalog, please write or phone or e-mail

iBooks
Manhanset House
Shelter Island Hts., New York 11965, US
Tel: 212-427-7139
ibooksinc.com
bricktower@aol.com
www.IngramContent.com

For sales in the UK and Europe please contact our distributor,
Gazelle Book Services
White Cross Mills
Lancaster, LA1 4XS, UK
Tel: (01524) 68765 Fax: (01524) 63232
email: jacky@gazellebooks.co.uk

Printed in the USA
CPSIA information can be obtained
at www.ICGtesting.com
CBHW032239240424
7491CB00012B/71